STUART DALY

BROTHERHOOD
OF THIEVES

THE FINAL BATTLE

WITHDRAWN

RANDOM HOUSE AUSTRALIA

To Ronan, my little buddy

A Random House book
Published by Random House Australia Pty Ltd
Level 3, 100 Pacific Highway, North Sydney NSW 2060
www.randomhouse.com.au

 Penguin
Random House
RANDOM HOUSE BOOKS

First published by Random House Australia in 2015

Random House Books is part of the Penguin Random House group of companies whose addresses can be found at global.penguinrandomhouse.com.

National Library of Australia
Cataloguing-in-Publication Entry

Author: Daly, Stuart
Title: The final battle
ISBN: 978 0 85798 538 5 (pbk)
Series: Brotherhood of thieves; 3
Dewey Number: A823.3

Cover illustration by Jeremy Reston
Cover design and typography by www.blacksheep-uk.com
Map by Stuart Daly and Anna Warren
Typeset by Midland Typesetters, Australia
Printed in Australia by Griffin Press, an accredited ISO AS/NZS 14001:2004 Environmental Management System printer

Random House Australia uses papers that are natural, renewable and recyclable products and made from wood grown in sustainable forests. The logging and manufacturing processes are expected to conform to the environmental regulations of the country of origin.

THE FOUR KINGDOMS

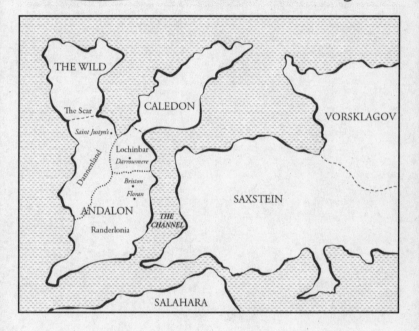

CHAPTER 1

HAVEN'S WATCH

The riders galloped along the snow-covered track.

They were perhaps two dozen in number, hastily equipped, the steel-grey half-light of dawn glistening off their piecemeal armour. Some wore padded gambesons or leather jerkins beneath their thick winter cloaks. Only a few had time to don iron chestplates or chain-mail hauberks. Even less were equipped with the conical helmets favoured by soldiers this far to the west. One man up front carried a lance, its shaft held high, bearing a banner of House Clayborne, its embroidered sea-eagle flapping in the wind.

Normally they would be decked out in the full panoply of war, but they had been woken early this morning by the plaintive moan of a signal horn. Stirred from the downy-warmth of his bed, Caspan had hurried to the window of the room he shared with Roland and Shanty above the stables in Castle Crag. His sleep-filled eyes had flashed with alarm when he saw the glow of the distant fire over to the west, at Haven's Watch.

He rode now in the middle of the company, a heavy sword strapped by his thigh and an iron-bossed buckler jostling by the side of his mount. He alternated his hold on the reins to blow warmth into his hands. He wasn't sure if he shivered due to the cold or the nervous anticipation of what awaited them at the headland.

War was coming.

Caspan could smell it in the waft of oiled mail that drifted in the breeze. He could taste it in the dry pit of his mouth. He could hear it heralded in the galloping hooves, the creaking of leather harnesses and bridles, the clanking of armour and weapons — swords that would soon enough be drawn and swung in defence of the west coast of Dannenland.

Caspan glanced at the young Baron of the High Coast, Saxon Clayborne. He rode bareback at the head of the band, his sable-lined cloak flapping in his wake. Sheathed by his side was a broadsword, its leather grip stained with sweat, and he wore a buckskin jerkin reinforced with patches of scale mail. In his haste to lead his troops he had failed to find his boots. His pale feet were a stark contrast to the dark flanks of his warhorse.

Saxon was seventeen; only two years older than Caspan, but the grim resolve in his eyes belied an experience well beyond his years. Only last month he had laid his father, the late Baron Cole Clayborne, to rest in the ancestral tomb beneath Castle Crag. Saxon had little time to bereave his loss and console his mother before a message arrived by raven, which bore the wolf seal of King Rhys MacDain. Saxon was to succeed his father and don the mantle of ruler of Castle Crag, the principal stronghold on the High Coast. It was a heavy burden assuming such a role at only seventeen, making him responsible for guarding merchant vessels from pirates along the western coast of Dannenland. Baron Cole had protected the territory for over two decades, ensuring trade and supplies reached their destinations. But the situation was very different now. Saxon didn't face raids from the pirates of the Black Isles — but a Roon invasion force.

Caspan thought back to when he had spied through the window of the central keep atop Tor O'Shawn, deep in Caledon, and overheard the meeting between the traitorous General Brett and Roy Stewart, the Laird of the Stewart Clan and leader of the combined highland army. They had discussed military tactics and revealed the location of their forces. The Caledonish army was to marshal in Sharn O'Kare Glen before heading south to conquer Lochinbar, the easternmost of Andalon's three duchies. Meanwhile, two Roon armies would advance deep into Dannenland: a force of seven thousand giants located in the Pass of Westernese; and a fleet of a hundred dragon-headed raiding ships hiding in the Black Isles. It was a deadly three-pronged attack, designed to stretch King Rhys's already exhausted and limited forces and lay siege to Briston. Once the royal capital was taken, the rest of the kingdom would crumble beneath their onslaught.

That was why Caspan had been sent to assist with the defence of the High Coast. Duke Connal had summoned several members of the Brotherhood to return from the deserts of Salahara. They had all gathered at Briston before being divided into three groups: the first, under Master Morgan's command, joined the army preparing to battle the Roon in the Pass of Westernese; Master Scott was sent with Duke Bran MacDain and Prince Dale to face Roy Stewart's highland army; and Shanty commanded the final band of treasure hunters, sent to assist Saxon in the defence of the High Coast.

Caspan and his friends had feared that they would be separated, assigned to different parts of the kingdom, but Duke Connal decided to keep them together. They worked well as a team and were familiar with Shanty's leadership after their mission to Caledon. But Lachlan had been asked to stay behind in Briston, and Caspan felt their team wasn't complete without him. Lachlan had stood by his side at the siege of Darrowmere, saved him at the skirmish at Mance O'Shea's Break, and ventured alongside him and Roland into the trap-riddled burial mound deep in the Caledonish highlands. Lachlan had insisted that he was fine and fully recovered from the effects of the Dray armband. It had covered him in an exoskeleton of black metal and had almost killed him. But Arthur, the physician who had saved his life, insisted the boy remain under his care for a few more weeks.

Caspan was drawn from his thoughts as the riders reached the headland at Haven's Watch and reined in near the signal fire. One of the three sentries who had spent the night in cold, silent vigil rushed over, saluted Saxon and pointed out to sea.

'It's the Roon, my lord,' he reported. 'They're coming!'

Caspan sat up in his stirrups, shielded his eyes against the falling sleet and looked to the west. There, barely visible against the distant Black Isles, were dozens of white sails. They didn't look threatening from this distance, more like children's toys. But in his mind's eye, Caspan pictured the dragon heads carved into the prows of the galleys, the battle-scarred shields slung over the sides, and the fierce, pale-skinned, tattoo-covered giants staring at the coastline, blades of black steel gripped in their hands. He swallowed and turned to Shanty, the slender, well-dressed dwarf, who'd pulled up beside him.

'It's a large force,' Caspan commented.

Shanty nodded grimly. 'Well, I'm glad, lad. We came here for a fight. I didn't think the Roon were going to disappoint.' The dwarf looked around the group, caught Kilt, Sara and Roland's attention, and motioned with a subtle jerk of his chin for them to join him and Caspan away from the others. They gathered near a copse of trees at the edge of the headland.

Roland rubbed the sleep from his eyes and yawned. 'Maybe staying up late to play cards with the guards wasn't the smartest thing to do.'

'You don't say,' Sara remarked. 'You knew the Roon were coming.'

'Yeah, but not so early in the morning. I was hoping for a bit of a sleep-in.'

Kilt rolled her green eyes. 'How dare they.'

'You're telling me. Still, there was no way I was going to call it an early night.' Roland jiggled his coin pouch. 'I was on a roll.' He stifled another yawn and pulled his cloak high around his neck. 'I just hope I wake up soon.'

Sara pointed at the waterskin hanging from his belt. 'Why don't you have some of your Slap Across the Face? That always seems to help.'

Caspan grinned, thinking back to Roland's impersonation of a squirrel the first time he drank the sickly sweet cider.

'I finished it off last night,' Roland moped and glanced at Shanty. 'You don't have any of your ginger cider left?' The dwarf shook his head, and Roland clicked his tongue disappointedly. 'I thought I'd be pushing my luck. Still, when cellars fail, nature provides.' He tilted back his head and caught some sleet on his tongue.

'It's just as well we're resting our Wardens,' Kilt said. 'They'll have a big day ahead of them.'

'We all will,' Shanty replied. One of Saxon's soldiers rode around the group to inspect the beach nestled in the cove beneath the headland. Shanty waited for him to move off before beckoning his companions to come closer. 'Just stick to the roles we've been assigned and hopefully we'll get through the day in one piece. I won't lie to you: the fighting's going to be fierce. Keep your heads down and your Wardens by your sides.'

Caspan nodded doggedly. They had to prevent the Roon navy from landing and gaining a foothold on the coast at all costs. They were part of a disparate band of defenders who had answered Saxon's call from all sections of the High Coast. There were units of militia raised from local fishing villages, the household guard of Castle Crag, and the veteran warriors of the First Legion, who had made the journey north from the southern city ports. Even a force of over a hundred pirates had rallied to Saxon's side, driven by the Roon from their haven of the Black Isles. The army was ostensibly under Saxon's control, being the new ruler of Castle Crag. But Caspan had attended several war councils since arriving in the stronghold last week, and whilst Saxon knew the terrain along the coast and had plenty of experience in skirmishes with pirate vessels, never before had he faced an invasion force of thousands and he wisely deferred to the advice of the experienced legion commanders.

Caspan looked across at the opposite headland, where a large group of riders gathered around a second burning signal pyre. A banner flapping at the head of a raised spear identified them as soldiers of the First Legion. They were camped in the leeward side of the headland, behind a sheltering stretch of trees on a field that bordered the road leading to Castle Crag. Caspan was learning more about battlefield tactics every day and believed it was a good location. It was within easy reach of the cove and allowed supply wagons to be brought up to the tents. Once the command was given, the legion could rally on the beach within a few minutes.

The plan was to stop the Roon from landing on the beach, but defences had been built regardless. Caspan nudged his mount closer to the edge of the cliff and leaned forward to peer down into the cove. It was low tide, revealing the massive wooden stakes driven deep into the pebble beach and pointing out to sea. Once the tide rose, the wooden stakes would be concealed beneath the waves and hopefully crack and disable the hulls of the Roon vessels. This would force the giants to leap overboard and wade ashore in a disorganised mess. They would then have the archers to deal with, who were positioned atop both headlands and the grassy hillock at the rear of the beach, the seaward side of which bristled with stakes. A deep trench dug immediately in front of this was filled with oil-filled pig bladders, which would erupt in flames once pierced with incendiary arrows. Trapped between the cliffs, the sea and the flaming trench, the Roon would perish beneath the feathered storm of death.

Caspan shifted his gaze to the opposite headland and studied the mounted figure at the head of the soldiers. General Liam White, the leader of the First Legion, sat straight in his saddle, staring out to sea, his gloved hands rested on the pommel of the great broadsword strapped by his side. If not for the slight stirring of his cloak he might have been mistaken for a statue, erected atop the cliff as a warning to all invaders of the proud warriors who defended these lands.

Liam was a tall, broad-shouldered man with narrow, dark eyes that revealed little warmth. His features were set permanently in a brooding scowl, hardened by a lifetime of soldiery. But he was nothing as terrifying as the Warden that waited dutifully by his side.

Liam had been awarded one of the magical guardians the Brotherhood had supplied to King Rhys. But unlike the treasure hunters' Wardens, which they befriended and treated with great respect, the General's giant bear was trained to kill. He had a starved, demented look in his eyes and growled whenever anybody other than Liam approached. His black fur was covered in countless scars, his left ear was missing, and one of his lower incisors jutted forward, over his jowl. The Warden was a hulking mass of muscle, larger than a draught horse, toughened by years of war to become the perfect killing machine. The General never dismissed him, instead keeping him as his constant guardian. He was called Maul.

Shanty had cautioned the friends that they should consider Maul as a sombre warning of what happens to a Warden when it was unable to return to the astral plane. The magical beast would be trapped forever in the Four Kingdoms. It would never be able to magically heal itself. Worst of all, it would become mortal.

Caspan fingered the metal figurine hanging around his neck and vowed that he would never misplace Frostbite's soul key. Nor would he do anything that would turn Frostbite into a cold-blooded killer. Today they would participate in the battle, but they were assigned a role that would hopefully keep them well away from the enemies' blades.

Roland touched heels to his mount's flanks and moved closer to Caspan. 'They're an impressive sight,' he commented, staring across at the General and his Warden. 'I pity the Roon that face them.'

Caspan nodded, thankful he wouldn't be anywhere near the beachhead, which was under the General's control.

'So you're sure these pig bladder thingies are going to work?' Roland asked.

Caspan drew his gaze from the General to regard Roland. He looked comical in the blue Strathboogie bonnet he had kept from their mission into Caledon and now wore everywhere. Caspan smiled in spite of his anxiety.

'The tactic worked fine during the siege of Darrowmere,' Caspan replied. He thought back to the night raid when he, Lachlan and Master Morgan took to the sky atop Talon, Lachlan's guardian griffin, and dropped ignited oil bladders onto the unsuspecting Roon army, causing chaos in their ranks. 'Only this time we're going to drop them on Roon *ships*. With any luck, we'll be able to stop them long before they get anywhere near the beach.'

Roland rubbed his hands excitedly and shifted restlessly in his saddle. 'This is going to be epic!'

Roland had a remarkable capacity for making light-hearted humour out of even the most serious of situations. In this instance, though, Caspan thought it was naive and dangerous.

'I'm not sure *epic* is the word I'd use to describe a battle,' Caspan cautioned.

Roland mulled his comment over for a moment before shrugging. 'Okay, how about "classic" then?'

Caspan drew a patient breath and gazed back at the Roon armada. He wondered if he, Roland and Sara would be able to stop so many ships. Even with their Wardens helping them, they'd only be six against what he could only guess must be over a hundred sleek and fast raiding vessels. Back in Tor O'Shawn, General Brett had revealed that three thousand Roon were aboard the ships. Caspan doubted they'd be able to take all of them out, but they had to try.

'We're the first line of defence against the Roon invasion force,' he said sombrely, mentally rehearsing the plan Saxon and the officers of the First Legion had finalised earlier this week. 'Should any ships get past us, they'll be intercepted by Saxon's fleet.'

'And don't forget the pirates who rallied to his side,' Roland added. 'I know we need to do the aerial attack and all, but wouldn't it have been great to have been posted with the pirates? Imagine standing beside Captain Panter Grinn on the deck of his ship, the *Mangy Dog*. Ah, it makes the blood stir just thinking about it.'

Caspan gave his friend a concerned look. 'He's a *pirate*, Roland. He makes a living out of plundering innocent merchant vessels. Saxon only accepted Grinn's offer of help because he's in desperate need of ships. Otherwise, he would have clapped him and his crew in irons and locked them up in the dungeon.'

'Yeah, I know,' Roland said dreamily. 'Isn't he great?'

This was more than Caspan could tolerate, and he leaned across and clouted Roland over the side of the head. 'You know, you really worry me sometimes.'

Roland grinned wolfishly as he readjusted his bonnet and motioned with a wave of his hand at the precipitous drop before them. 'What can I say, Cas — I like living on the *edge*.'

Caspan cringed. Roland's expression became serious and he studied the fingernails of his right hand fastidiously.

'For what the pirates and Saxon's fleet lack in numbers, they'll make up for in experience of naval combat,' he said. 'Whereas the Roon are skilled in using their galleys to sail up rivers and conduct raids, the pirates engage enemy ships at sea. They have large crossbows, called ballistae, set on their decks, which they shoot at enemy vessels, just below the waterline, smashing holes in their hulls and sinking them. Should that fail, they'll close in with grapples and board the enemy. I should also point out that nobody knows the currents and shoals along the High Coast better than the pirate captains, and especially Captain Grinn, who's prowled these waters on the *Mangy Dog* for the past two decades. It's hoped that the pirates' knowledge of naval warfare and maritime experience will give Andalon the vital edge it needs.'

Caspan gave him a baffled look. 'And since when have you been such an expert on naval strategy?'

Roland shrugged. 'I grew up in a fishing village not far from here. Stuff like that's general knowledge to me.' Caspan nodded, conceding his point, and Roland grinned ruefully. 'Oh, and I overheard two of Saxon's officers discussing naval tactics last night.' He laughed as he tugged his reins to the right, moving himself clear of the clout over the head he thought must be coming.

'You'd better stop goofing around once the battle starts,' Caspan warned. 'Remember that Shanty and Kilt are going to be aboard one of the ships.'

'Don't remind me,' Roland said enviously, prompting Caspan to take another patient breath. The black-haired jester gave his friend an earnest look. 'They'll have their Wardens with them, guarding their every move. I'm sure they'll be fine.'

Caspan wasn't so optimistic. 'Well, they'll only be put in danger if we let the Roon get past us. So let's make sure that never happens.'

Roland nodded determinedly and, standing up in his stirrups, spread his arms wide.

'Ah, I miss the sea,' he said wistfully, tilting his head into the breeze and closing his eyes. 'It's almost as if I can hear it calling me. Oh Roland, oh Roland, come back home. Oh Roland, oh —'

A seagull shot over the edge of the cliff and smacked into Roland's face, knocking him off his saddle. He lay on the ground, spitting feathers.

'What on earth was that?' he roared, clambering to his feet and drawing his sword.

Caspan laughed so hard it felt like his sides might split. 'A seagull hit you! I've never seen anything so hilarious!'

'A seagull! You've got to be kidding me!' Roland made a disgusted face and wiped his tongue on his sleeve. 'And thanks a lot, Cas. It might have been funny for you, but that hurt. I'm lucky I didn't split my lip.' He looked around for the bird, but it had flown away clear of sight.

Sara chortled from where she and Kilt waited on their mounts behind the boys. 'Only something like that could happen to you.'

Roland glared at her, then noticed his friends were laughing at him. 'Great! So you all saw it.'

Kilt gestured with a flick of her eyes over towards Baron Saxon and his mounted company. 'I think everybody did.'

Caspan heard their laughter and turned to see the soldiers staring at Roland. One of them was re-enacting the moment of the impact and doing a first-class impersonation of the dazed look on Roland's face when he lay on the ground.

'Some people around here have a very twisted sense of humour,' Roland muttered dourly.

Kilt grinned. 'Aw, lighten up, grumble-bum. It's not every day you get to see something as funny as that. In fact, I don't think I've ever heard of *anybody* being so unfortunate.'

'Well, there's always a first, isn't there.' Roland dusted himself off and climbed back onto his horse. He moved his mount further back from the cliff and opened his mouth to say something when Saxon called for everyone to gather around him near the signal pyre.

Caspan was appreciative of the warmth the pyre offered, and he positioned his horse as close to it as possible. He wasn't surprised when Sara drew her mount alongside his. She never coped well with the cold, and had done nothing but complain since the first snow of winter fell yesterday afternoon.

Caspan suppressed a wry grin at what she was wearing. While everyone else in the group had grabbed what armour and weapons they could find before riding out from Castle Crag, Sara had prioritised her cloak, her thick, fur-lined gloves and her feather and down bed quilt, which she'd wrapped around her shoulders. She was also carrying a heavy book.

'What?' she asked Caspan, looking at him askance. 'I'm not allowed to keep warm?' She followed his gaze to the book she held, shrugged and leaned across in her saddle to whisper, 'I couldn't find a sword. I thought this would be the next best thing.'

'I'm not going to argue with that,' Caspan replied, thinking back to when she had used a similar volume to crown the ruffian who had fought them in the Thirsty Wayfarer. It seemed a lifetime ago now. Caspan smiled fondly, his thoughts drifting back to his training at the House of Whispers and their beloved steward, Gramidge.

Sara placed the book in her lap, removed her gloves and raised her palms close to the fire.

'Go easy there,' Caspan cautioned. 'Get too close and you'll burn yourself.'

Sara snorted. 'Fat chance of that happening. I'll need to thaw them out first.'

Everyone had now gathered around Saxon, and the young baron addressed the group.

'This is the day we've been waiting for,' he announced. 'The Roon come in great numbers, and we are all that stand in their way. Yes, they are fierce fighters, but we've planned our defences and are ready for them. There's not a single man among us who doesn't know what role he'll play today. Not one of the wretched giants will step foot on the High Coast, for this is our territory!' He drew his sword and thrust it above his head. 'For King Rhys, the High Coast and Andalon!'

As one, the men of his household guard drew their swords, held them high and repeated the oath. Caspan was stirred by their iron resolve and felt there was hope for them yet. Saxon was right — they were prepared for the enemy, and were ready to defend their homeland. Caspan couldn't think of a more powerful motive.

Saxon stared defiantly at the coming giants. 'How long do we have?' he asked, addressing the grizzled warrior beside him who had been a close friend of his father's.

Fin looked skyward and studied the movement of the clouds. 'The wind is coming from the north. They'll make landfall by midday.'

Saxon flexed his fingers. 'Then we have a lot to do.' He beckoned one of his soldiers forward. 'Return to Castle Crag and send a message by raven to King Rhys. Inform him that the battle for the High Coast is about to begin.' The man saluted, dug his heels into his mount's flanks and galloped down the headland towards the stronghold. Saxon then commanded another soldier to ride to the cove to the south, where the Andalonian fleet and their pirate allies lay hidden, to warn them to get ready.

'Let's move to our stations and show the Roon what mettle Andalonian men are made of,' Saxon continued, addressing the group of riders. Kilt cleared her throat, and a smile played at the edges of the Baron's lips. 'My apologies. What mettle Andalonian men and *women* are made of.' He sought out Caspan, Roland and Sara. 'Ready to head out soon?'

Caspan nodded, suddenly feeling overwhelmed by the responsibility vested in him, his two friends and their Wardens. If they were successful with their aerial attack they could set the Roon ships ablaze and end the battle before it even started. But should they fail, hundreds — possibly thousands — of men would die and the High Coast might fall. The Roon would then head inland, slaughtering all in their way.

'Yes, my lord,' he replied. 'We'll cart the pig bladders up to Haven's Watch. That way we won't have to fly all the way back to Castle Crag to restock once the fight starts. It will save us precious time.'

Saxon gave a satisfied nod. 'Good idea. Now, let's see if we can send these giants to a watery grave.' He glanced down at his bare feet and grinned wryly, only now noticing that he'd forgotten his boots in his haste to assemble at the signal pyre. 'Although, I suggest we return to Castle Crag and get fully equipped first. I'd hate to greet the giants and not give them the proper welcome they deserve.'

'Well said, my lord,' Fin said, before digging his heels into his mount and signalling for the band to follow him back to the stronghold.

CHAPTER 2

THE QUIET BEFORE THE STORM

'Well, that's the last of them,' Caspan said, patting the final oil-filled pig bladder he'd placed in the wagon.

Kilt helped him tie a canvas over the top, then stepped back to inspect the three wagons they had stacked. She wiped sweat from her brow and gave Roland a disapproving look. 'You know, it wouldn't have killed you to give us a hand with those last few dozen bladders.'

Roland had been put off the activity when a bladder popped in his hands, spilling oil all over his clothes. It was more than he could stand, and he'd only just returned from his room atop the stable, wearing a new tunic and breeches. He pursed his lips as he inspected his friends' handiwork.

'Oh, I don't know. You seem to have had everything under control,' Roland commended, then stretched out his hands, inspecting the length of his tunic. 'Do you think this is a little short on me? I might go change again.'

He stepped aside to allow Shanty and Sara to hitch the three draught horses they were leading to the wagons.

Kilt glared at him. 'Don't even think about it. We're getting ready for a battle and all you're worried about is if your sleeves are too short! You're unbelievable!'

Shanty checked the leather tarps were secure, then beckoned Roland and handed him a leather halter. 'Here you go. Now be careful. Follow the trail up to Haven's Watch, but take it nice and slow. Make sure none of the bladders pop. Leave the wagon up there, but don't park it too close to the signal pyre. The last thing we want is an ember setting everything alight.'

Roland gave him a grieved looked. 'But I thought Kilt was going up with Sara and Caspan?'

Shanty nodded and smiled. 'That was the original plan, until you decided to shirk your duties.' He patted Roland on the shoulder. 'Oh, and don't forget to bring your horse back down.'

'I'm not stupid, you know,' Roland muttered sourly as he watched a group of Saxon's soldiers walk their horses towards the bailey, where the Baron's troops were marshalling. They wore chainmail hauberks and conical helmets with nasal guards, and carried battleaxes and kite-shields bearing sea-eagle motifs.

Roland regarded them for a moment before turning back to the horse and sighing. 'I suppose we should introduce ourselves, considering we've got a long walk ahead of us.' He extended a hand in welcome to the mare. 'I'm Roland.' The horse stared down at him blankly and flicked an ear at a fly. 'Well, if you insist.' Roland grinned as he shook the horse's ear. 'You seem like the strong, silent type, but that doesn't matter. I never stop chatting, so I'll talk enough for both of us. And you look like a Georgina to me. So, come on, Georgina. We've got some pig bladders to deliver. Oh, I know, things don't get much more exciting than this.'

Caspan smirked as he turned to Shanty and Kilt, who sat down on some barrels stacked beside the stable. 'You'll be here when we get back?' he asked.

Shanty nodded. 'Fin's delivering an extra wagon of quivers and arrows to General Liam. Saxon said he won't lead us around to the ships until Fin returns. He reckons that will be in about an hour.'

'Good. I'd hate to head off without saying goodbye,' Caspan said, then turned to Sara and Roland. 'We should get moving.'

'Please, the excitement's eating me alive,' Roland muttered.

Caspan took hold of a horse's halter and, with Sara and Roland following, led his horse and wagon around the soldiers marshalling on the far side of the courtyard. They passed through the barbican of Castle Crag and headed up the snow-covered track that led to Haven's Watch.

It would be about a forty-minute return trip at the pace he was going, but Caspan didn't want to risk disturbing their precious cargo. It would be better to be slow and cautious, rather than hurry up to the headland and find half of the bladders damaged.

Caspan's chest churned with nervous anticipation. There had been a lot to keep him busy over the course of the past week and he had welcomed the distraction. It kept him from thinking about the impending battle, but now it was all he could think about. In contrast, Roland whistled merrily as if he didn't have a care in the world, and entertained Georgina with tales of a pony he had owned as a child.

'And his favourite food was carrots,' Roland continued. 'I bet you like them too, hey? What? No comment? Well, not to worry. I'll make sure I find you some when we get back to the castle. So, as I was saying, Harry loved carrots. In fact, that's all he'd ever eat. It got so bad that one day he jumped the fence into the neighbour's garden patch, dug up all his carrots and had a jolly old feast.' Roland chuckled heartily. 'One got stuck up his nostril, which wasn't exactly a pretty sight, as I'm sure you can imagine. My mum chased Harry all around the village before she finally caught him and pulled it out. But that was only the start of things to come, because the next week he got out and ate my mum's pumpkin pies, which were cooling on the kitchen sill. Oh Georgina, if you could have only seen the look on my mum's face. There she was, screaming like a lunatic and chasing Harry down the street with a broom, with all the villagers staring out their windows. I don't think I've ever been so embarrassed in my life. A month passed before I thought it was safe to wander the streets again. Understandably, pumpkin pies were a delicate topic in my household for a while.'

'Aren't you worried at all?' Sara asked him.

Roland screwed up his nose and shook his head. 'Not really. I mean, a few villagers still talk about the incident, but I've learnt to live with it.'

Sara drew an exasperated breath. 'Not the incident with the pumpkin pies, you great big goose! I'm talking about the Roon. You do know that there's an invasion force approaching?'

'Yep, and worrying about the Roon isn't going to make them go away, is it?'

'I suppose so,' Sara replied reluctantly.

'So why worry at all?' Roland said cheerfully. 'It's better to fill your mind with happy thoughts then worry about the serious things when they finally happen.' He stretched out his left arm and inspected the length of his sleeve again. 'Mind you, I still think this tunic's too short.'

Sara shook her head at him in wonder. 'You have the most remarkable way of looking at the world.'

Roland bowed graciously at her. 'Why, thank you.'

'You're just so simple and uncomplicated,' Sara continued. 'It's as if you can just turn your brain off and carry on in blissful ignorance of everything that's going on around you.'

Roland frowned. 'I'm not too sure if you're paying me a compliment or insulting me. And I don't think *simple* and *uncomplicated* are the words I'd use.' He pursed his lips in thought. 'Debonair — now I'd definitely use that. And suave — that would be another one.'

'And don't forget *snow-covered*,' Caspan added.

Roland raised a finger in agreement. 'Yes, snow-covered, too.' He caught himself and gave Caspan a baffled look. 'Snow-covered? What on earth do you mean by that?'

'I mean *this*.' Caspan stepped away from his horse and pelted a snowball at Roland. It exploded on his chest, covering his friend in white powder. 'You see — snow-covered.'

Roland stopped walking, stared deadpan at Caspan and drew a patient breath. 'Do you see what I have to put up with?' he said, turning to Georgina. 'Surrounded by puddenheads, I am.'

———⊱⊰———

Three sentries had been assigned by Saxon to replace those that had done the night watch. Sara stopped them from pulling back the canvases covering the wagons. A wick was attached to each bladder, and she was concerned that the light snow might cause them to dampen and smoulder when lit. It was best they remain under the tarps until the friends needed to fill the wicker baskets they would attach to their Wardens.

They unhitched the wagons, mounted up and peered out to sea. The Roon fleet had travelled about a quarter of the distance to the High Coast.

'I guess it's a little late to tell them this kingdom's invite only,' Roland remarked.

'I wish it was that simple.' Caspan beckoned with a wave for his friends to follow him. 'We'd better head back and get our Wardens ready.'

Roland dug his heels eagerly into Georgina's flanks and galloped past his companions. 'It's about time,' he hollered, glancing over his shoulder as he sped down the track. His eyes glistened excitedly and he skilfully held his bonnet in place with his left hand. 'I told you once, and I'll tell you again — this is going to be epic!'

Sara gave Caspan a concerned look. 'I don't know what worries me more: the Roon, or flying next to Roland and Bandit, armed with dozens of incendiary bombs.'

'I was thinking exactly the same thing.' Caspan smiled encouragingly at Sara. 'Come on. We'd better catch up. I don't like the idea of leaving Roland unattended, and especially before a battle. There's no telling what mischief he'll get up to.'

Sara nodded worriedly. 'He'd more than likely start another war.'

They set off after Roland and caught him just before they rode into Castle Crag. The trio dismounted as soon as they reached the stable. Shanty and Kilt had readied themselves for combat, summoned their Wardens, and were about to join Saxon's soldiers in the bailey.

'Talk about cutting it fine,' Shanty said. 'A few more minutes and you would've missed us.'

Roland patted Georgina on the neck and grinned wolfishly at the dwarf. 'Are you sure you're not wearing enough armour? There must be a dozen poor fellows running around in nothing but their underwear thanks to you.'

Shanty beat a gauntleted fist against his iron chest guard. 'Laugh all you want, but I'm not taking any chances. It's better to be decked out to the nines than to find yourself in the thick of battle, wishing you had more protection.'

In contrast, Kilt wore her Brotherhood cloak and a leather jerkin. They didn't offer her much protection, but Caspan reckoned she didn't want to be encumbered with heavy armour. She was fast on her feet, and relied on her speed in swordplay. She looked at Caspan and opened her mouth to comment, no doubt to offer him some parting words, when Fin's voice bellowed throughout the courtyard.

'All right, men, it's time. Form up in your lines. Those on the right will follow me up to the headland; those on the left will follow Baron Saxon around to the ships. So stop chatting and hurry up. We've got a war to fight, and I don't want to keep the Roon waiting. They've travelled a long way, and my blade's eager to meet them.'

The soldiers cheered defiantly and banged their axes and swords against their shields as they formed into separate lines.

Saxon sat atop a black warhorse that neighed and stamped its front hooves impatiently on the cobbles. Its tail flowed in silken ripples in the slight breeze. The Baron was now fully dressed for war, wearing a suit of half-plate over a knee-length mail shirt. His chest guard, metal shoulder-guards, or pauldrons, and shield were embossed with the heraldic sea-eagle emblem of House Clayborne. He wore his chainmail hood, or coif, pulled back so that it clumped at the back of his neck, revealing his long blond hair tied back in a ponytail.

Fin raised a horn to his lips to give the signal to move off, but Saxon placed a restraining hand on the commander's shoulder. The Baron then rode through his parting men-at-arms to pull up in front of the members of the Brotherhood.

'All the soldiers who defend the High Coast have a valuable role to play today,' he said, his blue eyes resting on Caspan, Roland and Sara. 'But none more so than you. You can end this fight before it even starts. I only wish we had more magical flying guardians to assist you.'

'Geez, there's no pressure on us,' Roland muttered.

Saxon smiled doggedly, then turned to Shanty and Kilt. 'Are you ready to ride out?'

Kilt nodded and swung lithely atop her panther, Whisper. She turned to Caspan. 'I know you think you're going to be safe, flying several hundred feet above the Roon ships, but be careful. There's no telling what surprises they'll have in store for you.'

Roland snorted dismissively. 'This fight's as good as won.'

Saxon's expression was grim. 'I hope you're right, because if we don't win today the High Coast will fall. The Roon will press forward until they join up with the northern army. They'll then press on to Briston and lay siege to the capital.' He regarded Caspan, Roland and Sara earnestly. 'I wish you the best of luck. We're all counting on you.' Turning his stallion, the Baron rode back to join Fin.

'Well, I guess this is where we say farewell,' Sara said to Kilt and Shanty. 'Promise you'll be careful.'

Kilt smiled bravely. 'We'll see you back in the hall tonight to celebrate our victory,' she boasted before riding off to join Saxon's men-at-arms.

'Don't worry,' Shanty assured Sara. 'I'll keep an eye on her.'

Caspan was sure the dwarf would do his best, but he knew anything could happen in the chaotic thick of battle. Surviving had just as much to do with chance as skill with a blade. Still, Kilt would have Whisper fighting by her side, and he couldn't think of any better protector.

Caspan knew Kilt felt cheated that she didn't get to play a more active role in their previous mission into Caledon. The boys had infiltrated the highland fort, snuck into the tomb, discovered the hidden Dray weapon, then fought their way out. Meanwhile, Kilt had waited, twiddling her thumbs, back in the camp atop the bluff. She hadn't said as much, but Caspan could tell from the resolute glint in her eyes that she was determined to prove her worth this time and get her fair share of the action. She was a skilled fighter, but he worried that she'd be too eager to face the enemy and throw caution to the wind.

Fin's horn sounded, and Saxon led his troops through the barbican and beneath the portcullis. Shanty pointed a finger in warning at Caspan, Roland and Sara. 'Remember — watch each other's backs and don't do anything foolish. War is a cruel mistress; she rarely gives second chances.' He gripped his reins and steered his magical faun, Ferris, after Kilt and Whisper.

The friends stood silently as they watched the soldiers exit the fort. Soon all that could be heard of them was the distant crunching of their horses' hooves on the snow-covered track and the jingling of armour. It wasn't long before these noises faded and were replaced by the sound of the sea-eagle banners above the gatehouse, flapping in the slight breeze.

CHAPTER 3

FROSTBITE'S NEW TALENT

The friends summoned their Wardens. Roland's manticore, Bandit, and Sara's pegasus, Cloud Dancer, weren't particularly fond of the cold and snow. In fact, Caspan was certain they hated it.

In spite of his bulk and fearsome appearance, Bandit was a delicate thing. It was hard for Caspan not to laugh when the Warden whimpered as he tried to tip-toe around a puddle of icy slush that had formed near the stable. Cloud Dancer didn't fare much better. She shivered as soon as she was summoned and tried to warm herself by a fire in a nearby iron brazier. All the while she stared at Sara, as if pleading to dismiss her back to the astral plane.

In contrast, Frostbite took to the cold like a duck to water. Caspan's drake seemed invigorated and rolled about blissfully in a deep patch of snow at the base of the castle wall. He made an unusual grunting sound, like a dog makes when gnawing on a bone, and wiggled his tail joyously. Never before had Caspan seen Frostbite in such a playful mood, and he was reminded that drakes were distant relatives of the wyverns and dragons that lived in the icy wastes east of Vorsklagov. This was the first time he had summoned his Warden since the snow started falling yesterday, and he wondered if perhaps only now, after four months, he was really seeing the true Frostbite.

'There'll be plenty of time for frolicking about later,' Caspan said to his Warden, whistling for him to return to his side. The drake dutifully obeyed his command, and it was when Caspan was securing the drake's specially crafted saddle-blanket that he stopped and gave his Warden a curious look.

Roland glanced up from adjusting Bandit's straps. 'What's up?'

'I'm not too sure.' Caspan placed his palm in front of Frostbite's snout. Small clouds of grey air were puffing out of his nostrils. He withdrew his hand quickly and looked to his friends, baffled. 'It's scalding hot.'

'That's strange. He's never done that before,' Sara commented as she finished tightening Cloud Dancer's harness.

Caspan stared in wonder at Frostbite. 'You don't think . . .'

'No, surely not,' Roland interjected. 'If he was going to start breathing fire, then he would have done it long before now.' He turned to Sara. 'Wouldn't he?'

Sara shrugged. 'You'd think so. But then again, Frostbite is related to fire-breathing dragons.'

'Well, there couldn't have been a better time for him to start,' Roland said. 'Mind you, he could have been a little more considerate and started yesterday. Then we wouldn't have had to waste all that time filling and stacking the bladders. We mightn't even need them now.' He rubbed his hands excitedly. 'Hey, Cas, see if you can get him to burn something.'

Sara nodded eagerly and pointed at the snowman near the castle wall. Roland had made it yesterday evening, when Caspan and the girls had been busy preparing their aerial arsenal.

Roland was aghast. 'No! Not Mr Edmund J. J. Cold Toes!'

Caspan grinned. He led Frostbite over towards the wall, then tried his best to demonstrate how to breathe fire through his nose. He felt incredibly silly, especially with Roland laughing hysterically at his efforts, but then Frostbite inhaled, craned his neck forward, and shot twin geysers of blue-coloured fire out of his nostrils, incinerating the snowman.

Roland pouted his bottom lip sadly, removed his bonnet and held it over his heart. 'Poor Mr Edmund J. P. Cold Nose. His sacrifice will never be forgotten.'

Sara arched a curious eyebrow at him. 'I thought his name was Mr Edmund J. *J.* Cold *Toes*?'

Roland silenced her with a raised hand and suppressed a wry smile. 'Please, show a little respect, Sara, you cold-hearted woman. This is painful enough as it is.'

Caspan stared at Frostbite in amazement. 'Aren't you full of surprises?'

'Just make sure he doesn't sneeze on anybody,' Roland cautioned. 'Things could get a little *roasty*, if you take my meaning.' He reached into his pocket and pulled out Bandit's black face mask. He tied it around the manticore's head and patted him encouragingly on the neck. Roland winked at his friends, held Bandit by the cheeks, and stared hard into his eyes. 'I know breathing fire might be a bit much to ask for, but I'm sure you've got some hidden talents. So, what have you got for me, buddy?'

The corner of Bandit's lips curled mischievously. He then yawned in Roland's face, sending the boy staggering away, coughing and gagging.

'What on earth have you been eating?' Roland said as he dropped to his knees and shoved snow into his mouth. 'Forget Frostbite's fire-breathing. All we have to do is get Bandit within twenty yards of the Roon and get him to breathe on them!'

Caspan chortled, then turned to Sara. 'But why would Frostbite wait until now to do this? And why didn't Master Scott warn me? He also has a drake guardian, and he never said anything about Shimmer breathing fire.'

'Remember that Frostbite had been in hibernation for a thousand years,' Sara explained. 'Perhaps he'd simply forgotten how to breathe fire, and it's an ability that's been triggered by the cold. And Shimmer, well, maybe she's never seen snow before? It might be that Master Scott has spent every winter in the deserts of Salahara, searching for Dray tombs.' She rubbed her chin thoughtfully. 'But Roland was right: Frostbite's timing couldn't have been better. The Roon are going to get the shock of their lives.'

'And let's not even get started on what he can do to snowmen,' Roland said pointedly.

Caspan shoved Roland playfully. 'We'll stick to the bladders as planned,' he said. 'After what happened at Saint Justyn's, I'd like to keep Frostbite well and truly clear of Roon archers.' He quickly finished harnessing Frostbite. The friends then secured large wicker baskets to the sides of their Wardens. These would later be filled with the bladders, which awaited them at Haven's Watch.

Caspan climbed atop Frostbite and glanced solemnly at his friends. 'It's time.'

Sara swallowed and nodded wordlessly while Roland grinned wolfishly and hooted as he swung atop Bandit. He flicked his manticore's reins, sending him rising out of the courtyard with several powerful beats of his wings. The black-haired jester looked down at his friends and waved for them to hurry up and join him.

'Come on. What are you waiting for?' he hollered. 'This is going to be epic.'

Sara gripped her reins in trembling fingers and turned to Caspan. 'I stand corrected. He's not only simple and uncomplicated, but a complete and utter puddenhead.'

Chapter 4
AERIAL ATTACK

The friends first stopped off at Haven's Watch. Assisted by the sentries at the signal pyre, it didn't take long to fill the wicker baskets with the bladders. With lit lanterns attached to their belts, the treasure hunters then headed out to sea to attack the Roon fleet.

Caspan led, with Sara and Roland following close behind. Caspan was eager to climb sharply, to hide behind the low-lying clouds so that the Roon wouldn't see them coming and have time to prepare for their attack. But Cloud Dancer wasn't a particularly strong flier, and Caspan was concerned that if they rose too quickly not only might Sara struggle to hold position but they might also lose some of their precious cargo. With this in mind, Caspan guided his friends up gently, then levelled off once they reached the clouds.

It was like floating through a sea of mist, with Frost-bite's splayed tail snaking slowly behind, leaving a trail in their wake. Beneath his black hood, Caspan's sharp eyes spied through breaks in the grey blanket, studying the sea below. He doubted any Roon archers would be able to hit them at this height, but he wanted to remain hidden until he and his friends launched their attack.

It took them about a quarter of an hour to reach the Roon. Caspan alerted Roland and Sara, and flew Frost-bite into a large cloud that provided perfect cover. He pulled back gently on Frostbite's reins, slowing the drake down, then turned to the right, towards a hazy break in the grey screen, from where he could peer down at the enemy.

Since spying on General Brett and Roy Stewart back in Caledon, Caspan had known all along that they would face an invasion force of over three thousand Roon. Before, when peering from the headland, it had been difficult to spot the distant boats and appreciate the size of the fleet. But nothing could have prepared Caspan for the shock of seeing such a large force up close, and he shuddered.

Even from this height, Caspan could see the dragon heads carved into the ships' prows and the circular iron-rimmed shields slung over their sides. Each boat was equipped with a single sail, which billowed in the wind, driving its crew steadily towards the High Coast. The ships could also be propelled by oars, but these lay in rows on the decks, kept in reserve, Caspan reckoned, for when the giants needed an extra spurt of speed. A helmsman stood at the rear of each ship, steering the vessel by means of a great wooden rudder. They were assisted by navigators standing at the prow, who charted their course towards the cove. The rest of the crew sat in rows on storage chests and crates that doubled as seats, their swords and axes gripped in their hands, ready for combat.

Caspan selected a bladder and exposed its wick to his lantern's candle. He waited until Roland and Sara had done likewise, then, with his heart racing, began their attack. They kicked their heels into their Wardens' flanks, sending them diving out of the clouds. The foremost of the Roon vessels were almost directly below them, and the friends carefully timed their shots, compensating for the distance and the movement of the ships. They watched with bated breaths as the bladders fell towards their targets.

Roland cursed as his splashed into the sea several yards behind one of the boats, causing its helmsman and several crewmen to spin around in alarm. But Caspan and Sara had direct hits. Their bladders landed midship and exploded upon impact, engulfing the decks in fire. Ignited oil splattered onto the sails, which burst into flames, sending billowing plumes of smoke into the sky. Giants scrambled desperately for their lives and dived overboard, leaving the ships to drift aimlessly.

One vessel veered to the right and rammed into another ship with such force that the iron-rimmed keel of its projecting dragon prow almost cleaved the other boat in half. Wood splintered and giants screamed as they abandoned ship. Water flooded into the breach, and the shattered mid-section quickly sank into a frothing grave. Soon all that was left was the end of the stern and the dragon head, which slipped into the water like a sea serpent. Jubilant, the friends directed their Wardens back into the clouds and lit new bladders.

'Two down, only ninety-eight left to go,' Roland said, then sent Bandit swooping down for their next assault.

This time he carefully studied the speed of one of the lead ships and hooted triumphantly when the bladder hit its mast and exploded, sending a fiery shower over the deck. Sara again was successful, with a direct hit mid-deck. The Roon tried desperately to combat the fire with their cloaks and blankets, but these merely caught fire. Even buckets of water proved ineffective, splashing the oil about so that it spread to other parts of the ship, which was soon consumed by the uncontrollable blaze.

Caspan timed his shot to perfection, certain that he would hit his selected ship a yard or two in front of its mast, but the helmsman must have seen him release the bladder and pulled his rudder hard to the right. Assisted by a large swell, the boat sped ahead and veered away, avoiding Caspan's attack by several yards.

Vowing that he'd do better next time, Caspan kept Frostbite hovering above the ship and readied his next bladder. There was no point returning to the cloud for cover, now that the Roon knew they were up there. It was better they stay where they were and try to hit as many ships as possible.

Peering down, Caspan noted that many of the enemy vessels had now readied their oars. The giants wouldn't be able to outrun the Wardens, but they could at least try to steer clear of the falling bladders. And it was a tactic that worked effectively, with four of the next six targeted ships avoiding the oil attacks.

'This isn't working,' Roland yelled to Caspan and Sara. 'We need to go lower so they won't have time to evade us. It will also allow Frostbite to blast them.'

Sara shook her head. 'Their archers will pick us off. What we need to do is coordinate our attacks on one ship. We'll use more bladders, but at least one of us should hit our target.'

'It sounds like a great idea,' Caspan commented, leading Frostbite above a ship. 'Let's see how it works on this one.'

Sara and Roland organised themselves into position, hovering several yards on either side of Caspan and prepared their next bladders. Roland then moved Bandit a dozen body-lengths forward, looked back and nodded.

Caspan dropped first. As anticipated, the helmsman cried out in alarm and pulled hard to the right, steering his vessel clear of Caspan's bomb, but moving the ship into the direct path of Sara's. The helmsman steered sharply back to the left and the giants struggled on the oars. Those on the port side dug theirs deep into the water and pulled hard in reverse; those on the starboard put their backs into it and rowed frantically until the water churned. The boat barely managed to avoid Sara's attack, but it was now floundering with little speed and was an easy target for Roland. He thrust a clenched fist in the air and cheered when his bladder hit the front of the deck. The Roon that managed to escape the fiery blast abandoned their oars and scrambled to the rear of the ship, where they tried to combat the flames. But there was nothing they could do to save the vessel, and they leapt overboard.

Roland gave his friends a triumphant smile. 'That's how we do it.'

'But we won't have enough bladders,' Sara said. 'We planned on two per ship, not three.'

Caspan stared grimly at the Roon armada. 'We have no other choice. All we can do now is keep singling out ships and coordinate our shots to take out as many as possible.'

'Leaving the rest for our fleet to deal with,' Roland commented dourly. 'I don't have to remind you that Kilt and Shanty are aboard one of those ships.'

'I don't like it any more than you do, but there's no other option,' Caspan replied. 'Let's just make sure every bladder counts.'

Sara made a quick mental calculation. 'Meaning that if there are at least one hundred ships, we'll only destroy sixty at most.'

Caspan stared at her fixedly. 'As I said, make each bladder count.'

He glanced back at the distant coast, imagining all the soldiers watching the aerial assault, putting their faith in the three young Brotherhood members and their magical guardians to destroy the enemy fleet before it neared the cove. Never before had Caspan felt such accountability. He usually thrived under pressure — it sharpened his senses and forced him to perform to the best of his ability.

But now he and his friends carried the fate of Andalon on their shoulders. It was an immense burden, and he hoped they wouldn't let the kingdom down.

For another half hour the three companions and their Wardens continued attacking the Roon fleet. They followed the same battle formation as before, with Caspan dropping his bladder first. Sara would then move into position to cut off the fleeing ship, forcing it to steer sharply in the opposite direction and lose its momentum, leaving the enemy ship at Roland's mercy. Occasionally a boat would try to outrun Sara's bomb and fail, saving Roland from wasting one of his precious cargo. Still, by the time the friends exhausted their load, only thirty-five Roon vessels had been destroyed.

What was alarming was that the trio had now gone through half of the bladders they had prepared. They'd also wasted precious time flying back to Haven's Watch to resupply. The Roon had started to split up, giving themselves more room to manoeuvre, but this also meant that it took the friends longer to organise themselves into position above each ship. By the time they returned from the headland with their remaining bombs, there would be no telling how far the Roon would have dispersed from each other. Even more precious time would be wasted hunting down the vessels.

Caspan glanced back anxiously, and noticed that the Roon were drawing closer to the coast with each stroke of their oars. He hoped he and his friends would be able to resupply and make it back out in time to complete their attack. If they didn't, the Andalonian fleet would emerge from the next cove and intercept the giants. Having seen the fury of the Roon back at Saint Justyn's and Darrowmere, Caspan feared many men would lose their lives.

'Come on,' he said, urging Sara and Roland to follow him back to Haven's Watch.

Roland went to flick Bandit's reins, when he was distracted by movement on the horizon. Curious, Caspan followed his gaze and peered hard at the grey blanket of clouds, soon spotting what had alarmed his friend.

Sara saw it too and clapped a hand over her mouth in alarm. 'We've got to get out of here!'

Caspan stared at the dark shapes that soared towards them. 'You head back and reload. Frostbite and I will take care of them.'

Roland shot him a defiant look. 'There's no way we're leaving you to face them on your own. Even with Frostbite breathing fire, there are too many of them for you to handle.' He sneered and gripped the haft of the broadsword strapped by his side. 'Besides, Bandit and I've been itching for a fight all morning. Our blood's up, and there's no way we're running away now.' As if to add credence to his words, Bandit bared his teeth and growled ominously.

Caspan didn't know how much use Roland's sword would be against the new enemy they faced, but Bandit was a formidable fighter. He feared though that Sara and Cloud Dancer, who lacked the aerial manoeuvrability and fighting skill of the other Wardens, would be torn to shreds. He stared hard at Sara. 'You need to go back. Cloud Dancer won't stand a chance against them. And Roland and I won't be able to fight them if we're trying to protect you.'

Caspan thought Sara would stubbornly refuse to leave, but was relieved when she nodded, kicked her heels into her pegasus and headed back towards the coast. She looked at her friends, fear and worry etched on her features. 'For goodness sake, be careful.'

Caspan nodded, drew a steadying breath, and turned to Roland. 'Are you sure you want to do this? It's not too late to join Sara.'

Roland rolled his shoulders, removed his bonnet and tucked it under his belt. 'I'm going to pretend I didn't hear that, ye wee Jimmy.' He drew his sword and pointed at one of the approaching dark shapes. 'You and Frostbite can take care of that one over there. Leave the other five for me and Bandit.'

Caspan grinned crookedly before taking a firm hold on Frostbite's reins. 'Right, let's show them what our Wardens can do.'

The boys kicked their heels into their guardians' flanks and sped off to face the six approaching rocs.

CHAPTER 5

ROCS

Caspan had encountered a roc before during the siege of Darrowmere, and the memory filled him with dread. The enormous eagle had attacked him, Lachlan and Morgan whilst they dropped oil-filled bladders on the Roon army. All they'd been able to do was out-manoeuvre the bird, luring it into a deep dive, then turning sharply at the last moment, sending the roc ploughing into a forest. But it had been night then, and this time the friends wouldn't have the cloak of darkness to use to their advantage.

The rocs were much larger than the Wardens, with hooked talons the size of scimitars and powerful beaks that could snap through tree trunks. They were also faster; not even Talon, the fastest of the Wardens, could outrun the roc they faced at Darrowmere. But for what the Wardens lacked in size and speed, they were more manoeuvrable, and it was this that Caspan hoped would give them the edge in the ensuing fight. Frostbite and

Bandit could weave and dart through the sky, avoiding the cumbersome birds. They could then swoop back in and attack the rocs in their exposed flanks.

As they flew closer, Caspan was surprised to find that there were Roon sitting atop the rocs. Caspan knew that the Roon trained the enormous birds to hunt game in the icy wastes north of The Scar, but never before had he heard of a giant riding a roc. They didn't appear to be confident at it, hunched over the rocs' necks, clinging tightly to the saddle straps and reins. Perhaps the giants had been inspired to fly rocs after their encounter with Talon at Darrowmere, and Caspan hoped that their lack of experience in performing aerial manoeuvres would give him and Roland a distinct advantage. But it was Frostbite's ability to breathe fire that Caspan believed would win them the fight. The only problem was that he hadn't trained the drake to deliver his fiery attack, and he hoped Frostbite would use his initiative and attack at will.

'Stay behind me,' Caspan cautioned Roland, who was starting to pull ahead. 'Frostbite's going to need a clear line of fire. Stay on our tail and make sure nothing tries to hit us from behind.'

Roland nodded, pulled back and positioned Bandit a few body lengths behind the drake. The boys then sat low over their mounts' necks as they sped towards the rocs.

The giant eagles moved incredibly fast and were upon them in no time at all. They folded their wings close by their sides and jutted their legs forward to reveal their talons, which were splayed wide, ready to rake and tear. But Frostbite never gave them the chance to attack. The drake pulled up and hovered in an upright position. His leathery wings stretched wide, he drew a deep breath and craned back his head. Caspan hung tightly around Frostbite's neck as he watched the rocs soar towards them, only to fly into the twin jets of blue fire that shot from Frostbite's nostrils. Caught by surprise, the giants' eagles shrieked and turned away. But it was too late for two of them, which were engulfed in Frostbite's fiery blast. Their feathers ablaze, the rocs whirled downward to the sea. Their scorched riders tried desperately to control them and yanked back on their reins, but nothing could pull the eagles out of the dive. It wasn't long before both rocs and Roon plunged into the rolling swells.

Two of the remaining rocs veered to the right, then swooped back towards Caspan. Frostbite turned to face them, and delivered a second cone of fire. One of the birds was caught by the blast and reared back, throwing its rider clear. The giant clawed through the air, searching frantically for something to grab hold of, then plummeted from sight. Its tail feathers and right wing scorched and smoking, the roc turned and fled.

Caspan barely had time to react before he realised what had become of the other two rocs. Roland cried out in warning, and Caspan turned just in time to see one of the rocs tearing at him from the right. He swung himself instinctively around Frostbite's neck, almost slipping from his saddle in the process, and barely avoided the talons that slashed through the air near his head.

The roc was so focused on attacking the drake that it had forgotten about Bandit, who sped forward to intercept the bird. The manticore's front paws and Roland's sword lashed out, hitting both the roc and its rider. The Roon gave a gargled cry and slumped forward in his saddle. Clutching his chest, he steered his injured mount free of the fight and headed back towards the Black Isles.

Distracted, neither Caspan nor Roland saw the second remaining roc until it was too late. It shot out of the clouds directly beneath Roland and crashed into Bandit with incredible force, sending the Warden tumbling through the sky in a welter of flailing legs and wings. Roland's sword flew from his hand and he clung tightly to his saddle, but nothing could save him when his saddle strap, cut by one of the roc's talons, snapped.

A scream caught in his throat, he fell.

Caspan reacted instantly and kicked hard into Frostbite's flanks. The drake shot downwards in a near-vertical descent. Caspan held tightly to the leather hand grips sewn into his saddle and hooked his heels into the drake's wingpits. The wind howled in his ears and he feared he would be ripped free, but he grit his teeth and held on for dear life, determined to save Roland.

Closer and closer to Roland they dived. Frostbite extended his claws to catch him, when a massive dark shape swooped in from the side. The roc snapped at Frostbite and slashed with its talons, but the drake twisted away, narrowly avoiding the attack. Caspan almost fell, but locked his fingers around the saddle grip and urged

Frostbite to continue after Roland. The sea was drawing closer with each passing heartbeat, and he feared they wouldn't get another chance to save his friend.

Out of the corner of his eye, Caspan saw the roc turn and head back towards them. Roland was only five yards away now. If they were lucky, they'd be able to catch him and still have time to evade the roc. But it was going to be close.

Frostbite tucked his wings even more tightly against his body, streamlining himself and diving even faster. With only twenty yards to spare before they plunged into the sea, Frostbite caught Roland. Caspan thought they'd never pull out of the dive in time. His heart racing, he squeezed his eyes shut, no longer able to watch, believing this was the end. Then he heard Roland yell triumphantly, and he peeped through his right eye to see they were speeding a yard above the ocean. Promising he'd pamper Frostbite with the longest belly-rub in the history of belly-rubs once the battle was over, Caspan sighed and relaxed back in his saddle.

The roc swept in from the side and slammed into Frostbite, sending the drake careening towards a monstrous, white-crested swell. Somehow, miraculously, the Warden managed to hold onto Roland and avoid all but the forked tip of his tail from hitting the wave. He banked hard to the right, his lowered wing tip carving through the water like a rudder. Frostbite brought himself around until he was facing the roc's exposed flank. For an instant, Caspan and the roc's rider's gazes met. The giant sneered and yanked hard on his reins in an attempt to steer the roc around for another attack. Then all was eclipsed in a jet of scorching blue fire.

Frostbite pulled up and flew over the deadly blaze. Looking back over his shoulder, Caspan saw the stricken roc writhing about on the surface of the water, trying to douse its flaming feathers. Of the Roon, there was so sign.

In a manoeuvre they had practised during their training sessions back at the House of Whispers, Caspan leaned down, offered Roland his hand and swung him up onto the rear of the saddle.

'That was absolutely awesome!' Roland hooted as he strapped himself into the saddle. 'What's the chance of doing that again?'

Caspan shook his head in wonder and drew breath to tell Roland that he should thank his lucky stars he was still alive, when he heard a tremendous roar. Both boys looked skyward. The wolfish grin disappeared from Roland's face.

High above them, Bandit was locked in a vicious fight with the remaining roc.

The giant eagle dwarfed Bandit, but the manticore appeared to be holding his own. The roc had locked its talons around the Warden's torso and was trying to bite into Bandit's neck. But for what he lacked in size, Bandit made up for in aggression and fighting ability. He fended off the roc's snapping beak with his front paws, and scratched and tore into the bird's mid-section with his rear legs, filling the sky with a cloud of feathers. But it was Bandit's scorpion tail that he used to his greatest advantage — he whipped it around to stab the roc in the side. The barb on its end was poisonous, but it would take a few minutes for it to have an effect upon such a large opponent.

Before Caspan could give the command, Frostbite shot upwards and flew straight towards the combatants. One hand tightly gripping the saddle, Roland reached forward and drew Caspan's sword from his scabbard. The black-haired boy then slapped the flat of the blade against Frostbite's rear flank, urging him to fly faster.

They had almost reached the fight and were sure they'd make it in time to help Bandit when disaster struck. The roc forced its beak past Bandit's forelegs and tore into the side of the manticore's neck. Roland cried out and waved his sword furiously in the air, watching helplessly as Bandit was tossed around like a rag doll. The Roon atop the giant eagle leaned out and thrust his broadsword deep into the Warden, just below his right foreleg. Bandit roared, tore free from the roc and drove his tail forward, spearing the roc through the chest. The bird contorted in a spasm of pain and gave an ear-piercing screech before flying away.

Bandit tried to give chase but stopped after several yards. His wings and tail dropped, his right foreleg hung limply, and his mane was matted red. He roared one final time. His noble head slumped onto his chest and he fell from the sky.

'No!' Roland screamed, almost leaping from Frostbite to save his magical guardian.

Caspan reached back and grabbed him by the tunic. Knowing they'd never reach Bandit in time and that

Frostbite didn't have the strength to grab hold of the massive manticore and lift him to safety, he instructed Roland to do the only thing possible.

'Dismiss him!' he urged.

Roland was so lost in his despair that he didn't hear Caspan. He stared wide-eyed at his plummeting Warden, his lips trembling.

'Roland!' Caspan yelled and shook Roland, this time drawing his friend's gaze to meet his. 'Bandit's got one last hope. You have to dismiss him. Hopefully he'll be able to recover once he's back in the astral plane. But he'll stand no chance if he hits the sea from this height.'

Roland nodded dumbly, raised his soul key to his lips and whispered Bandit's secret name. Fifty yards above the water, the manticore disappeared in a cloud of luminous blue smoke. His black face mask fluttered down to the sea.

Roland stared blankly at where he had last seen his Warden. 'Do you think he'll make it?'

Never before had Caspan seen Roland so upset. He was reminded of the emptiness and grief that had consumed him when he had almost lost Frostbite back at Saint Justyn's. He had grave fears for Bandit, but for Roland's sake he tried his best to sound optimistic.

'It's going to take more than a roc to knock Bandit out of action,' he said softly. 'But I'd say he's going to need a lot of rest. I know you'd want him fighting by your side, but I think Bandit's played his part in this war.'

Roland sniffed and wiped his glove across his nose. He drew a deep, steadying breath, then reached into his tunic and replaced his bonnet atop his head. His eyes narrowed determinedly. 'I think we've seen the last of the rocs. We should return to Haven's Watch.'

Caspan gave him a concerned look. 'Are you sure you're okay?'

Roland nodded and grinned, but Caspan could sense the dark, seething rage that brewed beneath it.

'I'm just dandy.' Roland jerked his chin back towards the distant coast. 'Now stop worrying about me and let's hurry back to join Sara. We've still got time to load up and launch another attack on the ships.'

Caspan regarded his friend a moment longer. Knowing they had no option but to return to the headland to restock on bladders, he steered Frostbite around and headed for the coast.

CHAPTER 6

THE MANGY DOG

Their baskets full again with incendiary bombs, the friends flew back out to sea and tried to take out as many ships as possible. As Caspan had anticipated, the enemy vessels were even more dispersed, many sailing with a gap of one hundred yards between them. Valuable time was wasted as the friends hunted down individual boats. It was also made more difficult by the fact that they were missing Bandit. Caspan tried his best to steer Frostbite into position so that Roland, sitting in the rear of his saddle, could drop a final bladder, but the drake and pegasus were starting to tire.

To make matters worse, the wind had become a howling gale that whipped the sea into a frenzy. The Roon used this to their advantage, riding the massive swells that surged towards the coast. The powerful wind also buffeted the riders and their Wardens, and blew many of their incendiary bombs off target.

In spite of this, the friends managed to destroy a further two dozen boats before they exhausted their supplies and were forced to return to land. They dismounted at Haven's Watch and warmed themselves before the signal pyre. Nobody felt like speaking, particularly after what had happened to Bandit, and they stared grimly out to sea, watching the twenty Andalonian sloops head out to intercept the fifty or so remaining Roon boats.

'They won't stand a chance against so many.' Sara lowered her gaze. 'We failed them.'

Caspan stood motionless, wondering if perhaps they could have utilised their Wardens more affectively. 'We did the best we could. And we had no way of knowing the Roon were going to use rocs against us. When you think about it, we're lucky we came out as well as we did.'

'Tell that to Bandit,' Roland muttered, and brushed irritably at a fine layer of sleet on his shoulders. 'Well, I don't know about you lot, but I can't just stand here and watch. Can one of you give me a lift down there?'

Sara regarded him sombrely. 'Your sword won't change the outcome of the fight.'

'I know, but I can at least try.' Roland's eyes gathered darkly. 'Besides, I've got a score to settle with the Roon for hurting Bandit.'

Caspan too wanted revenge for what had happened to the manticore, but he also felt that he'd let Baron Saxon down. He'd hoped that his aerial attack would have destroyed the enemy fleet, but half of the Roon invasion force still remained. Caspan was tired and frustrated, but was determined to return to the fight. He felt he owed it to Bandit and the Baron.

'I'll take you down,' he said to Roland, then turned to Sara and placed a hand on her elbow. 'But I want you to stay here. I'm sure Saxon will appreciate an extra pair of eyes — if things don't go in our favour in the naval engagement, you can warn General Liam and tell him to get ready. You're also a good shot with a bow, and could join the archers further back down the headland.'

There were three signal pyre sentries, who stood in the shade of a tree near the cliff top, carefully watching the Andalonian fleet sail out. Their mounts were tethered nearby, and they would ride down to the beach to give reports to the General. But it was a distance of over a mile and would take a few valuable minutes to travel. In contrast, Sara could easily fly Cloud Dancer off the cliff and over the cove, arriving at the beach in no time at all.

Sara nodded in agreement. Caspan pointed at the longsword sheathed by her side.

'I might need that, though.'

Sara unbuckled her blade and handed it to him. 'You're probably sick to death of hearing me say this, but promise you'll be careful.'

Caspan smiled softly. 'I cross my heart.'

'And don't do anything foolish,' Sara warned Roland. 'I know you're worried about Bandit, we all are. But getting yourself killed isn't going to make him any better.'

Roland snickered and glanced at Caspan. 'I'm ready whenever you are.'

Caspan raised a wary eyebrow at Sara and strapped on the sword. 'We should get going.' He climbed atop Frostbite and gave Roland a hand up onto the saddle, then leaned forward to pat his Warden on the neck. 'I know you've done a lot today, Frostbite. Just one more flight, I promise. Then I'll give you a well-earned rest.'

Frostbite turned and stared at him flatly with his ruby-red eyes. He shook off the sleet coating his wings, leapt into the sky and flew towards the Andalonian fleet.

Caspan felt a twinge of dread as he gripped the haft of his new sword. Hopefully no more of his companions or their magical guardians would be injured.

It didn't take Caspan and Roland long to catch up to the sloops. They circled above them until they spotted Shanty, Kilt and their Wardens. Caspan set Frostbite down near the ship's bow, and they were quickly joined by their friends. Shanty greeted the boys with an outstretched, gauntleted hand. The dwarf's grip was as strong as a vice at the best of times, and Caspan winced as he shook his hand.

'Ah, toughen up,' Shanty said, grinning at Caspan's discomfort and reaching up to clap him on the shoulder. 'You've spent too much time thieving and picking locks. You've got the delicate fingers of a girl.'

Kilt cleared her throat, prompting the dwarf to raise a conciliatory palm. 'There's no need to get offended, lass. I was merely making a point.'

Kilt stared at him fixedly and held up her hands. 'Like it or not, these delicate things will be fighting by your side and might well end up saving your life.' Her panther, Whisper, stood beside her and growled disdainfully at the dwarf.

Shanty tugged uneasily at the collar of his cloak. 'Well said, and I wouldn't have it any other way. Spoken like a true shield maiden.' He turned to Roland, evidently eager to change the topic of discussion. 'We saw what happened to Bandit. I'm so sorry. If there's any consolation, at least you managed to dismiss him before he fell to his death. Hopefully he'll make a full recovery.'

'You two will be back to your usual pranks in no time at all,' Kilt added. 'Although, I'm not sure I'm looking forward to that.'

A faint smirk played at the edges of Roland's lips and he gave a slight nod of thanks. He looked around the boat, his gaze resting on a man dressed in scarlet leather and wearing a wide-brimmed hat. A fancy jewel-encrusted cutlass was sheathed by his side in a well-oiled leather scabbard. He stood at the helm, his gloved hands gripping the wheel, guiding the boat over a swell.

Roland's eyes flashed with recognition. He pointed, speechless, at the man.

Shanty chortled and clicked his fingers in front of the boy, snapping him out of his trance. 'Yes, it's your hero, Captain Panter Grinn, Lord of the Pirates of the Black

Isles. And in case you hadn't noticed, we're aboard his boat, the *Mangy Dog*. It's our command ship.'

'And a finer vessel you won't find anywhere,' a familiar voice commented, and the boys turned to find Saxon standing behind them. The young baron ran his hand across the side rail. 'We've been hunting this ship for over two decades and never once have we come close to catching it.' He chuckled wryly to himself. 'And here I am now, standing at its bow, sailing off to fight the Roon. Who would have thought it possible?'

'And with Captain Grinn at the helm,' Roland added, still staring admiringly at the pirate.

Caspan smiled, relieved to see Roland returning to his normal self. He leaned in close and whispered in his ear, 'Maybe you should see if he wants to trade hats.'

Roland shook his head adamantly. 'Not on your life. I'll never give up my Strathboogie bonnet.' He chewed his bottom lip thoughtfully as he regarded the pirate. 'Still, I reckon I'd look dashing in that get-up.'

Saxon barked some commands at a group of nearby soldiers, instructing them to secure pieces of loose rigging, then looked back at the boys. 'I'm glad to have you aboard. Feel free to help the men manning the ballistae. They're always in need of an extra pair of hands. Now, if you'll excuse me, I have to discuss tactics with Captain Grinn.'

Roland licked his lips eagerly. 'Um, you don't mind if I tag along? I promise I'll be as quiet as a mouse and won't get in the way.'

'I'll believe that when I see it,' Kilt muttered.

Saxon beckoned for Roland to follow him. 'I can't see any harm in that.'

'All right!' Roland said excitedly, and hurried after the Baron.

'The poor baron doesn't know what he's got himself into,' Kilt commented before turning to Caspan. 'Roland seems to be coping okay with what happened to Bandit.'

'He's doing better now, but there's no way I was going to let him come here by himself,' Caspan replied. 'He's been momentarily dazzled by Captain Grinn, but he's out for revenge. I was going to fly back up to the headland, but I'll stay to keep an eye on him.'

Kilt nodded, then pointed at Caspan's sword. 'I'm surprised you didn't choose a bow.'

Caspan pulled a sour face. 'I wish I did, but I didn't have time to find one.'

'I know where there's some. There's a particularly nice longbow I'm sure you'll like. Come on, I'll take you there.' Kilt glanced at Shanty. 'I'm going to take Cas below deck to the storage room.'

'Don't be long,' the dwarf cautioned, staring boldly at the approaching Roon ships, which were no more than three hundred yards away. 'Things are going to heat up very soon.'

Caspan instructed Frostbite to wait beside Shanty and his guardian faun, Ferris, then hurried after Kilt and Whisper. They climbed down a staircase beneath the forecastle and walked along a corridor until they reached a room full of barrels and sacks. A few weapons racks stood against the rear wall, and it was here that Caspan found the longbow. It was indeed a nice weapon, constructed from a single stave of yew, with a back of taut sapwood and a belly of pliant heartwood. He tested its draw weight and gave Kilt a satisfied nod.

'I thought you'd like it,' Kilt said.

Caspan slung the bow over his shoulder, grabbed two full quivers from a nearby hook and attached them to the side of his belt. 'I prefer not letting the enemy get too close. Although, I don't know how effective I'll be out here. I've never used a bow on a boat before, and certainly not in a gale. The bobbing might spoil my aim.'

'You'll do fine. Besides, the Roon present large targets.'

Caspan murmured in agreement and turned to head back up to the deck, when Kilt held him by the wrist. 'What's up?' he asked.

The green-eyed girl regarded him earnestly and slowly released his hand. 'I've never really said sorry to you, have I?'

'For what?' Caspan feigned ignorance, even though he'd often wondered if Kilt would ever apologise for how she had bullied him during the first few weeks of their training with the Brotherhood.

'Don't act dumb with me. What do you think I'm talking about? I treated you terribly when we first met, and you were so undeserving. You never did anything to hurt me. And for all the nasty things I did to you, you never once bit back.' Kilt lowered her gaze ashamedly. 'I don't think I've ever treated anybody so badly. That is, anybody who didn't deserve it. So I'm really sorry for how I behaved.'

Caspan punched her playfully on the shoulder. 'Hey, water off a duck's back.'

Kilt smiled softly. 'Thanks, Cas. You know, you were right about me.'

'About what?'

'Once, back at the House of Whispers, you asked me if I'd been wronged by a footpad. I can't remember what I said.' Kilt laughed softly to herself and gave Caspan a sheepish look. 'I probably tried to beat you up. But the truth of the matter is that my father and I were robbed at knifepoint by a street thief in Briston. We were on our way to purchase property, and had all our life savings on us. We'd even mortgaged the small hut where we were living. We lost everything in an instant, and there was absolutely nothing I could do about it.' She stared hard at the ground. 'Until then, everything had been fine between me and my parents. But the next month they decided to marry me off to a rich merchant in exchange for a large dowry. That's when I ran away and hid in a cadet academy.'

'I don't blame you.' Caspan reached out, lifted her chin, and waited patiently for her to meet his gaze. 'But that's behind you now. My life wasn't exactly all sunshine and roses before I joined the Brotherhood. I often think back to what my life was like and I'm amazed I managed to survive. But that was the past. I've got a new life now, with great friends who I trust and respect. We're about to fight the most feared enemy to have ever invaded these lands, but I'll be standing alongside my closest friends, and I wouldn't change that for the world.'

Kilt's eyes softened. 'I saw how you saved Roland from falling to certain death. You risked your life to save me once too, back at the House of Whispers, when I fell from the rope. You're always looking out for us, prepared to put your life on the line to help us out. You're a good person, Cas. Don't let anybody ever tell you otherwise.'

Caspan had forgotten that Whisper had accompanied them down to the weapons racks. The snow panther had watched them from the shadows near the doorway. She now padded over to Caspan and did something that left him stunned.

She nuzzled against him and licked his cheek.

Kilt grinned. 'You see. Even Whisper thinks you're not too bad.'

Caspan smiled proudly and, for the first time, patted the great cat. Whisper purred, rubbed her flank against him and let her tail brush against his neck. Caspan grinned at Kilt and opened his mouth to comment, when a horn sounded from the deck, signalling everybody to prepare for combat.

The treasure hunters rushed back up the stairs.

CHAPTER 7

DRAGON SHIPS AND SQUALLS

Caspan was alarmed at how close the Roon boats were. Riding the enormous swells, they had come close to within fifty yards of the Andalonian sloops. He slipped the longbow from his shoulder and nocked an arrow as he raced after Kilt and Whisper to the front of the ship, where they joined Shanty, Ferris and Frostbite. Soldiers bustled all around them, manning ballistae, tightening rigging and readying their weapons. Officers strode by, barking commands and maintaining order. At the helm, Captain Grinn steered hard to the right, turning the *Mangy Dog* around until its starboard side faced three approaching Roon vessels.

Their dragon-headed bows burst over the waves like sea serpents rising out of the deep. The Roon handled their oars expertly, their strokes synchronised, setting a fast pace through the churning water. Several giants stood at the front of each boat, spears and axes gripped in their hands, ready to hurl at the crew of the *Mangy Dog*. They would then throw grappling hooks over and draw their boats alongside the pirate sloop. Once boarded, the slaughter would begin.

But they never got close enough to put their plan into action.

Rising over the crest of a large swell, the three Roon boats in perfect view, Baron Saxon bellowed the order for the ballistae on the starboard side to shoot. They fired, sending iron-headed bolts the size of harpoons soaring through the air. Two missed their targets, but the rest hit the fronts of the Roon ships. One smashed a wooden dragon head into a thousand splinters. Another skimmed off the curved side of the bow with no impact, but the others punctured gaping holes into two of the ships' hulls. Giants abandoned their oars and tried to stop the vessels from flooding, but water gushed on board and it wasn't long before the boats sank beneath the waves.

The Andalonian soldiers and pirates reloaded the ballistae in time to set off another round of shots at the remaining enemy boat. The Roon were only twenty yards away by now and closing fast, and the giants at the bow hurled their spears, one of which hit a *Mangy Dog* crew member in the chest and knocked him overboard. As the giants readied their grappling hooks, the ballistae targeted the sides of the boat. Upon Saxon's command they fired. This time all six metal-headed bolts blasted through the hull of the enemy ship. By the time Captain Grinn steered away to engage another pack of Roon boats, all that was left of the stricken ship was its mast, which sunk slowly into its watery grave.

The crew of the *Mangy Dog* cheered, but not all the Andalonian sloops fared as well. Six other Roon boats were sinking, their hulls breached, but three had managed to draw alongside Andalonian ships and board them. Their crews fought valiantly, but the Roon were too powerful and swarmed across their decks, cutting down those who stood before them.

His features set in a fierce grimace, Panter set a course between two enemy ships. The Roon helmsmen saw him coming and tried to intercept the *Mangy Dog*. They dug their rudders deep into the water, bringing their boats around and driving them through large swells, which showered their crews with spray. The Roon turned sharply, but the pirate sloop was sleek and faster, its sails full of wind and its keel slicing through the water like a knife. Saxon roared, giving the order to fire again. Ballistae bolts shot simultaneously from both sides of the *Mangy Dog*, blasting gaping holes into the enemy vessels.

Caspan held tightly to the bow rail with his free hand and stared grimly about him. Although the naval battle had only just begun, it had already degenerated into a chaotic mess of hurled spears, streaking ballistae bolts, ploughing oars and billowing sails. Everywhere he looked ships were being boarded or sinking, their crews being cut down or leaping overboard and swimming for their lives in the rough sea.

The sloops were larger and quicker than the enemy vessels, but they were completely dependent upon having the wind in their sails. Once they tried turning too sharply or changed direction they ran the risk of momentarily stalling. And this was when they became easy prey for the Roon.

Caspan was brought back to his senses by a gargled cry. He turned to find a soldier lying near his feet, killed by an enemy axe. Alarmed, he looked up, wondering from where the attack had come. His blood turned to ice. A Roon boat had skilfully concealed itself in a deep trough between two large swells and was heading straight for the *Mangy Dog*. Its crew straining on their oars, the Roon vessel burst out, barely twenty yards from the unsuspecting sloop.

Panter yanked his wheel hard to the left, trying desperately to avoid the dragon-headed bow, which threatened to slam into the side of the sloop. Roland leapt to the Captain's assistance and pulled on the wheel with all his might. The sloop's timbers groaned, and barrels and crates that hadn't been lashed down rolled dangerously across the tilting deck.

The *Mangy Dog* turned, but Caspan feared they'd never make it in time. The Roon vessel was almost upon them. Its dragon head raced down the side of a passing swell and reared like a great beast. Many of its crew abandoned their oars and gripped their swords and shields, ready to board the pirate sloop.

Caspan stood up dexterously and took aim with his bow at a giant straddling the dragon head. The Roon roared savagely and hammered the pommel of his broadsword against his bare chest, stirring himself into a berserk-like rage. Carefully timing his shot with the rocking boat, Caspan drew back the bow string to its full tension, exhaled slowly and released. The giant howled as the arrow hit him in the shoulder. But he merely snapped off the shaft and tossed it aside. His gaze locked on Caspan, and he snarled as he pointed his sword at him. The Roon climbed high up on the dragon head and made ready to leap across to the sloop.

Caspan stood his ground and set another arrow to his bowstring, but the Roon boat slid back behind the towering swell and disappeared from sight. As luck would have it, Panter and Roland steered the *Mangy Dog* around to catch the rolling wall of water, and the sloop sailed safely away.

The naval battle raged for well over an hour. Panter was an exceptional pilot, skilfully avoiding all enemy vessels that swarmed around them, and positioning the *Mangy Dog* so that its ballistae could deliver maximum damage.

Kilt grabbed a bow and quiver from below deck and joined Caspan in trying to pick off giants on approaching ships, but she wasn't that good a shot at the best of times, let alone aboard a rocking boat. Tossing her bow aside in frustration, she manned the ballistae at the prow. It was attached to a swivel base, allowing it to not only shoot straight ahead, but swing around to cover the starboard and port. For someone who had never fired a ballistae before, she performed admirably. Her first shot sailed way over the mast of a Roon boat, but the next seven were direct hits, puncturing deep holes into the hulls of enemy ships.

Shanty paced the deck irritably, complaining that he got all dressed up for nothing. Whenever an enemy ship looked as if it might get close enough to throw over its boarding lines, he gripped his sword and positioned himself so that he would be the first to engage the Roon. But Panter always managed to steer the *Mangy Dog* clear before bringing it around to expose the sides of the enemy ships to its ballistae.

'Blood and thunder!' Shanty bellowed when the sloop ploughed through a wave, drenching him in spray. 'All I'm going to do is rust out here!'

Caspan instructed Frostbite to keep low behind the bow rail, but the drake took up a lot of room. Frostbite often craned his head up, nostrils flaring as he searched for an enemy ship to incinerate. But Caspan quickly pulled him back down, fearful that the ignited Roon vessel might collide into the *Mangy Dog* and set it alight. When a spear thudded into the bow rail barely an inch from Frostbite's head, Caspan dismissed his drake. Frostbite growled and shot him an aggrieved look just before he disappeared in a cloud of blue smoke, but Caspan didn't want to run the risk of his Warden getting hurt unnecessarily.

Whisper remained by Kilt's side, but the panther was smaller than Frostbite and hunkered down behind the ballistae when in danger. During these moments she scraped her claws across the deck, sharpening them for battle. Ferris, meanwhile, chased after Shanty. When the sloop slid down the side of a mountainous swell, Shanty tripped over the faun.

'Damnation!' he roared as he lay on his back, weighted down by his armour. He tried to push away his Warden, who for some strange reason had decided to lie on top of him. 'How am I supposed to fight with you lounging all over me, you great big sack of fleas? Get off me!'

Wary of puncturing the hull of the *Mangy Dog* on a sunken ship, Panter ordered Roland to run to the prow and keep a careful eye out for submerged obstacles. Roland had spent his childhood aboard small fishing boats and knew exactly what to look for, guiding the sloop skilfully through the water. But nobody saw the Roon vessel that got behind the *Mangy Dog* until it was too late. Riding the swell the sloop left in its wake, the giants closed in on the ship.

Caspan and several soldiers rushed to the rear quarter deck of the sloop and loosed arrow after arrow at the giants. Several of the Roon were hit and slumped over their oars. The boat was soon bristled with feathered shafts. But the giants rowed at a furious pace until they drew alongside the *Mangy Dog*. Boarding lines were thrown, locking the boats together. The Roon then swarmed aboard the pirate ship.

'Finally, something I can attack!' Shanty yelled over the giants' battle cries.

Fighting erupted across the deck as the crew of the *Mangy Dog* tried to drive the giants back. But the Roon were too strong. The giants carved through the Andalonians with their broadswords and battleaxes, littering the deck with the dead and wounded. Shanty, Ferris, Saxon and a small group of soldiers and pirates gathered around the central mast and formed a defiant ring of steel. Caspan and the archers on the quarter deck shot arrows down at the Roon and tried to provide as much cover as possible. Some of the Roon tried to rush up the stairs to stop them, but a stalwart group of Andalonians formed a shield wall halfway up the stairs, blocking their path. Another blocked access to the elevated bow forecastle, from where another band of crewman armed with bows fired down at the giants.

Caspan sent a shaft thudding into the shoulder of a Roon facing Shanty, forcing him to lower his shield. The dwarf brought his sword down in a gleaming arc, sending the giant staggering back. Caspan dexterously nocked another arrow and finished off the Roon with a shot to the chest. But no sooner had the enemy slumped to the ground than two more giants pushed forward to take his place. They rained blow upon blow down on the dwarf, who braced his back against the mast and fended off their attacks with his sword.

Saxon cut down the giant directly in front of him and came to Shanty's aid, thrusting his sword into one of the Roon. The giant fell to his knees, and Saxon extracted his blade and delivered a wild swipe at the other Roon. The giant twisted and raised his axe to block the attack, leaving himself open to Shanty. The dwarf knocked the giant to the floor in a crumpled heap with a swing of his sword.

By now only a dozen Andalonian soldiers and pirates remained around the mast. A terrifying growl suddenly rose over the sounds of combat. Everybody froze and turned to the forecastle.

Whisper stood with her front forelegs against the balustrade, her fangs bared in a savage snarl. Atop the Warden sat Kilt, her blade gleaming and her green eyes blazing. She stared down at the Roon, then flicked her reins, sending the panther leaping over the railing and crashing into the enemy. Many were knocked aside and were cut down by Whisper before they could regain their feet. Roland and a band of pirates followed after Kilt, hurdling over the balustrade and launching themselves at the Roon.

Whisper tore through the giants, her claws slashing like daggers and rending through their armour. Kilt swung her sword in sweeping arcs, cutting down any giants that tried to attack her Warden in the flanks. Together, they cut and cleaved a path to Shanty and Saxon, allowing Roland and the pirates to join them.

'I'm glad you could make it,' Saxon said to the black-haired boy and ducked as an axe sailed past his helmet and thudded into the mast. As the giant struggled to free his weapon, the Baron drove his blade deep into the Roon's torso. 'I thought all was lost, but then *she* arrived.' Saxon stared admiringly at Kilt. 'I've never seen anyone like her before.'

Roland squeezed in between Shanty and Saxon. 'Kilt's one of a kind; I'll give her that. And if there's one thing I know about her, it's that you don't want to get her angry.'

'Perhaps someone should have told that to the Roon,' Shanty yelled over the clamour of clanging blades. He watched Kilt slay a giant with a powerful upper-hand swing of her sword, then screwed up his nose. 'Then again, maybe not.'

With Kilt and Whisper slaying all they came across, and Caspan and the archers loosing shafts until their quivers were empty, the Andalonians eventually gained the upper hand and drove the Roon back to their boat. Roland and Saxon severed the boarding lines, setting the Roon vessel adrift. Its sails full of wind, the *Mangy Dog* pulled away, leaving the enemy vessel far behind.

Shanty removed his helmet and wiped the sweat from his brow. 'That was well fought,' he said, turning to Saxon.

The young baron leaned against a side rail and cleaned his notched blade on a scrap of cloak. He nodded grimly and did a quick head count of the surviving Andalonians. Less than a quarter remained. 'But at a high price.' The Baron helped an injured soldier to his feet before beckoning over one of his officers. 'We have many wounded, Koln. See to it that an infirmary is set up in one of the storage rooms. Ensure there's clean water and bandages.'

'But what about the Roon, my lord?' Koln asked. 'We don't have many men left. Should we get boarded again I doubt we'll have the numbers to fight them off.'

'The injured are our priority now.' Saxon looked around at all the sinking and broken ships. Of the Andalonian fleet, four sloops remained. Only six Roon vessels had slipped past them and were now heading towards the cove. 'I think our part in this fight has come to an end.'

'Yes, my lord.' Koln saluted, and trudged off to do the Baron's bidding.

'I'll give you a hand,' Shanty called out to the officer. 'But not before somebody helps me out of this armour.'

He tried to reach behind his back to untie the leather cord of his chest plate, gave up and kicked the mast in frustration. Hearing laughter, he spun around and glared at Roland, who was chortling into his sleeve. 'Oh, that's right. Go ahead and chuckle.'

'Hey, don't get angry at me. I told you not to put on so much armour.'

Shanty smiled humourlessly. 'Well, I want to take it off now, don't I? And I'd appreciate a little help, if it's not too much to ask.'

Roland yawned and inspected his fingernails for a moment, before glancing questioningly at the dwarf. 'Sorry, did you say something?' He hooted and ducked as Shanty hurled his helmet at him. 'That's one piece off. Only seven hundred left to go. At this rate, you should be out of it by the end of the month.'

Caspan carefully inspected the surrounding sea, his final arrow still set to his half-drawn bow. Spotting no enemy boats in the area, he returned the arrow to his quiver and slung his bow over his shoulder. He made his way down to Shanty.

'Here, I'll give you a hand,' he said and started tugging at the strap.

'You see.' Shanty glared accusingly at Roland. 'You should pay close attention to Caspan. He knows how to respect his elders. There's a lot you can learn from him.'

Roland humphed, then assisted Koln as he searched for injured soldiers. Kilt, meanwhile, slid wearily from her saddle and hugged Whisper. The panther reciprocated by purring and licking her on the cheek.

'I'd hate to interrupt this special moment,' Saxon said, coming over to join them, 'but I'd like to thank you. We owe you and your Warden our lives. Never before have I seen such bravery. You were . . . well, remarkable.'

Kilt pushed Whisper gently away and bowed before the Baron. 'You're too generous, my lord.'

Saxon noticed she was cut on the arm and reached to inspect the injury. 'You're hurt!'

Kilt flinched at his touch, then saw the reassuring look in his eyes and relaxed. 'I hadn't even noticed. I'm sure it's nothing.'

'Still, I insist on letting my private physician tend to it when we return to Castle Crag. I'm not taking "no" for an answer.'

Kilt smiled softly. 'As you wish, my lord.'

Saxon returned her smile. 'Good. You don't want to risk infection.' He held her gaze for some time before he remembered he was still holding her arm. He cleared his throat and let go. 'I'm sorry.'

Kilt grinned. 'I was wondering when you were going to give me that back.'

Saxon quickly looked up at Panter, who stood at the helm, steering the *Mangy Dog* back towards the coast. The Baron pointed at the six Roon boats heading towards the cove. 'Are we going after them?'

'We'll follow them up to the headland,' the pirate replied and nodded to a crew member holding up a red flag. The man waved it above his head, signalling for the remaining ships to follow them. 'But we'll hold position in the cove entrance, trapping the Roon on the beach. If they try to escape, we'll sink them with our ballistae.'

Saxon grunted in approval and stabbed his sword into the deck. He leaned on the pommel and smiled ruefully. 'General Liam shouldn't have too much of a problem dealing with six boats. I know it's a little early to celebrate, but I'd say we've successfully defended the High Coast.'

Roland, who had been helping a wounded soldier to his feet, looked up and rubbed his hands excitedly. 'So there will be a celebratory feast in your great hall tonight?' The Baron smirked and nodded, and Roland added, 'With lots of sausages?'

Saxon slapped his thigh in mirth. 'Yes, there will be sausages galore.'

'Now that's my type of feast!' Roland said, licking his lips.

CHAPTER 8

THE FINAL BATTLE FOR THE HIGH COAST

The battle for the beach was brutal. All but one of the Roon boats came to a jarring halt when their hulls were impaled on the sharp stakes hidden beneath the waves. Surf swamped over the stricken ships and jostled them about, knocking Roon overboard. One of the vessels was flipped over by a towering wall of foam that surged towards it like an avalanche.

Many Roon that had trudged out of the surf onto the beach were injured or had lost their weapons. But they were far from beaten. Salvaging what weapons they could find, they formed up in three lines and advanced up the beach.

Those in the front line and on the sides raised their shields against the storm of feathered shafts loosed from the Andalonian archers, who were positioned at the grassy hillock at the end of the beach and atop the flanking cliff tops. Some Roon were hit and fell, but the rest closed ranks and pressed forward. Soon their shields were bristled with arrows and the dead littered the ground, but onwards the giants marched until they reached the trench in front of the berm. Into the ditch they swarmed, heedless of the sharp stakes and pig bladders stacked in its base. Andalonian soldiers tossed flaming torches into the trench, but they smouldered and fizzled out in the snow.

The Roon scrambled up the side of the ditch and launched themselves into the men of the First Legion. The Andalonians greatly outnumbered the Roon, but the tattooed giants fought like maniacs, smashing through the shield wall and slaughtering all they faced. Such was their bloodlust that some even slew their comrades.

No longer able to loose arrows upon the Roon for fear of hitting their own men, the cliff-top archers mounted up and galloped back along the headlands, determined to add their swords to the defence of the beach. Carefully watching the battle unfold from the prow of the *Mangy Dog*, Caspan caught a glimpse of Sara. She rode at the head of the troop upon Cloud Dancer, her black Brotherhood cloak flying in her wake. He lost sight of her when the riders rounded a copse of trees.

One of the Roon commanders saw the reinforcements riding along the cliff tops and roared for his men to fight harder. Their black-bladed swords and battleaxes hacked relentlessly into the Andalonians, until gradually the First Legion began to falter and withdraw. Before panic spread through their ranks, General Liam pushed through his troops on his warhorse and smashed into the Roon. His great blade carved a path through the enemy, and in his wake came Maul.

Nothing could stand before the ferocious bear, whose foot-long claws cut through mail armour like a heated blade through butter. The General's soldiers rallied behind him and his Warden, and re-formed their lines. Once a shield wall had been established, they pushed forward, forcing the Roon back towards the trench. The General and his men were making good progress until Liam, fighting in the front line, was cut down from his horse and disappeared amidst the slashing blades and slamming shields. One of his officers, wielding a shadow blade and carrying a flag, cried out in alarm. Word of the General's death spread like wildfire through the ranks of the First.

Separated from the General in the chaotic press, Maul gave a bloodcurdling roar and reared onto his hind legs. The Warden towered over the Roon and sent them flying through the air with tremendous swipes of his claws. But with Liam lost, the Andalonians' morale withered. Their right flank crumbled and men started to retreat.

But then, like a phoenix rising from the ashes, the General clambered to his feet. His armour was dented and stained red, but he was far from finished. He cut down the nearest Roon with a powerful swipe of his sword, then scrambled onto his horse and thrust his blade high above his head. A triumphant cheer rose from the ranks of the First Legion, and again they tightened their formation. Inch by agonising inch, they pushed the giants closer towards the trench.

The Roon made a defiant last stand at the edge, heaving their swords and axes until bodies piled before them, but they could not break through the opposing shield wall. The Andalonians pushed forward again, knocking the surviving giants into the pit. Those that managed to avoid the sharp stakes tried to scramble back up, but they met stiff resistance. Swords cut them down, and soon the trench was a mass grave for Roon.

The enemy defeated, an eerie silence descended over the battlefield. Where men and giants had fought only moments ago, snow drifted gently from the sky, blanketing the fallen in a fine white sheet.

General Liam swung gingerly out of his saddle, drove his sword into the ground and removed his helm. Two of his soldiers lifted him onto their shoulders. The rest of the First Legion amassed around them, chanting and cheering and thrusting their weapons triumphantly in the air.

Back aboard the *Mangy Dog*, Roland clapped Kilt and Caspan jubilantly on the shoulder. 'Now, didn't I tell you this was going to be epic?'

Kilt grinned and pushed him away. Caspan noticed she was unable to divert her gaze from Baron Saxon, who, upon seeing the celebrations upon the beach, passed around a waterskin.

'I don't think there's anything we can't do as a team,' Roland continued. 'Not even a Roon invasion force is too much for us.'

'Um, haven't you forgotten something?' a gruff voice asked, and the friends turned to see Shanty lying on his back, trying in vain to untie a leather thong securing one of his iron greaves.

'Let's not get ahead of ourselves,' Roland replied, and placed a hand on Caspan's arm to stop him from offering the dwarf assistance. 'A Roon invasion force is one thing, but taking off all those bits of armour is biting off more than we can chew. Besides, I don't know about you, but I'm feeling a little faint-hearted. Perhaps I've over-exerted myself.' He winked at Caspan and Kilt, pressed the back of his hand on his forehead in feigned exhaustion, and sat against the port rail. 'Ah, that's much better.'

Shanty glared at him. 'Duke Connal's going to have to look for a new Brotherhood member by the time I've finished with you!'

Roland yawned. 'Which means I've got about a decade left, given that's how long it'll take you to remove all that armour. Now do be a nice chap and keep the noise down. If it's not too much trouble, I might have a little nap.'

Shanty flushed red with rage, and Caspan and Kilt turned away and laughed into their sleeves. Roland might have survived the Battle of the High Coast, but they very much doubted he'd last long once Shanty got his hands on him.

CHAPTER 9

THE VICTORY FEAST

As promised, Baron Saxon put on a celebratory feast like no other. The great hall of Castle Crag was transformed from a spartan, lightless chamber into a dazzling display of colour and splendour. Gilded candelabra bedecked tables and chandeliers hung from the ceiling rafters, filling the hall with golden light. Sea-eagle tapestries draped down the walls, and satin-backed chairs provided comfortable seating for the guests, who milled near the central hearth with tankards in hand, or sat around the eight large tables laden with trays of suckling pig, roast quails, warm loaves of bread and jugs of sweet cider. Much to Roland's delight, there were plates full to over-spilling with sausages. Minstrels played lively tunes on lutes and pipes, and court jesters juggled balls and performed balancing tricks with chairs and swords, much to the guests' mirth.

'Now this is the type of life I could very easily get used

to,' Roland said, lounging back in his seat and rubbing his tummy contentedly.

Caspan grinned at him and motioned with his tankard at Roland's plate. 'How many servings is that? Three?'

'Three? Please, give me a little more credit than that. Try *six* full plates.' Roland burped indulgently and unbuckled his belt. 'Ah, that's better.' He eyed a platter of tarts at the far end of the table and licked his lips. 'I wonder if I can make room for some of those?'

'Eat as much as you want,' Caspan remarked. 'But don't think you'll be sleeping in my room tonight. You're belching like a pig!'

'So I'm destined for the pigpen?'

Caspan smirked and nodded. 'If you keep eating like that.'

'Where do you put it all?' Kilt asked Roland from across the table. 'There's nothing of you.'

The black-haired jester patted his belly. 'All in here, my dear Kilt.'

Kilt pushed aside her half-eaten plate. 'Well, I've had more than enough. And unlike you, I know when to stop.'

Roland chortled as he decided he would try the tarts after all and waved his fork to have them brought down to his side of the table. 'Glutton is as glutton does,' he announced proudly.

Caspan rolled his eyes and turned to Sara. She sat beside him, but had barely said a word all night. He wondered if perhaps she was thinking about the battle against the Roon. Caspan was no novice to combat now, having seen his fair share of fights since joining the

81

Brotherhood, but even he found himself distanced from the merriment at times, staring off into space, scenes of the battle flashing through his thoughts. It was during these moments that he wondered about Lachlan, who was left behind at the royal capital, too injured to participate in the fight. Since joining the Brotherhood, the boys had stood side by side during every battle. Caspan could picture him, standing atop the castle battlements, staring to the west, frustrated and angry.

'I bet he's glad he's out of his armour,' he said, and motioned towards Shanty with a flick of his eyes. The dwarf was standing on a table, waving his hands above his head as he danced a jig.

Sara grinned. 'I can't believe he finally coaxed Roland to help him.'

'"Coaxed" isn't the word I'd use. More like "threatened".' Caspan lowered his voice. 'Speaking of Roland, how do you think he's coping with what happened to Bandit?'

'He's putting on a brave face.' Sara leaned in close and whispered, 'One of the sentries up at Haven's Watch told me that Roland rode Georgina up there this afternoon.' She smiled sadly at the black-haired boy, who was devouring his second mince tart. 'He stayed there until sunset, staring out to sea, crying. I've also seen him pull out Bandit's soul key several times tonight and hold it against his heart when he didn't think anybody was watching. I'm sure he's hurting deep inside.'

Caspan nodded. 'That's what I think. Distraction is just what he needs.'

Sara smirked as she pointed at Shanty, who almost toppled off the table but flapped his hands about madly and made a quick recovery. Roland saw the display in the corner of his eye and laughed so hard he almost choked on his food. He banged his tankard on the table and bellowed, 'Encore! Encore!'

'Well, Roland's in the right place,' Sara remarked. 'There's no shortage of distraction here tonight.'

Caspan nestled back in his chair and sipped slowly at his drink as he regarded her. Again, he saw Sara's smile fade, leaving her with a sombre, almost troubled expression.

'Something's on your mind,' he said. 'Care to tell me what it is?'

Sara chuckled dismissively. 'I'm fine.'

'No, you're not. You've barely touched your meal and you've had a distant look on your face all evening.' Caspan nudged her and smirked. 'I know I can be boring at times, but please, you're crushing my self-esteem.'

Sara grinned and pushed him playfully. Then she sighed and gazed around the hall. 'Don't get me wrong — I really appreciate the feast Baron Saxon's thrown. It's worthy of royalty.' She clapped her hand to her mouth when Roland burped so loudly it left everybody at the table staring at him in stunned silence. 'Roland! My goodness, remember your manners.'

Roland's expression was one of roguish innocence. 'What? It's a sign of appreciation for the great food.'

Sara rolled her eyes and glanced back at Caspan. 'All this is fine, but don't you think it's a little premature?'

Caspan frowned. 'We defeated the Roon fleet and saved the High Coast. I think we have every reason to celebrate.'

Sara murmured in half-hearted agreement. 'I wonder if Master Morgan and Scott, and Oswald and Raven are celebrating too?' She turned to look at a nearby window. A cold wind rattled its shutters. 'They might be out there somewhere to the far east right now, fighting for their lives.'

The merriment drained from Caspan. He'd been so focused on defending the High Coast today that he hadn't had time to think about the other members of the Brotherhood. He suddenly felt incredibly selfish and guilty. 'You're right,' he muttered.

Sara placed a hand on his arm. 'I'm sorry. Now I've gone and spoiled your evening. I should have just kept my big mouth shut. I'm sure everything's fine and I'm worrying unnecessarily.'

Caspan shook his head, unconvinced. 'Saxon ordered messenger ravens out to the other armies and King Rhys with word of our victory. He also sent a message before the battle, informing the King that the Roon fleet had been spotted and that the Battle of the High Coast was about to begin.' His eyes narrowed. 'But it's strange nobody has sent *us* any messages. The Roon have two armies: one here at the High Coast and the other further east, at the Pass of Westernese. Their plan was to attack simultaneously. So why haven't we received word of what's happened at the Pass?'

'They say that no news is good news,' Sara said hopefully, but Caspan could see the doubt in her eyes.

He shook his head grimly. 'Not in this case. The silence scares me, and I don't scare easily.'

The wind howled outside so loudly that it drowned out the minstrels and the joyful noise inside the hall. Caspan shuddered and looked anxiously at the rattling shutters, as if it was a grave omen.

'Look at you fun sponges!' Roland said from across the table, his mouth full of tart. 'You sure know how to drain the life out of a party. You should go and sit near General Liam. Have you seen the look on his face? You'd think we'd lost today's battle.'

'Say it, don't spray it!' Kilt reprimanded, flicking a piece of tart that shot from Roland's mouth and landed on her sleeve. 'Urgh, you're so gross!'

Roland smiled proudly. 'Just sharing the love, Kilt.'

'Is my food that disagreeable to you that you'd rather flick it around the hall than eat it?' a voice asked.

Kilt turned to find Baron Saxon standing behind her. Her eyes went as wide as saucers and she rose quickly from her seat and bowed. 'No, my lord. I . . . I . . .'

Saxon laughed heartily. 'Please, sit down. I was merely toying with you.' He waited until Kilt eased back into her seat, then leaned over her and filled her tankard. 'Have you tried this?' Kilt shook her head.

Saxon raised the cup gently to her lips and waited for her to take a sip. Kilt blushed and glanced at her friends self-consciously, particularly Roland, who raised his sleeve to his mouth to muffle his laughter.

'It's a cider we make along the High Coast,' Saxon explained, his passion for the drink reminding Caspan of

Gramidge and his homebrews. 'Its main ingredients are elderberries and strawberries, but there's a special nut we grind to add to the mixture. We age it for several months in small oak casks we store in the cellar.' He lowered the tankard and stared expectantly at Kilt, waiting for her opinion.

She licked her lips, savouring the flavour. 'It feels like there's a small fire in my belly. It's very nice.'

Saxon gave a contented nod and glanced at Caspan, Sara and Roland. 'I hope the food is to your satisfaction? It's the best we could scrounge up in such short notice.'

'It's perfect, my lord,' Caspan replied.

'And the sausages?' the Baron asked Roland.

'Absolutely sausage-tastic,' Roland said, but Caspan noticed a sad, faraway look in his eyes. Roland took a final swig of his drink and grabbed a serving girl by the hand. 'Now, if you'll excuse me, I need to get something out of my system,' he announced to his friends and the Baron, then led the girl to a free space between the tables to dance. The girl giggled, enthralled by Roland's unique dance style, which reminded Caspan of a dog chasing its tail.

Saxon extended his opened hand to Kilt. 'Would you like to join me?'

'To dance?' Kilt asked.

The Baron nodded, and Kilt smiled from ear to ear. 'I'd love to.' She held up a finger in warning. 'But only if you give me your word you won't dance like *that*.'

Saxon regarded Roland and shook his head. 'I don't think I could even if I tried.'

Chortling merrily, Saxon and Kilt headed over to join Roland and the servant.

Caspan watched them for a moment then glanced at Sara. 'You don't want to?'

She turned up her nose. 'Not unless you want me stamping all over your toes. Sorry, Cas, but dancing's not my sort of thing.'

'That's fine.' Caspan filled his tankard and lounged back in his seat. 'I'm finding it entertaining enough just watching Roland.'

As if on cue, the black-haired jester performed an ambitious leap in the air, but slipped and did the splits. The servant reached out to help him to his feet, but ended up falling on top of him instead. They lay on the ground, laughing hysterically.

The celebration carried on late into the night. It was when fresh logs were being added to the hearth that Sara nudged Caspan, drawing his attention to a soldier who had just entered the hall. He stood beside the door, scanning the hall, then crossed brusquely over to General Liam. He whispered something in the commander's ear and handed him a sealed letter.

Caspan and Sara watched carefully as Liam broke the seal and read the message. He stared at it for some time, his expression dark and foreboding, before he drained off his tankard, summoned his officers and hastily left the hall.

'That can't be good,' Sara whispered.

Outside, the wind howled again. Caspan nodded, his stomach knotting with dread.

CHAPTER 10

GRAVE NEWS

Dawn appeared bleak and grey as the friends gathered outside the stable the following morning. The wind had died down and the snow had stopped falling several hours before. Still, the castle was blanketed in white and it was bitterly cold, forcing the friends to wear the collars of their cloaks high around their necks. They warmed themselves around a crackling fire set in an iron-strapped brazier.

'I can barely keep my eyes open,' Sara said, yawning. 'I barely slept last night.'

'None of us did,' Caspan remarked.

Roland flicked the snow off the top of a barrel beside the stable and sat down. 'What did you expect after the news General Liam dropped on us? Talk about killing the party.' He snorted bitterly before staring hard into the fire. 'It feels as if all we've done here was for nothing and we're right back where we started.'

Shanty gave him a reproachful look. 'It's not as if the northern legions sat on their behinds and let the Roon stroll through the Pass of Westernese. They would have fought hard and done everything possible to try to stop the giants.'

Roland's expression softened. 'Yeah, I know. I'm just frustrated, that's all.'

'We're all feeling like that,' Kilt said, then turned to Shanty. 'Have we heard anything about the survivors?'

The dwarf was solemn. 'I overheard General Liam talk to Saxon last night after the feast. Only several hundred soldiers managed to make it out of the Pass.'

Roland gasped. 'Several hundred! That's barely any. Weren't there over four thousand men in the army that went north?'

Shanty met his gaze and nodded slowly. 'They've retreated to Rivergate and will join with the reserves that have been pulled up from the south. General Liam will also lead the First Legion over to support them. Together they'll battle the Roon somewhere near Chester Hill.'

'But they'll only be about two thousand strong!' Roland said. 'If an army of four thousand couldn't stop the Roon, what chance will they have?'

'They'll do whatever they can,' Shanty replied. 'We can't ask for anything more.'

'We stopped the Roon here, and Caspan and Lachlan defeated them at Darrowmere,' Kilt said pointedly. 'If we've done it twice already, we can do it again.'

Roland looked at her dourly and mumbled something under his breath. Then he pulled out a package from the inside pocket of his cloak, ripped off its paper wrapping, revealing the chunk of pork inside, and tore off a slice. He proffered it to his friends, who all declined, then shrugged and shoved it into his mouth. He chewed for a moment before turning up his nose and spitting it out. 'Ugh, that tastes like leather. What more could go wrong today?'

Caspan gave Roland a sorrowful look. The black-haired jester could always be counted on to lighten the mood of a situation, no matter how grim. But everybody had a breaking point, and what had befallen Bandit and the military defeat at the Pass of Westernese was evidently too much for Roland. He'd tossed and turned all night, and called out to Bandit many times in his sleep. At one point he woke, sat up in his pallet and buried his head in his hands. Caspan asked him if he was all right and if there was anything he could do to help, but Roland shook his head. Caspan watched him in the pale moonlight that shone through the window, wishing there was something he could do to ease his friend's pain. A long time passed before Roland's heavy breathing became calm and regular, and he lay back down.

Caspan smiled softly at him now. 'I never thought you'd lose your appetite.'

'Yeah, well, I never thought we'd find ourselves in this situation.' Roland ran a finger along the edge of his dagger. 'If that Roon army isn't stopped, it'll march all the way down to Briston. And if the capital falls, we might as well start looking for somewhere else to live.'

'There's been no news about Duke Bran?' Caspan asked Shanty hopefully.

The Duke had led a third army off to face Roy Stewart's highland force in Lochinbar. Under his command were the men of the Sixth, Seventh, and the survivors of the Eighth Legion, along with his son, Prince Dale, and Master Scott. Caspan had formed a strong friendship with Dale during the siege of Darrowmere, and he often wondered how the Prince and Master were faring.

The capital of Lochinbar, Darrowmere, had fallen to a surprise attack from Caledon. The Prince had been lucky to have escaped and for several weeks had conducted guerrilla-style hit-and-run attacks on the highlanders. He returned quickly to Briston upon hearing that his father had been rescued from Tor O'Shawn.

'No messenger ravens have been received from them as of yet,' Shanty replied. 'But there's no reason for alarm. Remember that Roy Stewart had planned on moving only after the Roon launched their attacks.'

Roland frowned. 'But why do that? It'd be in his best interest to attack at the same time as the giants. We wouldn't have stood a chance against all of them at once.'

Sara shrugged. 'Maybe Roy's suspicious of Brett and the Roon.'

Caspan nodded in agreement, thinking back to when he had spied upon Brett and Roy in Tor O'Shawn. The traitorous Lady Brook — the dark-eyed, black-haired lady Caspan had first laid eyes on back in Darrowmere — had also been present, and didn't hold back in trying to cut down the highland laird with curt comments. At one point she even remarked that he had done such wonders in bringing the disparate highland clans under his control that he should give her kennel master some advice. Likewise, General Brett's and Roy's discussion on military tactics had been riddled with snide remarks, revealing a deep distrust between the men.

'I'd say you're right,' Caspan commented. 'Perhaps Roy Stewart's holding back until he's sure that Brett and the Roon have stuck to their side of the agreement.' He looked worriedly at Shanty. 'But now that they have, it will only be a matter of days before Caledon marches.'

'And that's when the real fun and games begin,' Roland muttered. He sheathed his dagger and looked at the dwarf. 'So General Liam and the First Legion have been ordered to march west, but what of Baron Saxon?'

'He'll stay here and guard the High Coast,' Shanty replied, much to Kilt's relief, who smiled thankfully. 'We've repelled the main invasion fleet, but for all we know some Roon may have stayed behind in reserve at the Black Isles and are planning on raiding the coast. That's why Saxon's left sentries up at Haven's Watch, ready to raise the alarm at the first sign of trouble. He's also going to send Fin and over a hundred of his soldiers north today to man the keeps up near Howling Head.' He exhaled wearily. 'If any good has come out of this rotten situation, it's that Captain Grinn and his pirates have promised to maintain their alliance with Saxon. They're going to patrol the area and keep an eye out for any Roon raiding parties.'

Kilt gave Roland an encouraging look. 'So all our hard

work here wasn't for nothing, after all. We hold the High Coast. That has to count for something.'

Roland nodded reluctantly. 'Yeah, I suppose so.'

A crow perched high up on the battlements squawked, drawing the friends' attention. They stared at the bird for some time, lost in their own thoughts, before Sara added a stick to the fire and rubbed her hands before it.

'I hope our friends are okay,' she said, voicing the concern that had weighted heavily on Caspan's thoughts all night. She glanced at Shanty. 'You haven't heard anything?'

As one, Caspan, Roland and Kilt turned to regard the dwarf, their anxious expressions revealing that perhaps they didn't want to know the answer to Sara's question. Master Morgan, Raven, Oswald and Thom, the mute swordsman Caspan had met on the rooftops of Floran, had been sent to the Pass of Westernese to aid the legions.

Shanty shook his head. 'King Rhys's message didn't go into such particulars. We can only hope that they and their Wardens managed to get out safely out of the Pass.'

Roland shifted uneasily. 'Master Morgan and Raven are skilled fighters. I don't know much about Thom, but he looks as if can take care of himself. But Oswald . . .'

'I know,' Caspan said tensely, believing the elderly treasure hunter was more suited to researching in archives and libraries than wielding a sword against Roon. 'I've worried about him ever since he was sent to the Pass.'

'There was no stopping him, though,' Kilt remarked. 'Remember that Morgan gave him the option of remaining in Briston with Lachlan, but he wouldn't hear of it.'

Caspan smiled sadly, thinking back to the meeting in Duke Connal's quarters, when the Brotherhood had been assigned to defend different parts of the kingdom. Oswald, who was normally so calm and even-tempered, had turned livid at Morgan's suggestion that he stay in the capital with Lachlan.

'But Morgan's no fool,' Kilt continued. 'I'm sure he would have kept Oswald back in their base camp, well away from the fighting.'

Caspan nodded, knowing that the Master would have done everything possible to protect his companions. He glanced expectantly at Shanty. 'And what are we going to do?'

'I thought I'd put that question to you. Duke Connal's provided no further instructions, so we're free to do as we like. We can stay here and ensure there are no further attacks along the High Coast, or —' Shanty regarded each of the treasure hunters in turn '— we can head east with General Liam and face the Roon at Chester Hill.'

'What do you think we should do?' Caspan asked. 'You've had far more experience than us at this sort of thing.'

Shanty pursed his lips in thought, then announced, 'I think we should head east. The final battle of this war will be fought at Chester Hill. I don't know what role we'll play in it, or if we'll have any impact on its outcome, but I'd hate not to try. Not all of us will go, though.' He paused, leaving the friends hanging off his next few words. 'I'd like at least one of you to remain here to help Baron Saxon.'

The friends exchanged shocked looks.

'Is that wise?' Sara asked. 'We were trained to work together as a team.'

Caspan was quick to support her. 'We've done practically everything together since joining the Brotherhood. We know each other's strengths and weaknesses and work well together. Making one of us stay here might cause that to fall apart.'

'You seem to have coped well without Lachlan,' Shanty countered. 'Look, I knew you weren't going to be happy about this, but I thought about it a lot last night and believe it's the right thing to do.' Roland drew breath to comment, but the dwarf silenced him with a raised hand. 'And before you start arguing the matter with me, just give me a moment to explain my reasoning. If there are more Roon hiding out in the Black Isles, Saxon's going to need all the help he can get. And we all know the impact one of our Wardens can have on a fight. They also travel much faster than horses and are invaluable for reconnaissance. That's why I'm asking one of you to stay behind. Yes, I know you work well as a team, and nobody likes my suggestion one bit. But Saxon needs at least one member of the Brotherhood to remain.'

Roland stared coldly at Shanty and folded his arms across his chest. 'Don't even think about asking me. Bandit's injured, so that rules me out.'

'I suppose it does.' Shanty regarded Caspan, Sara and Kilt. 'It wouldn't be for that long; perhaps a week or two. Just to ensure there are no further threats to the High Coast.' He sighed deeply. 'I like this no better than you do, but I've made up my mind and we're going to stick to it.' When no further opposition to his plan was voiced, he asked, 'Would somebody like to volunteer?'

Caspan, Kilt and Sara quickly avoided the dwarf's eyes and looked down, afraid that they'd be singled out.

Roland stared challengingly at Shanty. 'What are you going to do now — make them draw straws?' Shanty glared his disapproval at him, and Roland lowered his eyes shamefully. He drew a shaky breath, then said, 'I'm sorry. I'm not myself. I haven't been since I lost Bandit. I've never felt so alone before.'

Shanty's features softened and he reached over to tousle the boy's hair. 'The last few days have been tough on everybody. Let's just not forget who our friends are. Bickering amongst ourselves will get us nowhere. And I'm sure Bandit's going to be just fine.' Roland nodded and smiled softly. Shanty looked back at Caspan, Kilt and Sara. 'I won't make anybody stay against their will. If you want —'

'I'll do it,' Kilt said.

Caspan was stunned. 'Kilt, are you sure?'

The green-eyed girl nodded determinedly. 'Shanty's right: there might be more Roon in the area. One of us needs to stay behind with our Warden.'

Roland cocked a curious eyebrow at her. Caspan was relieved to see a mischievous glimmer in his eyes.

'And this decision has absolutely nothing to do with a certain young baron, does it?' Roland asked.

'Oh, shush up, you goose,' Sara chastised, hurling a snowball at him. 'I think it's very noble of Kilt volunteering to do this.'

'Can you lot stop throwing snowballs at me!' Roland barked, dusting the white powder from his cloak and tunic. 'Seriously! It's cold enough without you giving winter a helping hand.'

A smile played at the edges of Shanty's mouth, as if this is what he'd hoped for all along. 'I agree with Sara: I think it's very noble of you, Kilt.' He cupped his hands and blew warmth into them, then motioned for the treasure hunters to follow him across to the central keep. 'Come on. We'll tell Saxon and Roy what we intend to do.'

'Not that anybody is interested in anything *I* have to say these days, but I think this idea stinks.' Roland pushed himself off the barrel and went after his friends. 'Friends should stick together, through thick and thin. That's all there is to it.'

Kilt pouted her bottom lip and placed her arm around his shoulder. 'Aw, you're nothing but a big softy, aren't you? Behind those spindly legs and snide comments beats the heart of a lamb. You really do care about me.'

Roland looked down at his legs and frowned. 'Spindly? What are you talking about?'

'I think he really does care about you, behind all of his teasing,' Sara said, nudging Kilt. 'Maybe it's been nothing but a great facade to hide his true feelings.'

Roland pointed a finger at her in warning. 'Don't push your luck, bookworm.'

Laughing, the girls ran ahead to join Shanty.

CHAPTER 11

LACHLAN

A messenger raven arrived later that afternoon, revealing that the survivors of the Battle of the Pass of Westernese had withdrawn to Rivergate. It was a strong defensive position, which was based at a small castle on a causeway that spanned the Mooryn. The small force was to hold there until General Liam and the reserves from the south got into position at Chester Hill, several miles to the south.

Caspan and his friends had hoped that the message, which bore the royal seal of King Rhys MacDain, would reveal if Morgan and the other members of the Brotherhood were safe, but it said nothing as to their fate. Resigned that they most probably wouldn't find out until they arrived at Rivergate, Caspan, Roland, Sara and Shanty said farewell to Kilt and Baron Saxon, then climbed atop Frostbite and Cloud Dancer and flew east.

General Liam had already started the long march to Chester Hill, and the treasure hunters passed the First Legion as it trudged along the principal road, which led from the High Coast. The line of soldiers stretched across the countryside for over a mile. Several hundred yards ahead of the army rode a company of scouts, hooded and clad in forest greens, longbows strapped to their saddles in calfskin covers. At the head of the main column was a vanguard of heavily armoured cavalry, pendants flapping on the ends of their raised lances. General Liam followed behind, his wolf-skin cloak splayed across the back of his black stallion. Maul walked by his side, the bear's girth taking up so much of the road that the General was almost forced to ride off the trail. Then came the legion's officers, followed by a company of mounted lancers and a stalwart unit of veteran infantry, clad in mail hauberks and with shields slung over their backs. Columns of archers and light infantry came next, and finally wagons transporting the injured and the baggage train.

It looked a formidable force, winding its way across the countryside like an enormous iron snake. But Caspan knew that even once they joined the reserves from the south and the survivors from the Pass, they would face an army twice their size. The odds would be stacked heavily against them — they had no choice but to face the Roon. It would be the greatest battle of the war and determine the fate of Andalon.

As eager as the friends were to arrive at Rivergate to find out what had become of their fellow Brotherhood members, they decided to make a detour to the capital to visit Lachlan. The sturdy boy had wanted nothing more than to join them in their mission to the High Coast, but he had been forbidden to leave Briston by the physician, Arthur, who had insisted he needed at least another two weeks' rest before he'd be fit enough to fight.

Caspan could still picture the look on Lachlan's face on the day they parted. He'd seemed so disappointed, almost betrayed, to have been left behind. Paying Lachlan a visit would be the least the friends could do. It would certainly lift his spirits. With any luck, Lachlan might also be strong enough to join them. He was the best fighter out of the recruits. Even in a weakened state, he and his magical guardian, Talon, would be a welcome addition to their team.

It was almost midnight when the treasure hunters arrived in the city and were escorted by guards into the royal precinct. Believing Lachlan would be asleep, they decided to wait until morning to surprise him. A servant showed them to their rooms and, tired from the day's flight, they dismissed their Wardens and went straight to bed.

Caspan slept like a log and woke refreshed the next morning. To his surprise, golden sunlight streamed through his drawn window. He lay there for a while basking in its warmth, before he finally dressed and went down for breakfast. He hadn't realised how late he'd slept in until he reached the deserted hall and found out from a kitchen hand that Sara, tired of waiting for him to wake, had decided to visit her father in the library. Both Shanty and Roland had accompanied her.

Eager to meet Lachlan, Caspan gulped down two bowls of porridge then hurried through the castle corridors to his friend's room, only to discover from a passing servant that Lachlan had gone outside to train.

Caspan found Lachlan whacking a blunt practice sword on one of the padded pells in the courtyard between the armoury and the stable. Caspan decided to surprise him. He snuck around to the weapons racks, selected a sword and tip-toed up behind Lachlan. He waited for him to complete a six-swing technique that had been taught by the Masters back at the House of Whispers, then, trying hard not to laugh, poked him in the back with the point of his blade.

'Get yer hands in the air and give me all yer gold, ye knock-kneed vagabond!' Caspan demanded in a gruff voice.

Lachlan froze, then spun on his heel, bringing his sword around to swat aside Caspan's. He brought his sword up above his head, ready to deliver a crunching blow, but froze when he realised who it was.

'Caspan! What on earth do you think you're doing? I could have killed you!'

Caspan was laughing so hard he dropped his weapon. 'I'm sorry. But I couldn't resist.' He wiped tears of mirth from his eyes. 'You should've seen the look on your face.'

Lachlan grinned and patted him on the shoulder. 'Yeah, you're a barrel full of laughs. Just don't come whingeing to me next time I run you through.'

Caspan darted playfully around his friend and tousled

his short-cropped hair. 'You'll never be fast enough to catch me, Timmity Tom.'

'Oh, yeah!' Lachlan dived and tackled Caspan to the ground. He wrestled on top of him and pinned his arms down with his knees. 'Say "surrender" when you've had enough.'

Caspan tried to push him off him, but Lachlan felt as heavy as a mountain. 'I'll never yield,' he said defiantly.

'Really?' Lachlan gripped Caspan's right hand and used it to punch him playfully in the face.

'Oh, come on!' Caspan complained, moaning and laughing at the same time. 'You can't do that.'

'Show me where it says that in the rules. Now, do you surrender?'

'Never, you great big puddenhead!'

'Calling me names as well? You're a right sucker for punishment.'

It was when Lachlan started using both of Caspan's hands as weapons that the former street thief finally yielded. Lachlan gave him a hand up. They laughed as they dusted themselves off and crossed over to a nearby bench.

'Ah, it's good to see you again, Cas.' Lachlan removed the waterskin from his belt, took a quick drink, and proffered it to Caspan. 'When did you get back?'

Caspan took a long draught and wiped his sleeve across his mouth. 'Last night. We wanted to surprise you, but it was too late.'

'We?' Lachlan looked quizzically around the courtyard.

'I slept in, so rather than hang around and wait for me Sara popped over to the library to see her father. Roland and Shanty went with her.'

Lachlan's eyes narrowed. 'And Kilt?'

'Don't worry. She's fine. She stayed behind at Castle Crag.'

Lachlan exhaled a breath of relief. 'For a moment there I thought something terrible had happened to her. But why did she stay behind?'

'Quite a lot has happened since we left. If you've got a spare hour, I can fill you in.'

'I'm all ears.'

Caspan grinned. 'Yeah, I know. But I didn't want to say anything about that and hurt your feelings.'

Lachlan shoved him playfully. 'Knock it off, you clown.' He stood up, pulled on his black Brotherhood cloak and produced his red night-cap from his tunic pocket. 'Arthur says I need to get my strength back, but he also insists I go for walks every morning and evening. Care for a stroll along the battlements? The view over the city's fantastic. You can tell me everything that's happened.' He reattached the waterskin to his belt and plonked his cap atop his head. Its pompom dangled comically down the side of his face.

Caspan rose and smirked. 'You're seriously going to wear that in public?'

'Why not? It's cold and it keeps my head warm.'

'Whatever keeps you happy, Timmity Tom.' Caspan chortled as they made their way up a flight of stairs leading to the castle fortifications. 'Mind you, you're starting to remind me a lot of Roland and his silly blue Strathboogie bonnet.'

'He's still hanging on to that thing?'

Caspan grinned. 'And still playing his bagpipes. Or rather, still *trying* to play his bagpipes.'

'I can't believe he hasn't given up on them yet.'

'I think he delights in annoying everyone too much.'

'So there's been no improvement in his playing?' Lachlan asked.

Caspan shook his head. 'No, he still sounds worse than a flatulent cow.'

Lachlan roared with laughter as the boys stepped aside to allow a group of guards through before walking across the battlements. 'The past few weeks have taken an eternity to pass,' Lachlan muttered as he paused by a crenellation and looked across the rooftops of the sprawling city. 'It's been so frustrating, being cooped up in here, whilst the rest of you have been off fighting.'

Caspan cocked an eyebrow warily at him. 'It hasn't been all fun and games.'

'You think I don't know that?' Lachlan sighed. 'But I wish I could've been there to help. When the first messenger raven arrived yesterday, informing us that the Battle of the High Coast was about to begin, I felt like summoning Talon and flying over there to join you. But Arthur wouldn't hear of it, so I went down to the training yard and took my anger out on one of the pells. I imagined it was an army of giants. After two minutes I was so tired I could barely lift my sword.' He gave Caspan a wounded look. 'Fat lot of good I'd be on the battlefield at the moment, having to stop every few minutes to take a breather.' He stared back across the rooftops. 'Later in the evening the next message arrived, telling us that the Roon fleet had been defeated.' He glanced at Caspan. 'What was it like?'

Caspan shrugged. 'Not much different to the past few fights we've been in, only on a much larger scale.' Then he told Lachlan all about the battle. The muscular boy smiled proudly when he heard of Caspan's plan to drop incendiary bladders on the Roon ships. But when Lachlan learnt what had happened to Bandit, his features darkened.

'How's Roland holding up?' he asked.

The boys warmed themselves by one of the fires in the iron braziers. The dawn had held the promise of a sun-filled day, but heavy grey clouds had rolled in from the west and now blanketed the sky. Caspan expected it might start snowing within the hour. He leaned against a merlon and peered across the city, mentally charting a course across the rooftops. He caught himself and smiled wryly, surprised that the instincts he had honed during his time with the thieves guild in Floran, the Black Hand, were still second nature to him.

'He's doing okay, but he's not his normal self,' Caspan replied. 'He has a lot of pent-up anger, and doesn't have much patience for a lot of things.'

'Which is only to be expected, given what he's going through.'

Caspan turned to Lachlan. 'And how are you? You look fit enough.'

'Yeah, but looks can be deceiving.' Lachlan rested his elbows on a merlon and cradled his chin miserably in his hands. 'I walk every day and train on the pells, but it leaves me exhausted. I've never felt so weak, Cas. It's as if the Dray armband we found beneath Tor O'Shawn drained the life out of me. I'm recovering, but at this rate it's going to take forever before I'm back to normal.'

'Just be patient,' Caspan said sympathetically. 'You'll get there. The last time I saw you, you barely had the strength to walk, let alone train with a sword.'

Lachlan sighed and flexed the gloved fingers of his right hand, as if willing the strength to flow back into them. 'That's what I keep telling myself, but it seems like the war will be over before I leave this castle. King Rhys took pity on me and invited me to attend one of his military councils. But other than that, this —' he motioned to the courtyard with a wave of his hand '— is all I've got to look forward to every day. Talon and I are bored out of our brains. Arthur won't even let us go for a ride. I have dizzy spells, and he's afraid I'll fall off.'

'He's only being cautious.'

'There's a fine line between being cautious and over-protective, if you ask me.' Lachlan's shoulders slumped. 'The other day I summoned Talon down in the courtyard and scared the wits out of a group of serving maids. They complained to the guards and I was called into the Captain's office. I assured him that Talon wouldn't hurt a hair on anybody's head, but he said people were terrified of him and that I wasn't to summon him in the royal precinct again. I've got no choice now but to call upon Talon in my private quarters. The poor thing; he can barely move without knocking something over.' He regarded the magical Dray armband attached to his forearm. 'I wish I'd never put this thing on in the first place.'

'We'd all be dead if you hadn't,' Caspan replied sombrely. 'It won't come off?'

Lachlan shook his head and smiled softly. 'It's attached tighter than Roland clinging to the final sausage at a banquet.'

Caspan smirked, glad that Lachlan could still make light of his predicament.

The smile faded from Lachlan's lips. 'I feel like a caged animal; I can't wait to join the war.' He looked at Caspan grimly. 'But after what happened at the Pass of Westernese yesterday, I might never get a chance.'

'So you know about the defeat?'

'It'd be hard not to, given that I've been confined to the royal precinct,' Lachlan replied. 'It's been all the talk since a raven arrived last night. It was strange. One minute everybody was celebrating your victory at the High Coast; the next there was widespread panic in the streets and a steady flow of people heading south, running for their lives.' He ran his left palm over his armband. 'But I won't run. I'll meet the giants here and give them the shock of their lives.'

Caspan's eyes narrowed with concern. 'You wouldn't activate the armband again?'

'I'll do whatever it takes, Cas.'

'But it almost killed you!'

Lachlan shrugged and squared his shoulders boldly. 'Like I said; I'll do whatever it takes.' He forced a smile. 'Enough talk of war. I'm sure you've seen enough of it to last you a lifetime.' He gave a mysterious smile at the sound of approaching footsteps. 'On a happier note, here's somebody you'll be delighted to see.'

'I hope he's referring to me,' said a familiar voice.

Caspan turned to find Gramidge hurrying across the battlements, his arms held wide, ready to embrace him.

'Gramidge!' Caspan beamed, barely believing his eyes as he was swept into the steward's bear-like hug. 'What are you doing here?'

'Arrived two days ago, I did. Not even a hundred wild stallions could have kept me away from the capital once I heard Lachlan was here.' Gramidge stepped back and inspected Caspan. 'Now, let me check you're all in one piece. Battles have a tendency of stealing limbs from people. Two arms, two legs, a torso, a neck and head. Yes, everything seems in place.'

Caspan grinned.

'And your friends and their Wardens?'

In spite of his gruff appearance, Gramidge had a soft heart. Caspan didn't want to worry him unnecessarily by telling him what had happened to Bandit. For all he knew, the manticore would make a full recovery and soon be dining alongside his fellow Wardens at a celebratory feast back in the Great Hall at the House of Whispers.

That was, of course, if King Rhys's armies managed to defeat both the Roon and Roy Stewart's highlanders.

'They're all fine,' Caspan replied, uncomfortable with lying to his friend, but believing it was for the best. He felt less guilty when Lachlan gave him a furtive nod of approval.

The steward exhaled a relieved breath and smiled from ear to ear. 'I'm glad to hear it. Been worried sick, I have. Barely been able to sleep a wink since I heard you'd all gone off to defend the High Coast. And poor Lachlan — injured by that thing he put on his arm. That's why I came here, to keep an eye on him.'

Lachlan clapped Caspan on the shoulder. 'If you'll excuse me, I might use this as an opportunity to return to my quarters. I forgot to take my medicine this morning. Arthur will skin me alive if he finds out.'

Caspan smirked. 'Your secret's safe with me.'

'Now, you'll be there in ten minutes, won't you?' Gramidge asked Lachlan. 'Remember, you did promise. One final attempt.'

'I wouldn't miss it for the world,' Lachlan replied as he made his way across the battlements. He glanced over his shoulder at the steward. 'I take it you'll be recruiting a certain individual to help us?'

Gramidge tapped the side of his nose. 'All in good time. Now, don't forget.'

'Don't worry. I'll be there.'

'What's all this about?' Caspan asked the steward as he watched Lachlan descend the stairs back to the courtyard.

Gramidge shrugged. 'Oh, nothing special. At least, it's nothing *you* need to worry about.'

Caspan cast a suspicious eye at the steward. He was about to ask what sort of mischief he and Lachlan were up to and, more importantly, how it would involve *him*, when Gramidge blurted, 'Ah, but it's good to see you, Cas.' His look became sombre and he sighed. 'I'd be lying if I said I wasn't worried about Lachlan. He's a bit down in spirits at the moment. I do my best to keep him distracted and entertained, but he says it's like being locked inside a prison cell in here. It's a good thing you came by to visit. It means a lot to him.'

Gramidge smiled cheerfully and hooked an arm around Caspan's shoulder as they walked along the parapet. 'And he's not the only person who's glad you're here. You see, there's a little problem I've been trying to fix. And you'll be perfect for the job. Lachlan's been helping, but with you — well, the task's as good as done.'

'What is it?' Caspan asked, wondering if the steward had transported his skeps with him to the capital and needed help extracting the honey.

'Rats.'

Caspan stopped and stared deadpan at the steward. 'Rats?'

'That's right — rats.'

'I don't like the sound of this . . .'

Gramidge tilted his head in a curious manner. 'I'm surprised to hear that.'

'Oh?'

'Well, you spent half your life with the Black Hand in

Floran's sewers. You can't tell me you didn't come across the odd rat down there.'

Caspan thought back to the dark, fetid labyrinth of tunnels beneath Floran's cobbled streets, and the vermin that infested it. Some were as large as feral cats, with incisors that gleamed like stilettos in the darkness. They didn't scurry away when approached, but reared on their hind legs, bared their fangs and hissed. In spite of the folktales, Caspan had never heard of anybody being killed by the rats, though they did spread disease. He'd seen fellow thieves laid low by a single bite.

'I've met more than just a few, but it doesn't mean I *like* them,' he said.

'Then that makes two of us — three, actually, if we include Lachlan.' Gramidge leaned in close to Caspan's ear. 'Between you and me, nothing scares me more than rats. They're worse than spiders, and that's saying something. There's something about their whip-like tails and their beady little eyes that makes my skin crawl. Disgusting creatures, they are, scurrying about in the dark and getting up to all sorts of mischief. Urgh!' He shivered and rolled up his sleeve to reveal his forearm. 'Take a look at this! I'm covered in goosebumps at the mere thought of them.'

'So what am I being dragged into exactly?'

'It's nothing too serious,' Gramidge said. 'Just a slight territorial dispute I need your help to resolve.'

'With *rats*?'

Gramidge nodded. 'They've overtaken a section of the King's cellar. Normally it wouldn't be an issue, but they've built their nest right next to a particular keg of cider I'm keen to get my hands on.'

Caspan was glad to help the steward — it would be a welcome distraction from the war. 'So you're hiring me as your bodyguard?'

'You could put it like that. And if we succeed, you'll be rewarded with a tankard of the most amazing cider you will have ever tasted. Now, I bet that's caught your interest.'

Caspan laughed heartily. 'Okay, count me in.'

Gramidge smiled. 'Good, now let's get started. We'll make our way down there and wait for Lachlan outside the cellar door.'

The steward led the way across the battlements and ushered Caspan inside a tower. Gramidge took a lit lantern from the wall, and they descended a spiralling flight of stairs. They passed through a nail-studded door at the end and walked along a broad corridor, its walls lined with tapestries.

'The King won't mind?' Caspan asked, his voice and footfalls echoing along the passageway. 'We're not going to get into trouble?'

'I'll lay King Rhys across my knee and give him a good old smack on the backside if he objects. He might be the ruler of the kingdom, but that's no excuse for poor manners. Remember that I served as a steward here before I headed over to manage the House of Whispers, or Hampton Hall as it was known back in those days. I've known the King my entire life.' Gramidge brushed his fingers along a window ledge, a wistful expression on his face. 'I know every inch of this place as well as the back of my hand. There are over sixty rooms in the castle, and that's not including the cellar, which, I should add, the King's let go to rack and ruin. I have a right mind to give him a good old smack just for the way he's let it go. Honestly — some of the ciders stored down there are worth more than this castle. And now they're covered in spiderwebs and have rats sleeping all over them.' He shuddered and showed Caspan his arm. 'You see — goosebumps again. This is intolerable!'

He stopped outside a door and led Caspan down another spiralling staircase. 'This will lead us straight to the cellar,' Gramidge said, his voice lowered. 'Best we keep the noise to a minimum from here on. We don't want the rats to hear us and ruin our element of surprise.'

Caspan nodded and suppressed a wry smile. He felt as if he was part of an elite covert operation, deep behind enemy lines. This feeling was amplified when they emerged from the stairwell and found Lachlan waiting for them by the cellar door. Caspan tried hard not to laugh.

Lachlan wore a chainmail vest, metal greaves and a conical helmet over a thick leather hood. A lantern hung from his belt and he held a mop in a two-handed grip.

Caspan looked at Gramidge warily. 'Just exactly how *big* are these rats?'

'Big enough,' he said, handing Caspan a mop. 'There you go. You're all set.'

Caspan frowned as the steward untied a sack near the door and pulled out pieces of armour, which Lachlan helped him put on. 'So I don't get anything to wear?'

Gramidge glanced up from strapping on his greaves. 'You won't need it. You're going in stealth, so it would only slow you down. The plan is for Lachlan and me to take care of the rats. While we distract them, your job is to go into thief-mode, sneak around behind them, find the keg and lightfoot it out of there. What do you think?'

'Thief-mode?' Caspan asked, wondering what he'd got himself dragged into. Gramidge nodded enthusiastically. 'Just smashing.'

'Hopefully we won't *smash* anything in there. Some of these ciders are worth their weight in gold. The particular one we're looking for is stored against the rear wall. It's in a keg about this big.' Gramidge held out his hands, indicating its size. 'And it's marked with a bright red X just above the tap. You can't miss it.'

Caspan smirked. 'You really want it, don't you?'

'Do you think we'd be going to all this trouble if I didn't? It's the final keg of Lip Smacker.'

Caspan chortled. 'Lip Smacker? Let me guess: it's one of your homebrews?'

Gramidge's eyes glistened excitedly. 'That's right. But it's not just *one* of my homebrews. It's the *finest* I've ever made. I crafted it over two decades ago, but I cannot for the life of me remember the ingredients. I wrote the recipe down somewhere, but I've been searching for years and can't find it. That's why we've got to save it. It'd be a crime to just leave it in there, rotting away, with rats all over it.'

'So this is a rescue operation,' Caspan whispered.

'Spot on. And the most important one you'll ever go

on. All those relics you go searching for might be important, but the quest for Lip Smacker goes well beyond that.' Gramidge pulled on a mail vest, gripped his mop and glanced at Lachlan. 'We don't want a repeat performance of what happened yesterday.'

'It didn't go down well?' Caspan asked.

Lachlan grinned. 'You can say that again. We were swarmed and overwhelmed.'

Gramidge gave him a reprimanding slap across the shoulder. 'I don't know what you're smirking about. We barely made it out alive. I even had a rat crawl up my trousers, of all places.'

'It was terrible,' Lachlan added, hiding his grin behind his sleeve.

Gramidge gave the large treasure hunter a reproachful look. 'Remember, we don't want to *anger* the rats. The last thing we want is a full-scale battle on our hands. Things could get very messy. All we need to do is *distract* them long enough for Caspan to sneak around behind them. Besides, I could never bring myself to hurt an animal. I won't have any of you committing violent acts when under my command.'

Lachlan gave the steward an incredulous look. 'But they're *rats*!'

'And they're guarding the final keg of Lip Smacker!' Caspan added with a smirk. 'Don't forget that.'

'They can't help that they're rats,' Gramidge replied pointedly. 'How do you think you'd feel if you'd been born a rat? Imagine it: living in disgusting sewers, eating rubbish that not even a . . . well, a *rat* would eat.

It would be enough to drive you crazy.' He wiggled a finger at the boys. 'You see, it puts it all into perspective when the glove's on the other hand, doesn't it?'

Lachlan frowned. 'Don't you mean when the *boot's* on the other *foot*?'

Gramidge cuffed him across the shoulder again. 'Don't get smart with me. Now, are you ready?'

Caspan held out his mop and nodded, feeling quite ridiculous.

Gramidge took a steadying breath as he reached for the door handle. 'Right, let's do this.'

CHAPTER 12

THE QUEST FOR LIP SMACKER

Their lanterns concealed behind their cloaks so as to not alert the rats, the friends inched open the door and entered the cellar. Lachlan parted his cloak, providing just enough light to see by, and they waited in silence, allowing their eyes to adjust to the darkness.

Lachlan led the way forward. They crept down an aisle flanked by towering shelves stacked with barrels and bottles. Reaching a T-intersection, they turned left and, brushing past a silken screen of spiderwebs, continued for another twenty yards before turning right into another aisle.

Lachlan beckoned Caspan forward with a jerk of his head. 'The keg's down the end of this corridor.'

'It's on the rear wall, at about chest height,' Gramidge added, whispering into Caspan's ear. He drew back the folds of his cloak, illuminating their immediate surroundings in a dull orange glow so that Caspan could get his bearings. 'It looks quiet enough, but the rats are down there, hiding in the dark. Urgh!'

Caspan studied the corridor for a moment, then handed Gramidge his mop.

'Are you sure?' the steward whispered.

Caspan nodded. 'You can dual wield. Besides, I can hardly climb when I'm carrying that.' He tested his weight on the lower shelf of a rack then scaled it all the way to the top. Crouched near the vaulted ceiling, he looked down at his friends, waiting for them to advance down the aisle and draw the rats' attention.

Lachlan glanced up at Caspan, nodded, and pulled his cloak back behind his shoulders, flooding the cellar in flickering light. Scurrying and chattering noises echoed ominously from the far end of the cellar. Peering into the darkness, Caspan saw dozens of black shapes moving in the shadows.

Lachlan advanced warily down the aisle. Gramidge huddled behind him, his mop held in a two-handed grip. They had barely moved further than ten feet when Gramidge froze and took a sharp intake of air.

'Brace yourself!' he yelled. 'Here they come!'

Dozens of large black rats stormed out of the shadows and swarmed the steward and the treasure hunter. Lachlan delivered a wild swipe at one on a nearby shelf. The rodent darted away, but the head of Lachlan's mop smacked heavily into the side of a keg, dislodging it and sending it crashing to the floor.

'Be careful!' Gramidge hollered, staring woefully at the liquid spilling across the flagstones.

'Easier said than done,' Lachlan yelled back, kicking aside one rat and trying to swat another pack away with his mop — which again ended with another smashed barrel.

'Stop breaking the kegs!' Gramidge bellowed.

'The kegs?! What about *me*? I don't want to get bitten!' Lachlan whirled his mop behind his head, forcing Gramidge to duck, then swung it around and smashed a stack of bottles.

Gramidge moaned. 'The rats are the last of your worries, you over-muscled, mop-wielding maniac! Break another bottle or barrel and I'll sink *my* teeth into you!'

Trying hard not to laugh, Caspan darted along the top of the rack. He quickly reached the end and was lying on his chest, his legs dangling over the edge, preparing to climb down, when something dropped from a ceiling rafter and landed with a heavy thud barely a foot from his head.

Caspan froze.

Dreading what he was going to find, he raised his head slowly and gazed into the eyes of the biggest, meanest rat he had ever seen. He gulped. He'd seen rats the size of small cats before in Floran, but this one was as large as a medium-sized dog. Its yellow-stained incisors glistened like daggers. Its tail slashed through the air like a whip.

Caught at the rodent's mercy, Caspan forced a nervous smile. 'There's a nice little ratty,' he muttered.

The rat hissed, tensed and launched itself at Caspan's face.

A scream caught in his throat, Caspan pushed back, launching himself in the air. The rat's fangs and claws slashed barely an inch from his nose, and Caspan flew through the space between the racks until his back slammed into the opposite shelf. The wind exploded from his lungs and he dropped to the ground. Remarkably, he managed to land on his feet. Immediately in front of him was a keg with a red X painted on it. The barrel of Lip Smacker! But looking up, he saw the rat leaning over the edge of the rack, ready to pounce.

Caspan snatched the barrel and turned to bolt out of the cellar, but then he caught himself. An ominous creaking sound came from behind him. He spun around to see that the rack he had slammed into was teetering back. Holding the keg of Lip Smacker in the crook of his left arm, he grabbed hold of one of the rack's support beams and tried desperately to stop it from falling. But his effort was futile.

A mighty bang shook the foundations of the castle as the rack crashed into the one behind it, sending barrels and bottles smashing onto the flagstones. The next six racks were also knocked over like a set of falling dominoes. The sound of splintering wood was deafening.

Cringing, Caspan watched helplessly as the chaos unfolded before him. Terrified rats screeched and ran for their lives. Cider flooded the floor like a wave racing across a beach. It only took a matter of seconds, but it seemed to Caspan that an eternity had passed before the final rack crashed into the cellar wall, bringing an end to the destruction.

Dust swirling around him, standing ankle-deep in cider, Caspan looked back at his friends. They stood, mouths gaping, their mops lowered, staring at him in complete and utter shock.

CHAPTER 13

IN THE COMPANY
OF FRIENDS

The trio hurried back to Lachlan's quarters, where they were joined shortly by Shanty, Sara and Roland. No sooner had Roland greeted Gramidge and Lachlan than he grabbed the big treasure hunter's night-cap and took off around the room, hooting joyously as he bounced across the bed. Lachlan chased after his friend, tackled him to the ground and held him in a headlock until he handed back the cap.

Shanty couldn't resist joining in, exacting revenge, he claimed, for Roland's refusal to help him remove his armour after the Battle of the High Coast. Roland tried to fend off the dwarf, but Shanty was too strong and only let go of the boy once he had ruffled his hair into such a state it resembled an old mop.

'Thanks a lot, Shanty!' Roland moped, inspecting his reflection in a window. 'How am I supposed to get around looking like this?'

'Isn't that what that silly highlander bonnet's for?' Shanty replied, grinning from ear to ear.

Roland snorted as he tried to fix his hair, then replaced his bonnet. He tilted it jauntily to one side, and checked his reflection out of the corner of his eye. 'Call it what you will, you great puddenhead. It's just very apparent that you have no understanding or appreciation of style.'

'Style?' Shanty guffawed and pointed at the bonnet. 'Is that what you call *that*? It looks more like a bright blue cowpat plonked on your head.'

Roland laughed in spite of himself. 'How are you holding up, Lachlan?'

'I'm slowly getter better.'

Shanty nudged Roland. 'He's still strong enough to beat you in a wrestle.'

'And wield a *mop*,' Caspan added with a grin.

Gramidge moaned, burying his head in his hands. 'Let's not mention that again. I can't believe we made such a mess. It'll take me months to clean it up.'

'Did we miss something?' Sara's eyes narrowed suspiciously as she pointed at Caspan's breeches. 'And why are you all wet?'

'Best you don't know,' Caspan replied, then gave Gramidge an apologetic look. 'I really am sorry.'

'Is that why you can't stop grinning?' Roland asked.

'I know, lad,' Gramidge said to Caspan. 'It wasn't as if you did it on purpose.' He patted the keg on the small table in front of him. A broad smile crossed his lips. 'Still, it was well worth it.'

'What is it?' Roland asked, leaning across the table to inspect the barrel.

'Only the finest cider you'll ever taste,' Gramidge replied.

'It's called Lip Smacker,' Caspan explained. 'Gramidge made it when he worked here, many years ago. Only he's forgotten the ingredients.'

Gramidge lowered his head ashamedly. 'I can't for the life of me remember.' He counted off the ingredients on his fingers. 'I think there were plums, boysenberries, honey, goosenberries —'

'Goosenberries?' Shanty queried. 'Does such a thing even exist?'

Gramidge whined. 'You see — I'm doomed! I'll never remember how to make it.'

Lachlan took six tankards from a shelf on his wall, filled them to the brim with Lip Smacker and distributed them. 'Then let's make this last keg count. Here's to lost recipes.'

'To lost recipes,' the friends repeated as they clanked their tankards together and drank.

'Mmm. It's absolutely delicious,' Shanty said. 'It's similar to October Cider, but even fruitier.' He licked his lips. 'Is that peach? And maybe even a hint of passionfruit?'

'I don't know,' Gramidge moped. 'Don't make this any worse than it is.'

They sat in silence for a while, savouring the cider. Caspan felt increasingly sorry for Gramidge. Lip Smacker was undoubtedly the finest drink he had ever tasted. He also knew how much pride the steward took in making ciders and cordials. Along with taking care of the House of Whispers and looking after his bees, creating home-brews was one of his greatest passions.

'How's Braggarts' Reward coming along?' he asked, hoping to distract Gramidge with happier thoughts.

Roland's ears pricked up. 'Braggarts' Reward? What's that?'

'Whatever it is, it sounds like it's tailor-made for you,' Shanty commented.

'It's my latest cider,' Gramidge explained, interrupting Roland before he could respond to the dwarf's quip. 'I've been working it on for several months now. The hardest part was deciding on which barrel to mature it in. Oak gives drinks a distinctively vanilla flavour, but I wanted a minty flavour, so went with cedar.'

Roland stared at him deadpan. 'You're serious, aren't you?'

'I've never been more serious in my life,' Gramidge replied. 'The flavour of the wood seeps into the cider and enhances its flavour.' He held his chin high with pride. 'Making great cordials and ciders is an artform. It takes years of trial and error.'

'All the more reason you should take better care of your recipes,' Roland muttered under his breath as he raised his tankard to his lips.

The friends chatted for over an hour before they discussed the impact of the war on the capital and the steady flow of people abandoning the city and heading south.

'What are your parents going to do?' Caspan asked Sara.

'I wish they'd flee the city and head south to Floran, but Father will never leave the library,' she replied. 'Those books are his life. Some of them are hundreds of years old and contain the history of the Four Kingdoms. To him they're just as valuable as the Dray artefacts we seek. He'll never risk stacking them in the back of a dirty old wagon and damaging them. And if he doesn't go, neither will my mum. They'll stay here and tough it out.' She sighed and smiled sadly. 'I just want them to be safe, that's all.'

'That's why we have to crush the Roon at Chester Hill,' Roland remarked with a grim resolve that prompted Lachlan to raise an eyebrow at Caspan.

They ate a late lunch, and the treasure hunters left shortly after. It was a sad farewell, leaving Lachlan and Gramidge behind in the courtyard, who waved up at them as they flew over the battlements and climbed high above the city. Caspan wished desperately that Lachlan could have joined them, but he knew it was for the best. By his own admission, Lachlan was not yet ready to wield a sword in combat for a prolonged period of time. He'd be more of a liability than an asset, with his friends having to keep a constant eye over him. Still, Caspan couldn't help but feel as if their team was starting to fall apart, and it upset him greatly.

Caspan had learnt to trust and depend on his friends. Lone wolves, he now knew, never survived long without the support of the pack. But now his pack was dwindling; being cut back after each successive mission. Bandit had been severely injured, Kilt had remained at the High Coast, and Lachlan still wasn't fit for travel, let alone charging onto a battlefield. Caspan's greatest fear was that he would lose everyone he cared about, leaving him alone and abandoned. There had been a time when he cherished solitude, but he had come a long way since then. Now he didn't think he'd be able to survive on his own.

He hunkered down in his saddle and drew the hood of his Brotherhood cloak over his head to ward back the chill, dreading what he might discover when he arrived at Rivergate.

CHAPTER 14

RIVERGATE

The treasure hunters arrived at Rivergate just as darkness fell. The stronghold was a solid defensive position, set in the middle of a causeway that spanned a swift-flowing river. A barbican guarded the northern causeway, its portcullis lowered and its drawbridge raised. Lit torches were set along the battlements, where cloaked sentries kept watch. They looked up in alarm and nocked arrows to their bows when they saw the friends and their Wardens approach from the south. But Caspan heard an officer call out, assuring the guards that they were reinforcements, and Shanty directed Caspan and Sara to land their Wardens in a small courtyard.

They were greeted by a soldier clad in a torn chainmail vest, a stained bandage wrapped around his forehead. The lion clasp on his cloak identified him as an officer of the Third Legion.

'Welcome to Rivergate,' he said, shaking the treasure

hunters' hands as they dismounted and dismissed their Wardens. 'I'm Captain Jace. I'm sure I speak for everybody here when I say I'm glad to see you.'

Caspan observed the injured soldiers lying on cloaks and makeshift straw beds around the courtyard. It looked more like an infirmary than a military stronghold. He hated to think how fierce the fighting must have been in the Pass.

'You have many wounded,' Shanty remarked, as if reading Caspan's thoughts.

'And these are those still fit to fight. The rest were sent south to safety.' Jace sighed wearily. 'We're all that remains of the Second, Third, Fourth and Fifth legions: two hundred and thirteen men, all bruised and battered, but we hold a strong defensive position here and we'll hold out until the First and southern reserves are in position. Although, I was hoping we'd be sent more reinforcements.'

'We've flown ahead of the First,' Shanty said. 'They should reach Chester Hill by sunset tomorrow.'

'Meaning we've got to hold out here for one day.' Jace cocked an eyebrow at the dwarf. 'Please tell me the First Legion is still commanded by General Liam.' Shanty nodded and the Captain breathed a sigh of relief. 'I'm glad to hear that. We lost all our commanders and senior officers back in the Pass, leaving me in charge.' He regarded the black coats worn by the treasure hunters. 'You're not from the First?'

Shanty shook his head. 'We're members of a special order created by the King.'

Jace folded back the lapel of Shanty's cloak, revealing the silver wolf embroidered in the collar. 'The Brotherhood,' he said matter-of-factly.

Shanty's eyes flashed, surprised as to how the soldier knew the name of the secret order.

'There's no need for alarm,' Jace reassured him. 'I only know because some of you fought alongside us in the Pass. They wore the same black cloaks and rode magical beasts into battle. I'm not certain what your order does, but there isn't a soldier here who doesn't owe his life to the Brotherhood. Your friends performed a delaying action, allowing what was left of the legions to escape.'

'And what of our friends?' Caspan asked, fearing the worst as he failed to see any sign of them or their Wardens in the courtyard. 'Did they make it out alive?'

'They can tell you that themselves.' Jace jerked his chin towards a stairwell leading to the central keep, from which three black-cloaked figures emerged.

Caspan held his breath as the people pulled back their hoods.

It was Master Morgan, Raven and Thom.

'I never thought I'd be so glad to see you!' Roland rushed over to hug the Master.

Morgan gave one of his rare wry grins and pushed him gently away. 'My thoughts exactly, Roland. Although, I think we can skip the hugging in future. A handshake will suffice.'

Roland nodded. 'Okay, manly handshakes it is from here on.'

The rest of the treasure hunters greeted one another then moved over to a quiet section of the courtyard.

'We were worried you didn't make it out of the Pass,' Caspan said to Raven. 'We heard the fighting was fierce, but never received any news as to who survived.'

Raven smiled sympathetically. 'I knew you'd all be worried, but we didn't have any ravens to spare on private messages.' She tousled Caspan's hair. 'It's great to see you.'

'So what happened exactly?' Shanty asked. 'We heard it was a massacre.'

'We ambushed the Roon when they were deep inside the Pass,' Raven explained. 'We chose the perfect area for it, where the walls of the ravine closed in.' She gestured towards Morgan and Thom. 'We took position up on the ledges with the archers. We thought that in the bottle-neck the sheer size of the Roon army would work against them, but they were too strong. They swarmed down the Pass under the cover of their shields. We took down as many as we could, but we couldn't stop the giants. They just kept coming and coming until they smashed into our infantry. Initially the legions' lines held, and they started to force the Roon back. We thought victory was ours. But then the Roon sent forward a company of berserkers.' She shuddered and swallowed. 'I've never seen anything like them. They cut down the Roon in front of them in order to reach our lines.'

Caspan's eyes narrowed and he looked at Morgan. 'Just like the berserker we encountered at Saint Justyn's.'

The Master nodded. 'They're the fiercest of the Roon. They have no fear of death and stir themselves into an uncontrollable bloodlust. One of them is bad enough, let alone a company of hundreds.'

'They crashed into our soldiers like an avalanche,' Raven continued. 'Our lines crumbled, and it turned into a desperate race to escape. Some pockets of resistance held out, but everywhere men dropped their weapons and ran for their lives. In the panic, many soldiers fell and were trampled to death. Some managed to scramble up the sides of the ravine to reach us, but most were dragged back down by the Roon and slaughtered.' Raven lowered her eyes. 'I loosed arrows until my fingers bled, but there was nothing I could do to save them.'

Morgan patted her on the shoulder. 'General Bryan of the Third Legion was one of the last to fall. He and his personal guard, all armed with shadow blades, held out for half an hour. But then the General's Warden fell. It wasn't long after that Bryan was slain and the Roon swarmed over his guards.' He stared grimly ahead, envisaging the scene. 'That's when Raven, Thom and I summoned our Wardens and came down from the ledges. We held the giants off for as long as we could. The men you see around you here were lucky to make it out, but thousands weren't so fortunate. Several hundred were also captured and taken prisoner.'

Shanty pointed at a slash across the Master's leather vest, and a torn section of chainmail on Thom's shoulder. 'By the look of it, you just made it out.'

Morgan shrugged, as if his wound wasn't even worth consideration.

Raven slipped her bow from her shoulder and inspected

a frayed section of string. 'And now we've got to hold this position until the First Legion reaches Chester Hill.'

'I spoke to General Liam before leaving Castle Crag,' Shanty said. 'He'll be there by tomorrow nightfall. Hopefully he'll be in position before the Roon reach this river.'

Raven looked doubtful. 'Roon scouts have been spotted in the woods barely a mile north of here, and that was over an hour ago.'

Morgan clicked his tongue. 'Meaning they could be spying on us from the northern bank of the river right now.'

'And what of Oswald?' Caspan asked worriedly, wondering where the elderly treasure hunter was.

Raven smiled reassuringly. 'He's up in the keep studying maps of the region, planning a route to Chester Hill for when we eventually need to pull back.'

'I should go and help him,' Sara offered. 'I mightn't be that handy with a sword, but show me a map and I can easily plan an escape route.'

Roland frowned. 'Won't we just follow the most direct route south?'

'It mightn't be that simple with several thousand Roon hot on our heels,' Raven replied, then smiled at Sara. 'I'm sure Oswald would like that.' She shifted her gaze to Caspan and Roland. 'Why don't you each grab a bow and a quiver from that wagon over there and join Thom, Shadow and me on a scouting mission? We're keen to find out just how close the Roon are and would appreciate the help.'

Roland frowned. 'Shadow?'

'She's my guardian dire wolf.'

'Ah, that's right.' Roland cocked his head to the side. 'I've never really thought about it until now, but it's surprising how many of the Brotherhood have dire wolves. There's you, Master Morgan and Duke Connal. Let me guess — Oswald has one too?'

'No,' replied Raven. 'He has a unicorn named Legend.'

'A unicorn! I didn't know they came in that.' Roland regarded Shanty. 'And Legend — what a great name. You should've consulted Oswald when you were thinking of a name for Ferris.' Before the dwarf could reply, Roland glanced questioningly at Thom. 'What magical guardian do you have?'

Thom hand-signalled Raven, who chuckled softly. 'Thom would like me to tell you that he'd love to have a Warden, but he'd never be able to whisper its name and summon it. He's mute.'

'Oh, I'm sorry,' Roland apologised. 'I never knew.'

Sara pouted her bottom lip at Thom. 'So you're the only member of the Brotherhood who doesn't have a magical guardian?'

Thom tapped Raven on the shoulder and made another series of hand signals, but this time Caspan paid close attention. He hadn't been watching Thom the first time he signed, but he'd caught the final movement of his hands in the corner of his eye and thought he recognised the symbol. Studying him closely now, he was surprised to find that he understood every word the treasure hunter was saying with his hands.

Caspan turned to Raven and signed. *He just asked you*

to tell Sara that there's no need for him to have a Warden. *He has us to watch his back.*

Roland chortled and nudged Caspan playfully. 'Yeah, good one.'

Thom's eyes widened at Caspan. *I didn't know you could sign*, he signalled.

'I didn't know I *could* sign', Caspan replied out loud so that everyone could follow the conversation. 'At least, not until now. The Black Hand used secret hand signals when thieving at night. I thought they were a code that only members of the thieves' guild understood, but we must have been using common sign language.'

I often wondered if that was the case, Raven messaged him. *Do you know of Master Scott's past?*

Yes, why? Caspan signalled.

Raven smiled. *I'm glad he confided in you. You have a lot in common.*

Cast from the same mould, I'd say, Thom signed.

Caspan was surprised at how liberating it felt using a language system he had only previously used when on thieving missions. *So Master Scott can also sign?*

Thom nodded. *Scott and Oswald are the only other members of the Brotherhood I can communicate with. It's a skill Scott mastered when working for the thieves' guild in Briston.*

Caspan gave Thom a quizzical look. *And what of Oswald? Don't tell me he was once a member of a thieves' guild?*

Thom gave Caspan a wry look. *I don't think there's any language Oswald doesn't understand. He taught himself how to sign long before he joined the Brotherhood.* He grinned. *I hope your hands don't get too tired. I don't get many chances to talk to people, and I love a good chat.*

Raven smirked at Caspan. *Good luck to you. Thom never shuts up.*

Roland planted his hands on his hips and snorted. 'Well, isn't this nice. Look at you three, chatting away like there's no tomorrow and we can't understand a word of it.' He made a ridiculous series of hand signals, culminating with him almost accidentally sticking a finger in his eye.

Sara shook his head at him. 'What on earth do you think you're doing?'

Roland grinned and shrugged. 'Just trying to join in on the conversation.'

Raven laughed as she drew her dagger and severed the frayed string on her bow. She untied it at the ends, attached a fresh string and tested the tension. Satisfied, she slung her bow over her shoulder.

'So what about it, boys?' she asked, looking at Caspan and Roland. 'Care to join us on a scouting mission? I know Shadow will appreciate Frostbite and Bandit's company.'

The grin slowly faded from Roland's lips. Sensing his friend's reticence, Caspan was about to explain on his behalf what had happened to Bandit, when Sara cleared her throat, drawing everyone's attention. She then gave a detailed account of the fight against the rocs. Raven lowered her eyes, her expression grave, and Morgan placed a sympathetic hand on Roland's shoulder.

'I'm so sorry, Roland,' he said softly. 'I'm sure Bandit will be fighting by your side in a few weeks' time.'

Caspan gave Roland a reassuring smile. 'That's exactly what I told him.'

Roland glanced at Raven. 'Sorry, I don't think I'll be going on any scouting missions for a while.'

'Nonsense,' she replied. 'You can ride tandem with me. Now hurry up and grab a bow and quiver before I change my mind.'

Roland smiled appreciatively. 'Thanks, Raven.'

Morgan turned to Shanty. 'I'm about to help Captain Jace inspect the battlements and work out a plan of defence. Care to help?'

Shanty slapped his thigh. 'Is a Roon as ugly as a toad?' The others chortled and the dwarf gave Morgan a questioning look. 'But where's the garrison's commander? Surely he'd know best how to defend this stronghold.'

'He and his soldiers fell in the Pass,' Morgan replied. 'We were lucky he left four men back here to raise the drawbridge and let us inside.'

'Just keep Shanty away from the armoury,' Roland warned the Master. 'Not unless you want every soldier in this fortress running around in nothing but their underwear.'

Shanty chuckled and opened his mouth to reply, when one of the soldiers atop the barbican gave a gargled cry and toppled off the side, a feathered shaft lodged in his chest. The treasure hunters and Jace each grabbed a bow and quiver and raced up the stairwell to the battlements.

'I don't think we'll need to do that scouting mission after all,' Caspan muttered to Raven as they hid behind merlons and set arrows to their strings.

They peered through the embrasures and spotted black shapes moving through the trees on the far side of the river. Bowstrings hummed and arrows zipped out of the darkness to thwack into the fortifications. Raven took cover behind a merlon just in time to avoid a shaft that whistled past her head. She drew back her bowstring and tested its tension. 'I can make out six of them.'

'Let's see if we can reduce that number.' Caspan pulled back his string. In one fluid motion he rolled his shoulder around the merlon, brought his bow up and loosed his arrow at one of the Roon. There was a pained cry from the trees and a heavy thud.

Raven nodded, impressed. She then darted into the crenellation and her bowstring hummed. A second later there was another cry from beyond the river. 'That leaves only four,' she said, sliding back behind cover.

'And I haven't even started yet,' Roland announced as he stepped out from behind a merlon and took aim. His arrow went high, skimming through the tops of the trees.

Shanty cocked an eyebrow at him. 'You were saying?'

Roland inspected his bow. 'Ah, just as I suspected. It's bent.'

Caspan rolled his eyes, nocked another arrow and took aim. This time his shaft thudded into a tree, and he leapt back to avoid an enemy shot that zipped barely an inch above his head.

'Be careful,' Morgan cautioned. 'Remember, these parapets are lit up by torches, making us easy targets.'

Sara grabbed the closest torch and stamped it out. 'Then let's even the odds a little.'

'That won't make any difference to the Roon,' Morgan said. 'The giants can see in the dark. But extinguishing the torches will at least acclimate our eyes and let us spot the Roon more easily.'

The companions scurried along the battlements, putting out torches and drowning the parapet in darkness, before returning to the crenellations to scan the far bank.

Sara's eyes narrowed. 'There's one.' She raised her bow, drew back the string and slid into the gap between the merlons. Her bow twanged and a giant slumped to his knees, clutching the shaft that punctured through his chainmail vest.

'Nice shot,' Raven commended as she swiftly set an arrow to her bow and loosed, killing the giant before he could climb to his feet.

'That's exactly what I would've done — if I had a bow that wasn't *bent*,' Roland muttered.

Eventually the treasure hunters dispatched the remaining Roon. The woods to the north of the river fell silent, and the friends studied the trees for a while before Raven headed out to check that the area was clear.

Caspan, Roland, Sara, Shanty and Ferris accompanied her. Raven led the group, gliding through the darkness like a fleeting shadow over the forest floor. An arrow was set to her bowstring, pulled back at half draw, ready to shoot at an instant's notice. But not even she was as skilled in woodlore as Ferris. The faun quickly picked up the Roons' tracks, confirming that there had only been six giants and that there were no more in the area. The treasure hunters then returned to the stronghold to report back to Jace.

The Captain had set up a makeshift headquarters in a large chamber in the central keep. A map of Andalon was spread on the table and weighted down with a helmet and daggers. Studying the map, Caspan finally came to understand the strategic importance of Rivergate. Situated on the swift-flowing Mooryn, it was the only crossing to the south between Westford and Hollen; the final obstacle in the Roon's way to Briston. And this was why it had to be held at all costs until the First Legion and the southern reserves could get into position at Chester Hill.

'It's good you took care of the Roon scouts,' Jace said upon hearing Raven's report. 'They won't be able to report back to the main army and tell them we're here. We can use that to our advantage.'

Raven leaned over the map. 'If we destroy the causeway to the north, that would force the Roon to travel around to Westford or Hollen. It would buy the First Legion several more hours to get ready. More reserves might even be mustered.'

Jace shook his head. 'It's a good idea, but it won't work. I've inspected the causeway, and it would take a hundred men a week to break it apart.'

'Then we'll hold them off with arrows,' Shanty suggested. 'They can't storm this fort if we don't let them get any further than ten yards across the causeway.'

Jace looked at him sceptically. 'If we had the arrows we could, but we only managed to salvage one of the supply wagons before leaving the Pass. We'd be lucky if we have fifty full quivers between us.'

'That should be more than ample to do the job,' Roland said.

'Not against an army of *thousands*.' The Captain glanced at Morgan, who stood silently by a window, staring at the woods beyond the river. 'What about your magical guardians? They saved us back in the Pass.'

'We'll do what we can,' Morgan said, turning to face Jace. 'But we've lost the element of surprise. The Roon will now be expecting our Wardens. We might not be so lucky next time.'

'I bet they won't be ready for Frostbite,' Roland commented. The Master and Raven gave him confused looks, and he elucidated, 'He can breathe fire.'

Morgan gasped. 'What?'

'I was wondering when that might happen,' a familiar voice said, and the friends turned to find Oswald standing in the doorway.

The elderly treasure hunter was wrapped in the same oversized black Brotherhood cloak he'd worn when he first met the recruits back in the Eagle's Eyrie for their first lesson of Dray relics. He pushed his spectacles higher up his hawk-like nose and beamed as the young treasure hunters rushed over to greet him.

'Not so hard. You'll snap my back if you're not too careful,' Oswald cautioned as he pulled away from Caspan's embrace. He shuffled over to plonk down on one of the seats around the table. 'I'm so glad to see you're all okay.' His smile faded as he studied the faces in the room. 'Where's Kilt?'

'She stayed behind at Castle Crag.' Roland leaned in close to Oswald and whispered in his ear, 'I think she's got a thing for a certain young baron.'

Oswald exhaled a relieved breath and patted his chest. 'Thank goodness she's all right. I don't think my poor old heart could have dealt with such sad news.' He nestled back in his chair, regarded the recruits and smiled. 'Just take a look at all of you — in your official Brotherhood cloaks. I couldn't be more proud.' He turned to Caspan. 'It sounds as if Frostbite's revealed a secret talent.'

Sara gave the grey-haired treasure hunter a suspicious look. 'You don't sound too surprised.'

'I always wondered if Frostbite could breathe fire,' Oswald replied. 'He is, after all, a drake.'

'But how about Master Scott's Warden, Shimmer?' Caspan asked. 'She's also a drake, but she's never done it. Well, not as far as I know.'

'Have you ever noticed the scar on her neck?' Oswald asked. 'I've suspected that she was injured a long time ago. Often she makes strange coughing sounds, and I've wondered if she's trying to breathe fire, but can't.'

Sara nodded. 'I've noticed that, but I just thought she had a cold.'

Roland grinned. 'And you never handed her a kerchief? Shame on you.'

Sara shoved him playfully, then looked questioningly at Oswald. 'But why didn't you tell Caspan about Frostbite?'

Roland folded his arms across his chest as he scrutinised the old man. 'Yeah, why not?'

'As I said, I've suspected that Frostbite could breathe fire, but I never knew for certain.' Oswald gave Caspan an apologetic look. 'I didn't want to get your hopes up for no reason.' Caspan nodded, conceding Oswald's logic. The elderly treasure hunter rubbed his chin in thought and regarded the map. 'We need to work out how to use Frostbite to our advantage.'

'Isn't it obvious?' Roland said. 'We can get Frostbite to stick his head up over the parapets and roast the Roon.'

Caspan shook his head. 'The trees are too close. Roon archers will no doubt take cover behind them and shoot at Frostbite.'

Sara nodded in his support. 'You saw what happened back at Saint Justyn's. All it will take is one arrow to hit him in the underside of his neck and Frostbite might be killed.'

'I can always hold a shield in front of him,' Roland offered.

Morgan gave the black-haired boy a dour look. 'And snatch arrows out of the air with your free hand?' Roland nodded enthusiastically and opened his mouth to comment, but the Master stopped him with a scowl. 'Don't be ridiculous. If you don't have anything sensible to say can you kindly keep your mouth closed.'

Roland lapsed into a brooding silence and turned up his nose at the Master when he wasn't looking.

Captain Jace exhaled wearily as he strode over to a window and peered down at the northern causeway. 'The trick is to work out how to prevent the Roon from crossing the Mooryn. We've raised the drawbridge, but that created a gap of only ten yards. That won't stop the Roon for long.'

Caspan's eyes narrowed. 'Then we need to stop the Roon before they get anywhere near the drawbridge.'

'Which is easier said than done,' Jace muttered dourly. 'We had an army of thousands back in the Pass, and we couldn't stop them then. What hope do we stand?'

They stood in silence for a moment, all staring at the map, trying to work out how such a small force with limited supplies could hold off the Roon. It seemed an impossible task to Caspan. Once the giants reached the causeway he couldn't see how they'd be able to restrain them for much longer than an hour, if at that.

Oswald suddenly sat up straight and blurted, 'Holstein Bridge!'

Sara stared at him, her eyes wide with sudden hope. 'Of course! Why didn't I think of it before?'

Roland looked back and forth confusedly between Sara and Oswald. 'What?'

'When in need of an answer to a quandary, look to the past for an historical example,' Sara explained.

'Well, now that you've put it like that it makes perfect sense,' Roland remarked sarcastically, throwing his hands in the air in frustration. 'What in the blazes are you two talking about? What's Holpton Bridge got to do with anything?'

'It's *Holstein* Bridge,' Sara corrected.

'Holstein — Holpenstekelstein — Holpiholpiholpis-patsnzoodlystein!' Roland blurted. 'What difference does it make?'

'Quite a lot, actually,' Oswald said calmly, an amused expression on his face as he regarded the irate boy. 'Especially considering the final two places you mentioned are non-existent, whilst the first is the location of a famous battle that took place in —' he glanced questioningly at Sara.

'765,' she replied assuredly.

Oswald clicked his fingers. 'Ah, of course. How silly of me.'

'You can try to impress me with dates until the cows come home, but it isn't going to work. I'm still waiting for an explanation.'

Sara gave an exasperated sigh. 'Maybe if you'd paid more attention during History class in your cadet academy I wouldn't have to waste my time explaining things to you.' Roland screwed up his nose and did a first class impersonation of her. Sara rolled her eyes at him, then said, 'At the Battle of Holpton Bridge —'

Roland's finger shot up in conjecture. 'I believe the correct term is *Holstein* Bridge, my dear Sara. Please, I know it can be difficult at times, but do try to get your facts right.'

Sara glowered at him. 'Argh! You can be so infuriating!' She took a few calming breaths before regaining her composure and continuing. 'At *Holstein* Bridge a group of thirty Saxstein soldiers held off an army of several hundred warriors from Vorsklagov for an entire day until reinforcements arrived.'

'Finally, we get to the relevant part,' Roland commented.

Sara did her best to ignore him. 'The Saxstein soldiers were held up in a fort similar to this. The causeway was about the same size as the one here, but it didn't have the defensive advantage of a drawbridge. Still, the Saxstein warriors used a tactic that prevented the enemy from coming across.'

Roland's eyes glistened roguishly. 'Let me guess: they shouted historical examples from the battlements and bored the enemy to death.'

Morgan gave him a stern look. 'That's enough from you. Sara can barely think straight with you constantly interrupting. Now, if you can't keep quiet, I'll send you to the parapets for guard duty.' He glared at the boy for a moment before motioning with a wave of his hand for Sara to continue.

She cleared her throat and sat down by the table. 'The defenders were outnumbered. They could never hold out for long in a protracted siege. Like the situation we face here, they knew they had to stop the enemy from getting anywhere near the fort.' She paused and glanced at the people gathered around the table.

The suspense was more than Roland could bear. 'And?' he blurted, at the end of his tether. Morgan glowered at him. The boy gave the Master a wounded look and sunk down in a chair.

'There was a large forest north of the river,' Sara explained. 'It was the middle of summer. The ground was littered with dried leaves and dead branches.'

'Providing perfect fuel for a *fire*,' Caspan said excitedly and, studying the map, located Rivergate. 'I didn't realise the woods on the northern bank stretched back so far.'

Jace leaned over the table and, with his dagger, traced their path all the way back to the Pass. 'It's called Huntingdon Hedge.'

'Hedge? That's a pretty stupid name for a forest,' Roland muttered, again drawing another glare from Master Morgan. 'Well, it is,' he insisted. 'Think about it: a hedge implies a row of shrubs bordering a field — not a forest that stretches back for,' he regarded the map, 'well, what must be several miles. Seriously, either this Huntingdon fellow didn't know what he was talking about or he had a very fertile imagination.'

Caspan ignored him and stared fixedly at Sara and Oswald. 'So you're suggesting we stop the Roon by setting fire to the woods?'

Sara nodded. 'Frostbite could simply fly along the river bank, setting the forest alight in a matter of minutes. The snow hasn't fallen particularly strongly here. I imagine the woods would go up in flames in no time at all.'

'There aren't any villages in the area?' Caspan asked, again studying the map. 'I'd hate for anybody to get hurt.'

'Other than *Roon*, you mean,' Roland said.

'Huntingdon Hedge is a royal reserve,' Jace replied. 'People can travel through it, but nobody lives there.' He pointed his dagger at a spot halfway between Rivergate and the Pass. 'The King has a hunting lodge here. We passed by it during our flight. No-one was there, and it didn't appear to have been used for some time.'

'Now all we need is the wind to blow in our favour.' Raven hurried over to a window and stared down at the battlements. She looked back at her friends gathered around the table, her eyes wide with excitement. 'The wind's picking up. And judging from the flags atop the barbican, it's a southerly breeze.'

Roland moaned and banged a clenched fist on the table in frustration. 'Isn't this typical of our luck? We finally come up with a half-decent plan of defence and the wind decides to blow the mother of all raspberries in our face.'

Shanty leaned in close and whispered in his ear, 'It's actually good news. It means the wind's blowing from the *south*.'

Roland frowned. 'Meaning the fire would spread *north*?' Shanty nodded, and Roland gave his friends a sheepish look. 'Well, that's all right then.'

Thom grinned wryly and signed to Caspan and Raven. They glanced at Roland and chuckled softly to themselves.

Roland pointed at Thom. 'Hey, I saw that!' He turned to Caspan and Raven, who tried to hide their laughter behind their raised sleeves. 'What did he just say?'

'Oh, he just made a passing observation that we should hand you over to the Roon,' Raven replied. 'The confused information you'd give them would be priceless.'

Roland smirked in spite of himself. 'That's not very

nice,' he said to Thom. 'I'd expect more from you, being a respected member of the Brotherhood and all.'

'Well, I guess we should stop talking about this and get started. Who's coming with me?' Caspan asked. 'My saddle's got room for two people.'

Roland sat up enthusiastically and opened his mouth to reply, when Master Morgan said, 'Sara should join you. It was, after all, her idea.'

Roland made a dour face and slumped back in his chair. 'If we're going to get technical, it was actually Oswald's suggestion.'

Sara beamed and winked encouragingly at Caspan.

'Come on then,' he said, making his way to the door. 'We've got an army to stop.'

CHAPTER 15

A STRANGER IN THE NIGHT

Caspan and Sara flew Frostbite downstream for several minutes before they turned around and drew close to the northern bank. Driven by the blustering wind, clouds raced past the full moon like tattered ghosts, and the pale moonlight shone upon the river surface, providing enough light for Caspan to navigate by. Huntingdon Hedge was ominously still and silent. Caspan was keen to finish the task and return to the safety of Rivergate. Even his sharp eyes couldn't see far into the dark wall of trees, and he feared there might be Roon scouts spying on him, their axes and spears poised, ready to throw.

He glanced back at Sara. 'Do you think we should start here?'

She nodded. 'We need to create a wide front so that the Roon won't be able to find a way around the fire. We must be at least a mile from Rivergate. I think that should be far enough.'

'Are you ready?'

Sara set an arrow to her bowstring. 'As ready as I'll ever be.'

Before setting off they'd planned that Sara would watch the woods and provide cover as Caspan steered Frostbite along the winding river and the drake focused on setting the forest alight. Sara had proven herself a competent archer during their training sessions back at the House of Whispers, and Caspan was relieved to have her keeping an eye on his back.

'Then let's do it.' Caspan dug his heels into Frostbite's flanks, sending the drake upstream.

They flew at a steady pace, wary of presenting an easy target to any Roon in the area, but also cautious of rushing the task and leaving gaps in the wall of fire. Caspan tapped Frostbite twice on the right side of the neck, directing the drake to turn his head towards the river bank but still fly straight ahead. It was one of the first commands Caspan and his friends had mastered during training, and his Warden responded instantly. They had just rounded a bend in the Mooryn and flew along a straight stretch, perfect for creating their deadly wall.

'Fire!' Caspan ordered.

Frostbite filled his lungs with a great breath, arched his neck forward and shot a geyser of blue fire from his nostrils, illuminating the river and the neighbouring section of forest in a turquoise light. Patches of snow lay at the bases of the trees and clumped on branches, but it had no effect on the magical fire. Within seconds, a fifty-yard section of the river bank was ablaze. Driven by the strong wind, the fire spread rapidly through the trees, driving deeper into Huntingdon Hedge.

Sara stared grimly at the inferno. 'It won't take the Roon long to spot that.'

'I don't care if they do, just as long as it stops them from coming anywhere near Rivergate.' Caspan steered Frostbite into the middle of the river, away from the scorching heat, then commanded the drake to deliver another fiery blast towards the woods.

Up the Mooryn they flew, setting the forest ablaze until the night sky had an eerie, blue glow. Caspan was surprised when they reached Rivergate. Barely any time seemed to have passed since they'd left the stronghold, which was good, for they didn't know how long they had left before more Roon scouts, or the main army for that matter, reached the fortress. Frostbite swooped over the causeway and set Caspan's mind at ease with a blast of fire that engulfed the forest to the immediate north.

They extended the fire front further up the Mooryn until Sara cried out in alarm and pointed at the river bank. Caspan pulled back on Frostbite's reins, bringing the drake to a sudden halt in the middle of the river. Peering down, he spotted a dark shape knee-deep in the water, hurrying away from the fire.

He tensed, fearing it was a Roon scout, and reached behind to tap Sara on the thigh, urging her to loose her shaft. He caught himself when he realised that the figure was in fact a man, clad in forest greens and gripping a bow.

'It's a survivor from the Pass! We've got to rescue him.' Caspan waved down at the man and yelled, 'Up here!'

The soldier looked up and, to Caspan's surprise, ran back towards the forest. When he was a few yards from the woods he hesitated, glanced back at the drake and treasure hunters, and waved his bow above his head, signalling for help.

Caspan flew Frostbite down towards the man, when two Roon burst out of the trees and charged towards him. The stranger set an arrow to his bow, turned and loosed the shaft, but it was a hasty shot and sailed several feet above the giants. But Sara had more luck. Skilfully twisting in the saddle to bring her bow around, she sent an arrow thudding into one of the giants' shoulders, forcing him to drop his spear and howl in pain.

Caspan let go of the reins and leaned over to the right, his outstretched hands reaching for the man, as he dropped his bow and leapt towards Frostbite. As they shot past, Caspan caught hold of the soldier and hauled him up. The man wrapped his arms around Frostbite's neck as the drake soared back into the sky, just as the remaining Roon threw his axe.

It sailed through the air, twisting head over shaft . . . until its haft thudded into the back of the soldier's head. Caspan felt the man go limp and start to slide off Frostbite.

His feet firmly secured in the saddle straps, Caspan pulled the man towards him and wrapped an arm around his waist. He heard Sara's bowstring hum behind him.

Caspan glanced down to see the second Roon fall face-first in the water.

'How is he?' Sara asked.

Caspan cradled the man's head against his shoulder. 'He's conscious, but he took a heavy hit. We'd better get him to Rivergate so someone can check him out.'

Sara nodded. 'We've finished here anyway. If that fire doesn't stop the Roon, I don't know what will.'

Caspan was about to reply when the soldier's hood rolled back, revealing their features. Caspan's eyes flashed with surprise.

'It's a girl!' he said, lifting a section of the plaid shawl from beneath her cloak. 'And she's wearing the tartan of a Stewart highlander!'

CHAPTER 16

THE ENEMY OF MY ENEMY

As soon as Caspan and Sara returned to Rivergate, the girl was taken to a chamber in the keep. Two soldiers were posted inside the room to keep guard and a medic was summoned to tend to her injuries.

The girl was quite an enigma and the topic of much discussion as the treasure hunters and Captain Jace waited in the makeshift war room for her to recover. They were intrigued as to why she had been running away from the Roon, who were meant to be her allies, and, as she appeared to be wearing the garb of a scout, how she'd been allowed to join the Caledonish army, which precluded women from military service. The most alarming thing though, was that this was the first sighting of a highlander this far west, and the companions wondered how many more Caledonish warriors were in the area.

They didn't have to wait long before there was a knock on the door and a sentry announced that the girl was ready to be questioned. They found her sitting up in bed, a bandage wrapped around her forehead. She glared at the soldiers keeping guard by the door and at the medic, who was tidying up on a side table.

Before entering the room the treasure hunters and Captain Jace had agreed that Oswald should do the talking, believing he was the least threatening out of them all and that his calm demeanour would help settle the captive.

'That was quite a knock you took to the head,' Oswald said as he sat on the edge of the girl's bed. He smiled reassuringly. The girl shuffled over to the far side and glowered at him. 'I'm glad you've recovered.'

The girl's eyes narrowed defiantly. 'What? So ye can torture me?'

Oswald chuckled softly to himself. 'Do I look like the torturing type, my dear? I've been called many things in my life, but never a *torturer*. Although, some of the initiates I've taught over the years may argue otherwise, saying I've tortured them to death with my boring lessons. But that's a different matter altogether.' He smoothed a rumpled section of his cloak. 'I just want to ask you a few questions, that's all.'

The girl glared contemptuously at everyone in the room. 'Then why do yer need so much backup? Donnae tell me yer afraid o' a *girl*?'

'It's merely a precaution,' Oswald replied calmly. 'I'm sure you'd do exactly the same to us if we were your captives. And we're hardly afraid, but very *intrigued*. You see, as far as we knew, Roy Stewart's forces were still in Caledon. So until we find out who you are and what you're doing all the way out here, you might as well relax and tell us what we'd like to know. Then we can return you to your people.'

The girl scowled and looked over at a jug on a nearby table. She licked her lips. 'Give me a drink.'

Oswald nodded, and Sara, who was closest to the table, filled a tankard and handed it to the highlander. The girl waited for Sara to step back before taking a sip.

'So, do you have a name?' Oswald asked.

The highlander gulped down the cider and wiped her sleeve across her mouth. She stared boldly at the elderly treasure hunter, clearly with no intention of answering his question.

Oswald shrugged. 'Name or no name, we know you're from the Stewart Clan.'

The girl gave him a surprised look, then noticed Oswald was observing the tartan shawl beneath her cloak. She drew her cloak close together and glared at the treasure hunter.

'An' what o' it?'

Morgan pursed his lips. 'As a matter of fact, it's a great interest to us. As I said, according to our scouts, Roy Stewart's army hasn't moved from Sharn O'Kare Glen. So either you're part of an advance unit — and most probably scouts, based on your green cloak and bow — sent to assist the Roon, or you've taken a very long stroll and got terribly lost.'

The girl snorted contemptuously. 'Save yer breath. Ye wonnae get a thing out o' me.'

Oswald clicked his tongue. 'That's a shame. I was hoping you'd tell us why the Roon were after you. It seems a strange way to treat an ally.'

'Why donnae ye go an' ask them?' the captive returned.

Oswald drew a patient breath. 'I was at the Pass yesterday, but I didn't see any Caledonish warriors. Did your company arrive after the fight?'

Again silence. Oswald sighed and looked across at Master Morgan, who stood, stoic as a statue, over near the table.

'I don't think we'll get anything out of her,' the Master muttered, turning to Caspan and Sara. 'You might as well put her back where you found her. The Roon seemed keen to get their hands on this girl.'

The highlander's eyes flashed. 'Ye wouldnae dare!'

Morgan stared flatly at her. 'Why not? You've made it perfectly clear you don't want to tell us anything. There's no point wasting our time here when there's a dozen other important things we need to do.' He beckoned for the others to join him as he crossed the room.

'Wait!' the girl called out.

The treasure hunters stopped in the doorway. Oswald winked at Caspan, then glanced back at the highlander. 'You've changed your mind?'

The defiance slowly faded from the highlander's gaze, revealing to Caspan what he believed to be a very frightened girl.

'Mah name's Skye,' she said.

'There, that wasn't too hard, was it?' Oswald smiled as he returned to her bedside. 'Now that you've told me

your name, it's only befitting I tell you mine. I'm Oswald.'
He introduced the other members of the Brotherhood
and Captain Jace.

Skye looked around the chamber. 'Where am ah?'

Oswald regarded her for a moment. 'How about we
make a trade? Every time I answer one of your questions,
you'll answer one of mine. Agreed?' Skye nodded slowly,
and he replied, 'We're in Rivergate, a fortress located on a
small island in the middle of the Mooryn.'

'What's yer strength?'

There was an urgency in her tone that Caspan found
surprising.

Oswald raised a finger. 'I believe it's my turn to ask a
question. Now, let me think. Ah, yes: are you part of
a band of Caledonish scouts sent to assist the Roon?'

Skye nodded, then asked, 'How many men defend
Rivergate?'

'That's hardly fair,' Roland interjected. He stood
beside Caspan over near the window, his features bathed
in the blue light from the fire blazing across the river. 'She
can't just nod. Anyone can *nod*. We need *details*.'

Morgan silenced him with a stern look.

'We are the survivors from the battle in the Pass,'
Oswald said. 'We number little more than two hundred
strong.'

'That's why ye created the fire front,' Skye said. 'Even
wi' yer magical beasts, ye'll never last long against the
Roon. Yer hopin' the fire will drive them back.'

'That's the general plan.' Oswald took Skye's empty
tankard, crossed to the table and refilled it. 'So you've

seen the size of the Roon army?' he asked, handing back her drink.

The highlander nodded and lowered her gaze. 'An' how they treat prisoners.'

Captain Jace stood beside the guards at the door. His eyes narrowed as he walked towards the girl. 'What do you mean? What's happened to them?'

Skye opened her mouth to reply, when she caught herself, her expression reticent. She looked in turn at each of the people gathered in the chamber, then glanced back at Oswald. 'If ah tell ye what happened — what ah saw — do ye promise tae help me?'

Oswald turned questioningly to Morgan, who studied the girl intently before giving a slight nod.

'We'll put it to consideration,' Oswald replied.

Skye took a long draught of her drink. She drew a deep breath, as if mustering her courage, and said, 'Ah was part o' a small band o' scouts sent by Roy Stewart tae assist the Roon. We'd been wi' them for the past three days, movin' ahead o' the main army, chartin' a safe route south. We suspected ye'd be waitin' in ambush in the Pass, an' advised the Roon tae proceed wi' caution. But they wouldnae listen tae us an' marched into the ravine regardless. We decided tae wait back, believin' Andalonian archers would be positioned up on the cliff tops. Ye know just as well as ah do what took place in the Pass.' Her eyes narrowed furtively. 'But it's what happened *after* the battle that will be o' particular interest tae ye.'

Perhaps it was just his imagination, but Caspan was sure the shadows in the room seemed to lengthen and darken, as if some sinister force had crept inside the chamber.

'Right from the beginnin', many o' the Caledonish lairds were critical o' Roy Stewart's decision tae join forces wi' the Roon,' Skye continued. 'Roy is normally a wise man, nae prone tae makin' rash decisions, but his judgement was clouded by his desire tae conquer Lochinbar. He should hae never formed an alliance wi' the giants. Yes, they fight bravely in battle, but they're also notorious for their cruelty tae prisoners. They give no quarter, both during an' after combat.' She regarded each one of them in the chamber. 'Think yourselves lucky ye werenae taken prisoner.'

Jace grit his teeth, as if steeling himself for what he was about to hear. 'What happened?'

Skye lowered her gaze again. 'Ah'm sorry, but the prisoners were put tae the sword.'

Caspan's heart was like a lead weight in his chest. *Hadn't Jace said that over three hundred Andalonians surrendered to the Roon?*

'None escaped?' Jace pressed.

Skye shook her head grimly. 'All were slaughtered.'

Stunned, the Captain stared off into nowhere, then set his piercing gaze back on Skye. 'I hope Roy Stewart's very proud of his alliance.'

'We tried everythin' possible tae stop the Roon,' Skye protested.

Caspan was moved by the sincerity in her voice. But not so Jace, whose features were as hard as stone. 'I bet you did,' he snarled.

Skye looked at the Captain beseechingly. 'Ah know we're enemies, but killin' unarmed an' wounded prisoners is nae the highland way.'

'But forming alliances with those who do is? You need to think more carefully about whom you share a battle-field with.' Jace stormed off towards the door.

'We didnae know,' Skye called after him. 'Ye hae tae believe me. Does it mean nothin' tae ye that mah friends were killed when we tried tae stop the Roon?'

The Captain stopped in the doorway and glanced over his shoulder. 'What?'

Skye's eyes welled with tears and her hands trembled so much she could barely hold her tankard. Oswald took the drink from her and placed a comforting hand on her shoulder.

'You don't need to tell us, my dear child,' he said.

Skye shook her head. 'No, ye need tae know the truth.' She took a moment to compose herself, then explained, 'We were in our tents when the executions started. By the time we made it tae where the prisoners were kept, nearly a quarter o' 'em had already been killed. My commander confronted the Roon leader responsible for carryin' out the slaughter an' tried tae stop him, but he was cut down. The next thing ah knew, the giants turned on us. Ah ran for mah life. Ah was the only member o' mah company tae escape. Some Roon gave chase. Ah managed tae pick two off with mah bow, but the rest trapped me down by the river.'

It was only now Caspan noticed that the highlander's hands were scratched and her cloak torn in several places, evidently delivered by branches as she ran through the forest.

'You're lucky to have made it this far,' Oswald remarked. 'It's several miles back to the Pass.'

Skye nodded. 'Ah know. Ah was down tae mah final arrow an' exhausted by the time ah reached the river.' She glanced across at Caspan and Sara. 'Ah'm very lucky ye came by when ye did.'

Caspan smiled softly at her. Skye drew a deep, calming breath as she lay back in her bed, letting the tension and weariness drain from her body. She closed her eyes and nestled against the pillow, then looked around the room again, her gaze pausing on Roland. She sat up straight, her eyes narrowing.

'Yer one o' the boys who snuck into Tor O'Shawn,' she said matter-of-factly.

Roland cleared his throat and shifted uncomfortably. 'Tor-o-what?' he muttered, trying his best to sound as ignorant as possible.

'Some Andalonian boys disguised themselves as Strathboogie clansmen an' snuck inside Roy Stewart's fort. They rescued the Iron Duke before escapin' on magical, flyin' beasts.' Skye jerked her chin at Roland's bonnet. 'That's an interestin' hat yer wearing. Care tae tell me where ye found it?'

Roland snatched the bonnet from his head and hid it behind his back. 'I don't have the foggiest idea what you're talking about.'

His curiosity getting the better of him, Caspan asked Skye, 'How do you know about what happened at Tor O'Shawn?'

'There's barely a highlander who *hasnae* heard o' yer exploits,' Skye replied. 'From what ah heard, the boys who snuck into Tor O'Shawn encountered General Brett in the corridors before escapin'. They knew one another, an' there was no loss o' love between them.' Skye's eyes narrowed conspiratorially. 'What would ye say if ah could persuade Roy Stewart tae reconsider his alliance wi' the giants?'

'Why would you do that?' Morgan said warily. 'You'd stand nothing to gain from betraying your allies.'

Skye snorted. 'Allies? They slew mah companions — mah friends!'

'But how could *you* possibly organise such a thing?' Roland asked.

Skye's lips formed a hard, tight line. 'What? Because ah'm merely a *girl*? Let me assure ye, yer nae the only one who can go in disguise. It was this same girl who dressed as a man an' joined the band o' Caledonish scouts sent tae join the Roon. Ah was also the only one tae escape from the giants.' She looked at Roland challengingly. 'Donnae make the mistake o' underestimatin' mah capabilities.' She held Roland's stare for a moment before turning to Morgan. 'Ye said ye'd consider helpin' me if ah told ye what happened back in the Pass. Well, ah've stuck tae mah side o' the bargain. Now ah'd like ye tae help me get back tae Roy Stewart. He needs tae hear o' what happened tae his scouts.'

Oswald eyed Skye suspiciously. 'How can you guarantee us that we won't be taken prisoner once we return you to your people?'

'Yer nae mah enemy,' Skye replied. 'If anythin', the way ye've treated me has only made me realise just how wrong this war is.' She clenched her fists determinedly. 'We need tae unite against the Roon. When Roy Stewart hears o' what happened tae yer prisoners an' his scouts, ah'm sure he'll reassess his alliance.'

'And why would he listen to you?' Roland asked.

'Oh, he'll listen all right,' Skye replied assuredly. 'Ah'm his daughter.'

Chapter 17

Caspan Volunteers

The members of the Brotherhood and Captain Jace gathered in the war room to discuss what should be done. They decided that, if Skye was indeed who she claimed to be, and she could persuade her father to reconsider his alliance with the Roon, then it would be in their best interest that she be escorted safely to the highland army camped at Sharn O'Kare Glen. They had little reason not to believe her, given that when Caspan and Sara found her she was being hunted by giants. Skye also knew military details that only someone with close connections to Roy Stewart would be privy to.

Once it was decided that they would return Skye to her father, Captain Jace suggested that a group of soldiers should escort her back. Morgan argued otherwise, stating that time was of the essence and it could take a group of men travelling by horse over a day to reach Roy Stewart's camp. By then the highland army might have already engaged Duke Bran's army.

'I'll do it,' Caspan offered. 'Frostbite can fly at ten times the speed of a galloping horse. If I head off now, Skye and I can be at Sharn O'Kare Glen before midnight.'

Morgan rubbed his chin. 'It will be risky, Caspan. Are you sure you want to do this?'

'We don't have many other options. As you said, time is of the essence, and none of the other Wardens can travel as fast as Frostbite. We've been given a chance to drive a wedge between Caledon and the Roon. We mightn't get another opportunity like this. This could be our only hope to save Andalon.'

'I'd feel a lot more comfortable if one of us accompanied you,' Raven commented. 'It's not that I doubt your ability, but it will be incredibly dangerous.'

Caspan shook his head. 'It'd only slow Frostbite down. Besides, his saddle's only designed for two riders.'

'What if Sara and I were to saddle up Cloud Dancer and come with you?' Morgan suggested.

'Cloud Dancer's a lot slower than Frostbite. I doubt she'd make it to the highland camp before sunrise. By then it might be too late, and Roy Stewart's army might have moved.'

'And what if the highlanders take you captive?' Captain Jace warned. 'They mightn't be as accommodating as we've been to Skye. Have you stopped to consider that?'

'I'll have Frostbite with me,' Caspan replied confidently. 'I can't think of a better guardian. Besides, I don't think Skye would let anything bad happen to me — she's given her word. And I know that Roy Stewart doesn't approve of torture. I remember he was critical of how General Brett treated Duke Bran.' He regarded the Master. 'You've got to let me do this.'

'I'd hate to see Caspan come to any harm,' Shanty said, smiling softly at the former street thief, 'but he's right. This might be our only chance to destroy the union between the Roon and the highlanders. It will be dangerous, but we don't have any other choice.'

'It will be no more dangerous than waiting here, hoping the fire stops the Roon,' Caspan added. 'All we need is for the wind to drop or change direction and the giants could be at Rivergate within a couple of hours.'

'That's really reassuring, thanks for that,' Roland said sarcastically. He crossed to the window and peered outside to make sure the wind was still blowing from the south. Nodding in satisfaction, he turned questioningly to Caspan. 'What are you going to do if Roy Stewart wants to negotiate a possible truce?'

'Then the highland laird can send an envoy or a raven to the King,' Shanty said flatly. 'That's not for Caspan, or any of us for that matter, to discuss. Besides, I think the possibility of peace talks is getting a little ahead of ourselves.'

'I have no intention of going anywhere near the highland camp,' Caspan added. 'I'll drop Skye off a mile or so from Sharn O'Kare Glen. She can then make her own way into the valley. If all goes to plan, I won't see the highlanders.'

Morgan exhaled wearily and paced the room. Caspan watched him anxiously, his heart racing, hoping the Master would agree to his suggestion. With his head held low, the Master stopped before the hearth and stared into the flickering flames. A faint smile formed at the edge of his lips as he turned to Caspan.

'It seems like it was only yesterday when you had your first sword-training session back at the House of Whispers. You barely even knew how to hold a sword. And now you're volunteering to undertake a mission that most soldiers would run a mile away from.'

Caspan held his gaze and licked his lips eagerly. 'So you're going to let me do this?'

Morgan sighed. 'It goes against my finer judgement, but yes, I'll allow you.' He raised a finger in warning. 'But you'll need to keep an eye in the back of your head. Skye may have given you her word that no harm will come to you, but you'll be going near an enemy war camp. There's no telling what type of reception you'll receive when you drop Skye off.'

Caspan nodded determinedly. 'I promise I'll be careful.'

Morgan turned to Jace. 'We need to send a messenger raven to the King, informing him of what's happened.'

'I'll see to that now,' the Captain replied, walking towards the door.

Morgan regarded Caspan. 'Now, I suppose we should start getting you ready for your mission.'

As they exited the chamber, Roland tapped Caspan on the shoulder. 'Hey, Cas, there's no chance of smuggling me inside one of your saddle bags, is there?' he whispered.

CHAPTER 18
ROY STEWART

Fifteen minutes later, Caspan and Skye climbed atop Frostbite down in the courtyard. Sara and Roland checked that the few provision bags, blankets and two full quivers were securely fastened to the rear of the saddle cloth, then stepped back to join the other treasure hunters in a doorway alcove. They huddled in their cloaks and crowded around the warmth offered from an iron brazier. The wind was now a howling gale, which threatened to rip the banners from the battlements.

Caspan was wary of slowing Frostbite down with extra weight, but he didn't want to take any unnecessary risks. If all went to plan, he'd drop Skye off around midnight then return to Rivergate. It would be a journey of around eight hours, and he hoped to be toasting his success with his friends back in the fortress several hours before dawn. Yet there was no guarantee all *would* go to plan.

Caspan would be flying into enemy territory, and there was no way of knowing what he might encounter. It would be an uncomfortable and cold trip at best in the strong wind, but that wouldn't impact too much on Frostbite. The drake would use the heavy gusts to his advantage, gliding on the currents like a ship sliding down a towering wave. Though it would be a different story altogether if heavy snow were to set in, causing them to seek shelter until it passed. There was also the chance they might run into a band of highland scouts patrolling the hinterland of Sharn O'Kare Glen. The supplies and arrows were therefore a necessary precaution.

Keen to get underway, Caspan bid farewell to his friends and commanded Frostbite to rise out of the courtyard. Buffeted in the strong wind, they turned east and headed off into the night.

Caspan was surprised at how far the fire front had moved. Driven by the gale, it had spread deep into Huntingdon Hedge, and he felt assured that the garrison at Rivergate would be safe for now. The fire also proved a valuable landmark, helping him keep his bearing as they soared through the sky.

Skye was as rigid as a statue, clinging fearfully to the saddle horn and wrapping her feet tightly around Frostbite's flanks. Caspan had forgotten how frightening it was to fly for the first time, particularly at night, and he tried to keep Frostbite at a low altitude. But it was dangerous in the driving wind, which at times threatened to push them into tree tops and hillsides. It wasn't long, though, before Skye relaxed and sat more easily in the saddle. Caspan eased Frostbite higher. From here they could ride the wind currents, and Skye even held her arms out to the side and hooted joyously as they swooped through the darkness.

Soon the fire was all but a distant glow on the western horizon. Eventually this was swallowed by the night, and Caspan navigated his way via the north star. Feeling hungry, he reached into one of the saddle bags and rummaged around until he found some chunks of salted pork and slices of crusty bread, which he and Skye gulped down. It was bitterly cold, and Caspan was grateful Roland and Sara had packed blankets, which he and Skye wrapped around their shoulders. Skye pointed out some landmarks, but for most of the flight they rode in silence.

A long time seemed to have passed, and Caspan was fighting back a tremendous yawn when Skye tapped him on the thigh and pointed to the black silhouette of a hill up ahead. 'Mah father's camp's just on the other side,' she announced.

Caspan nodded and set Frostbite down in a glade on the leeward side of a hillock. He waited for Skye to dismount, then tossed her an extra blanket and a lit lantern.

'I guess this is it,' he said, extending a hand in farewell.

Skye frowned. 'Yer nae comin'?'

Caspan shook his head. 'I know you've promised no harm will come to me, but I'm not so sure how the highlanders will react when they see me wandering through their camp.'

'But mah father will want tae talk tae ye,' Skye insisted.

'I'm not in any position to negotiate terms with Roy Stewart,' Caspan replied pointedly.

'Ah'm nae expectin' ye tae, but he might hae an urgent message for ye tae deliver once he hears o' what happened tae his scouts,' Skye said. 'Ah cannae say for certain what his reaction will be, but it might hae a huge impact on the war. Imagine if he decides tae call a truce between Caledon an' Andalon? He might need ye tae run an urgent message south tae the Iron Duke. What if yer nae here tae deliver that message, an' the Iron Duke marches north tomorrow mornin' tae attack? All o' this would hae been for nothin'. Ah donnae think ye'd want that guilt on yer shoulders.'

Caspan shook his head doubtfully. 'I don't know.'

'Ye've brought me this far. What harm will it do if ye hang around for a little longer?' Skye regarded him for a moment. 'Look, how about ye give me two hours? That's nae much tae ask. Wait here, an' if mah father doesnae come out tae speak tae ye, then ye can leave.' She considered Caspan earnestly. 'What happens here tonight might determine the course o' the war an' save the lives o' thousands o' men. Ye wouldnae hae brought me all the way out here if ye didnae believe in me.'

Caspan sighed and nodded. 'Okay. But I'm only giving you two hours.'

Skye smiled. 'Thanks. Ye wonnae regret this.' She then hurried off into the night.

'Well, it looks as if it's just you and me again,' Caspan

said, as he slid off Frostbite and rubbed some life into his thighs. He led the drake over to the shelter offered by a large oak on the edge of the clearing, then untied his bow from the rear of the saddle and pulled off its calfskin cover. Slinging a quiver over his shoulder, he glanced around the trees and selected a position that allowed him to peer back towards the stretch of open land that led to Sharn O'Kare Glen. Hopefully he'd be able to spot any highlanders before they snuck up on the copse.

As Frostbite nuzzled against him, Caspan reached around to pat the drake on the snout. 'Better to be safe than sorry,' he muttered. In the ghostly half-light of the crescent moon, Caspan noticed the almost pensive expression on the Warden's face. 'What? You think we should trust Skye?' Perhaps it was a coincidence, but Frostbite raised his chin in a nodding motion. Caspan smirked and wiggled a cautionary finger at his guardian. 'I know you're a lot older and wiser than me, and you probably think you've seen it all, but you've still got a lot to learn about people, my scaly friend. Especially high-landers. Here.' He reached into one of the saddle bags and placed a chunk of pork on the ground for Frostbite to eat. 'Keep your mind at ease by chewing on that.'

Again the drake regarded him thoughtfully, then, sitting back on his haunches, picked up the meat with his front claws and nibbled at it.

Caspan chortled. 'Well, I've seen it all now. Next thing, you'll be needing a plate and fork.'

The night dragged by. Caspan felt himself starting to drift off to sleep when he spotted the bobbing, wan glow of an approaching lantern. Suddenly alert, he reached instinctively for an arrow, then caught himself, believing confronting Roy Stewart with a readied bow mightn't be the best way to establish trust. Slinging his bow over his shoulder, he studied the dark shapes illuminated in the lantern-light, detecting four people.

'That was a wise decision,' a voice commented from behind the treasure hunter.

Caspan spun around to find a man standing by the trees, his bow aimed at him. As the stranger stepped forward, two other men emerged from the darkness surrounding Caspan, their swords half-drawn from their scabbards.

Frostbite growled and tensed, but Caspan grabbed the drake's reins and held him in check. If the highlanders wanted to attack, they could have done so long before now.

The highlander with the bow rested it against a trunk and lit the lantern attached to his belt. He waved it above his head, signalling the group approaching from Sharn O'Kare Glen. They waved theirs in return.

'We meet again,' the highlander announced, stepping closer to Caspan, all the while keeping a close eye on Frostbite.

Caspan studied the man intently, only now realising it was Ewan, the leader of the dreaded Gall-Gaedhil, the band of black-clad highland assassins who were acting as Roy Stewart's personal guards. The last time Caspan had seen the highlander was inside the central keep of Tor O'Shawn as Ewan battled Lachlan.

Caspan raised his hands. 'I mean you no harm. I've come here on a peace mission.' In spite of Skye's assurance, he feared he might be taken prisoner . . . or worse.

'Ah'll let Roy Stewart be the judge o' that.' Ewan retrieved his bow and set a precautionary arrow to the string. His dark eyes studied Frostbite as he waited for the other group of highlanders to reach the glade.

Caspan was relieved to discover that the person carrying the lantern was Skye. She hung her lantern on a branch as she entered the copse, and started when she saw the Gall-Gaedhil. She turned to the hooded man standing beside her. 'Ah told ye we could trust the boy an' his magical beast,' she said. 'Ah told them no harm would come tae them. Donnae ye trust me?'

'Ah'm merely being cautious,' the stranger replied calmly.

Skye exhaled disparagingly and glanced at Caspan. 'Ah'm sorry, but this is typical o' mah father. Ah invite him tae a secret meetin', an' he turns up with half a dozen bodyguards.' She strode over to a log on the far side of the clearing, sat down and gave Caspan a smile. 'But thanks for waitin'. Ah'm sure ye remember mah father, Roy Stewart.'

The stranger drew back his hood and set his piercing blue eyes on Caspan. 'Ah owe ye mah gratitude for returnin' mah daughter tae me. She's had her mother worried sick for the past week since she disappeared.' He considered his daughter, a faint smile playing at the edge of his lips. 'Unfortunately she takes too much after me in mah younger days. Fancy dressin' as a scout an' joinin' the band that went west tae join the Roon? Now there's a tale for mah grandchildren.' He cocked an eyebrow at his daughter. 'That is, o' course, if ah'll ever hae any.'

Skye bristled. 'Oh, be quiet.'

The Stewart Laird sat down beside Skye and motioned for Caspan to join them. 'Ah hope mah men didnae startle ye, but ah had tae make sure ah wasnae walkin' into a trap.'

'I would have done the same,' Caspan replied.

Roy nudged his daughter. 'Ye see — ah'm nae the only cautious one here.' Skye rolled her eyes and mumbled something under her breath as her father turned to Caspan, his expression serious. 'Yer no doubt keen tae return tae yer friends, so let's get straight tae the point. Ah hae a gift ah'd like ye tae deliver tae the Iron Duke. Ah'm sure he'll appreciate it.'

Roy jerked his chin at two of his company who were waiting at the edge of the clearing. Caspan was able to identify one of them as a member of the Gall-Gaedhil by the man's black shawl and kilt. The other person was cloaked and hooded. His hands were bound. He was shoved into the clearing by the highland assassin, who then reached up and pulled back the stranger's hood.

Caspan's eyes flashed with surprise.

It was General Brett.

'Circumstances forced me tae seize the opportunity tae form an alliance with the Roon,' Roy said to Caspan. 'But as o' this day, havin' heard what they did tae your prisoners and mah scouts, Caledon will hae nothin' further tae do with the giants.'

Brett snarled at the Stewart Laird. 'You traitorous dog!'

Roy regarded him calmly. 'Ah donnae think yer in any position tae make such comments.'

'Wait until the Roon hear of this! They'll invade Caledon, burn every village, and put every man, woman and child to the sword! Highlanders will live to regret the day Roy Stewart —'

Roy nodded slightly, signalling for the highlander standing behind Brett to shove a rolled up piece of cloth in his mouth. He secured it in place with a leather cord.

'What the Roon did to mah band o' scouts was nothin' short o' an act o' war,' Roy said to Caspan as the highland guard moved the General out of the clearing.

'So you'll side with Andalon?' Caspan could barely mask the surprise and hope in his voice.

Roy pursed his lips pensively. 'That remains tae be seen. Caledon an' Lochinbar hae been enemies for hundreds o' years. Ah donnae think a hatred that has spanned generations can be so easily overcome.'

'Yet you united the highland clans,' Caspan countered.

Roy nodded slowly. 'True, ah did. But a prudent man doesnae take bold steps. He inches forward, carefully considerin' each move. That way he doesnae make mistakes.' He reached beneath his cloak and produced a sealed letter from his shawl. 'Consider this mah first calculated step. Make sure the Iron Duke receives this. Hand it tae him personally tonight. Can ye promise ye'll see it done?'

Caspan nodded as he accepted the letter and tucked it inside his tunic. 'You have my word.'

Roy signalled for Brett to be brought back into the clearing. 'An' as mah second step, ah'm placin' Brett in yer custody. See tae it that he's also delivered tae the Iron Duke. Consider it a token o' mah good will.'

'It will be my pleasure,' Caspan said, overwhelmed by the responsibility the laird was placing in him.

'Ah would hae also given ye Lady Brook, but she's been wi' the Roon for the past week,' Roy said.

Caspan shuddered. There was something about Brett's tight-lipped, stern-featured co-conspirator that scared him. He remembered her sitting in a darkened corner of the great hall in the central keep of Tor O'Shawn. He hoped that would've been the last he'd see of her.

Roy patted Caspan on the shoulder and looked wistfully about the clearing. 'Life is a strange thing. Who would hae thought ah'd be out here tonight, discussing alliances an' treaties wi' one o' mah enemies.'

'He's nae an enemy, Father,' Skye said pointedly.

Roy Stewart looked deep into Caspan's eyes. 'Ah'm startin' tae see that.'

Skye snorted. 'Pity it's taken ye *forty years* tae do so. Still, better late than never.'

Roy smiled fondly at his daughter and nudged Caspan. 'Ye see what ah mean about her bein' just like me? She's as wild as the highlands she was born in.' He slapped his thighs, rose and extended his open palm to Caspan. 'Ah wish ye the best o' luck, lad. Ah'm sure we'll meet again, an' next time in more favourable circumstances. Remember tae give the Iron Duke that letter. Ah really donnae care what he does wi' Brett, although ah imagine a nice cold prison cell will suit him nicely.'

Caspan smiled as he shook the laird's hand. 'Don't worry. I promise I'll pass on your message.'

The highlanders made their way back across the glen, leaving Caspan and Frostbite with the prisoner.

CHAPTER 19

THE DUKE'S CAMP

Caspan kept a careful eye on Brett during the entire flight south. He made sure the former general of the Eighth Legion sat in front of him, gagged, his bound hands strapped to the thick leather cord that served as a saddle grip. Caspan also kept his longbow in its calfskin cover at the rear of the saddle, well and truly out of reach.

They weren't long into their flight when Brett made some plaintive wheezing sounds and slumped forward in his harness, but Caspan refused to remove his gag. The traitor was as crafty as a fox, and Caspan wasn't going to fall for any of his ruses. Caspan's suspicion was confirmed when, after several minutes, Brett stopped gasping, sat back and glared daggers over his shoulder at him. Caspan tried his best to ignore him, fixing his gaze on the land below, searching for Duke Bran's encampment.

It wasn't long before he spotted the distant glow of campfires glistening in the darkness like rubies on a black carpet, and he steered Frostbite towards the military base. They flew slowly over the camp until Caspan spotted a large central tent, which had twin banners that bore the royal wolf crest of House MacDain flapping above it.

Caspan saw the sentries start as Frostbite hovered above the Duke's shelter. No doubt the arrival of the large magical beast had raised the alarm. They dispersed when two familiar faces strode among them, urging them to lower their weapons.

Caspan set Frostbite down in a clear section to the side of the royal tent and slid off his saddle. The widest of smiles crossed his face as he hurried over to greet Master Scott and the Duke's son, Prince Dale.

Caspan barely recognised the Prince. It had only been a month or two since they had battled alongside one another on the parapets of Darromere against a Roon horde, but Dale seemed to have aged dramatically. His youthful blue eyes now looked grey and weary, and he had grown a thick beard. Although only eighteen, the Prince could easily be mistaken for a man in his mid to late twenties.

Dale smiled broadly as he approached Caspan, greeting him with a handshake. 'Ah, it's good to see you again,' he said, before pointing a finger in warning at him. 'But let's make sure that the next time we meet, it won't be in battle! I promised you we'd go hunting one day, and I mean to honour that.'

Caspan beamed. 'Just name the time and place.' He longed to take his bow and head off into the woods of Lochinbar to hunt game with the Prince, but with the country engulfed in war, such a carefree activity seemed all but a distant dream.

Scott clapped Caspan on the shoulder in greeting then stepped back to inspect his former student. 'You're looking well. A little worn and tired around the edges, but I'll let that pass.'

'That's only because I was trained by the best,' Caspan replied, grinning. Considering all that he'd been through over the past few weeks, it was nothing short of a miracle he hadn't been injured.

Scott chuckled. 'Now that's the answer I was hoping to hear.' The smile slowly faded from his lips and his forehead creased with concern. 'Don't get me wrong, I'm delighted to see you, Caspan, but what are you doing here? I hope nothing's happened.'

'Quite a lot has, actually, as I'm sure you can see.' Caspan jerked his chin towards Brett, who remained strapped into the harness on Frostbite.

Scott's eyes grew wide with shock. 'The General!'

'*Former* General, before he turned *traitor*,' Dale corrected. He ordered some soldiers to get Brett down from Frostbite, then glanced at Caspan. 'But how?'

'It's a long story, but it's been an even longer night.' Caspan rubbed his thighs wearily. 'Do you mind if I sit down for a minute and have something warm to drink? I'll fill you in on what's happened.' He looked around the camp questioningly, failing to spot Duke Bran amidst the crowd of curious soldiers. 'I hope the Duke's here?'

Dale nodded. 'He's inside his tent, discussing tactics with his officers.'

Caspan cocked an eyebrow. 'At this time of night?'

Dale's expression was solemn. 'At dawn we march to fight Roy Stewart. Father wants to make sure his commanders know where they'll be deployed on the field and what role they'll play in the battle.' The Prince strode over to a large tent with a banner of House MacDain flying from a spear near its entrance. As he drew back the flap, a cold blast of wind buffeted the camp, making a nearby group of tethered horses neigh and stamp restlessly. Dale shivered. 'This night isn't even fit for wolves, let alone men. We'll wait in my tent until my father's ready.'

Caspan shook his head. 'My drink will have to wait.' He reached beneath his tunic and pulled out Roy Stewart's letter. 'Duke Bran needs to read this right now.'

Dale inspected the letter's seal and looked at Caspan, confused. 'I don't recognise this.'

'It's from Roy Stewart,' Caspan explained, much to the Prince and Master Scott's disbelief. 'Like I said, a lot's happened. But this can't wait. I need to see the Duke right now before it's too late.'

A few minutes later, Caspan sat beside Dale inside the Prince's tent, a warm tankard of cider nestled against his belly. Opposite the table sat Scott and Duke Bran. The Duke's grim features were drawn and drained from lack of sleep, but he studied Roy Stewart's letter intently. His gaze lingered on the message for some time before he lowered it and stared at Caspan, dumbstruck.

'This changes things somewhat,' he muttered, a glimmer of hope in his weary eyes. 'I've been discussing battle tactics all night, and now we mightn't have to fight Roy Stewart after all.' He waved the letter before him. 'He's made an offer of *peace*.'

Prince Dale's eyes flashed with surprise. 'Peace?' He reached across the table. 'May I?'

Bran obliged, and Dale quickly read the letter. He handed it back to his father. 'How did you come by this?' he asked Caspan, stunned.

Caspan spent some time explaining everything that had happened during the past few days, from the Battle of the High Coast and Bandit's injury, to the defence of Rivergate, the chance encounter with Skye, and the subsequent meeting with Roy Stewart.

Bran rose from his seat and paced the tent once Caspan had finished. The wind howled outside and caused the candles on the table to flicker, but the Duke barely seemed to notice, his steel-grey eyes deep with concentration.

'Normally I wouldn't entertain the idea of meeting with the enemy,' he announced eventually, glancing at the three expectant faces that looked across at him, 'but this is too valuable an opportunity to turn down.'

'So Roy Stewart wants to meet with you?' Scott asked.

Bran nodded. 'There's a stone circle several miles from here. He's requested I meet him there an hour after dawn.'

'On your own?' Scott pressed.

Bran shook his head. 'We can each bring two people, but no more.'

'And you trust him? You don't think it will be a trap?'

'I know the area,' Dale commented. 'The stone circle lies on top of an exposed hill. The nearest trees are several hundred yards away. You'd be able to make your escape long before the enemy got close.'

Scott regarded him sceptically. 'Still, it doesn't mean they mightn't try.'

The Duke stopped pacing and turned to Caspan. 'What do you think? Can Roy be trusted?' Caspan shifted uncomfortably and gave Bran a blank look. 'You'd be the best judge of his character, seeing that you spoke to him less than an hour ago. How did he seem?'

Caspan hoped he didn't seem disrespectful, but he couldn't help but snicker at the irony that he should be the one being asked about trust. Trust was something fools placed in others because they lacked the ability to take care of themselves. At least, that's what he'd been conditioned to believe back in Floran, during his time with the Black Hand. *Trust no one* was the creed by which he had lived. There were no such things as friends. Only rivals, who'd sooner put a blade against your throat whilst you slept than share the day's takings. Greed and jealousy governed men's hearts. Not trust. That's why he'd become a lone wolf.

But now he knew otherwise. Barely four months had passed since he'd joined the Brotherhood, but he had learnt so much in that time. The Brotherhood Masters had honed his thieving and fighting skills, but the most valuable lesson Caspan had obtained had been that nobody could survive in this world alone. Even a lone wolf needed friends — to join the pack, where his skills would be complemented and strengthened. And that didn't come without having faith in your friends to watch your back.

Caspan cleared his throat. 'I think he can be trusted. He seemed honest enough, and was angered by what had happened to his scouts. He referred to it as nothing less than a declaration of war. And I know he doesn't like Brett. I learnt as much when I spied on their meeting back in Tor O'Shawn.'

'Roy's also given us General Brett,' Dale said pointedly. 'He gained nothing from doing that.'

Scott folded his arms warily across his chest. 'Other than earning our trust, which he might then use against us.'

'That might be so, but I can't refuse this offer,' Bran said.

Dale straightened on his stool. 'I'll come with you.'

The Duke regarded his son for a moment. 'No. If it's a trap, I can't risk having both of us captured or killed. And if anything happens to me, I need you to lead the army and govern Lochinbar.' He rubbed his grizzled chin, his eyes narrowing conspiratorially. 'I can only take two people with me, but what if they had the ability to summon magical guardians?'

Scott nodded his approval of the plan. 'This is sounding better. Even if it were a trap, you'd be able to fight your way out. So who will you take — Caspan and me?'

Bran gave Caspan a sympathetic look. 'I know you're tired, but Roy seems to trust you. If he didn't, he wouldn't have given you this letter or handed Brett over to you. You might have a calming presence on these affairs. And Frostbite and Shimmer will be able to deal with any surprises the highlanders have in store for us. One of the commanders in the Seventh Legion also has a Warden, and some others have magical Dray weapons, but I'd prefer to have you by my side.'

Caspan nodded, but he felt torn. He'd promised his friends at Rivergate that he would return before dawn, but one thing had led to another, and now he was being pulled even further from his original course. As desperately as he wanted to go back to his companions, he also didn't want to miss the meeting between the Duke and Stewart Laird. Bran was right: Roy seemed to trust Caspan, and the highland laird might be more comfortable in his presence. Besides, he could always fly back to Rivergate after the meeting. He took a long draught of his drink, felt its warmth fill his belly, and nodded.

Bran peered outside the tent flap. 'It will be dawn in a couple of hours. I suggest you get what rest you can. We'll need to be up at sunrise.'

'There's ample room in my tent,' Scott informed Caspan. 'I've get plenty of spare blankets, too.'

Caspan smiled as he stood up and stretched. 'Thanks, but I should dismiss Frostbite first. He's tired, too, and I'd like him fresh and ready for the morning.' He glanced at Duke Bran. 'But what of General Brett?'

The Duke's lips curled contemptuously. 'I've got enough to think about at the moment. I'll deal with him once we've returned from our meeting.' He turned and smiled softly at Caspan. 'Now, go and get some sleep. We've a long day ahead of us.'

CHAPTER 20

THE MEETING AT THE STONE CIRCLE

Dawn crept timidly across the land as Duke Bran, Scott and Caspan cantered out to the stone circle. The wind had died down, but dark clouds had settled in overnight, heavy with the promise of snow and painting the forest in shades of bone. It was still bitterly cold, and they all wore thick, padded jerkins beneath their cloaks. The Duke also wore a chainmail vest, pauldrons and gauntlets, which clinked and rattled as he guided his mount along the trail.

They rode to the accompaniment of birdsong, which Caspan found comforting. If enemy soldiers were waiting in ambush then surely the woods would be ominously silent. Still, he wasn't leaving anything to chance and he gripped his bow in his left hand. The heavy pommel of the longsword strapped to his side slapped reassuringly against his thigh.

Caspan had only had a few hours sleep, but he felt alert and ready for action. He'd always found the cold invigorating. It also helped that he'd washed his face in a bucket of freezing water as soon as he woke.

Reaching the end of the forest, the trio drew rein and peered up the open hill that rose before them. Cresting the slope was the stone circle, reaching into the sky like the outstretched fingers of a giant hand. It was a distance of perhaps three hundred yards up to the monoliths, and the companions studied the surrounding woods for some time before Master Scott nudged his mount forward and led the way up.

Caspan felt exposed and vulnerable as they rode up the grassy incline. He imagined dozens of highlanders hiding in the forest fringe, their bows drawn at him and his companions, waiting for the command to fire. Guiding his horse with the pressure of his knees, he set an arrow to his own bow and scanned the screen of trees, but not even his sharp eyes could detect any movement.

He drew a breath of relief and returned the shaft to his quiver when they reached the top. In the centre of the stone circle waited Roy Stewart, Ewan and, much to Caspan's surprise, Skye. Scott rode around the perimeter of the monoliths, a hand resting on the hilt of his sword, checking that no enemies lay waiting in ambush. Satisfied, he nodded at Bran. The Duke gave the command to dismount, and Caspan and Scott led their horses over to the side of the stones, allowing Bran to discuss matters with Roy in private. The treasure hunters were joined shortly by Skye, giving Caspan the opportunity to introduce her to Scott. Ewan came over halfway and leaned against one of the monoliths, his dark eyes carefully studying the Brotherhood Master.

'Ah'm glad ye trusted us,' Skye said to Caspan. 'Ah was worried the Iron Duke might hae laid an ambush or stormed this hill wi' an army o' hundreds.'

Caspan glanced at Scott and smiled softly at the irony of her words. 'We thought the same,' he replied, turning to Skye. 'It appears we're not that different after all.'

Ewan humphed and pulled his black tartan shawl higher around his neck. He looked back towards the centre of the monoliths, where the Stewart Laird and Duke Bran were sitting on a stone slab that had toppled over and now served as a makeshift bench. They were speaking in hushed voices.

'He doesn't look like the talkative type,' Scott whispered to Skye, motioning towards the leader of the Gall-Gaedhil with a flick of his eyes.

'He lets his sword do the talkin', as do all the Gall-Gaedhil. Still, they never leave mah father's side. They watch him like loyal guard dogs. I'm sure one sleeps at the base o' his bed.' Skye turned to Caspan. 'It didnae surprise us one bit when we saw ye ridin' up the hill wi' the Iron Duke. It was a wise choice, considerin' ye can summon yer magical drake.'

'Yet you waited regardless?' Caspan queried.

Skye shrugged. 'If ye wanted tae harm Father, ye could hae easily done so last night. He believes he can trust ye. As do ah.'

Caspan swelled with pride. Earning the trust of the leader of the highland army and his daughter was quite an achievement for a former street thief who once had no greater ambition in life than to scrounge enough food out of alleyways so he wouldn't starve.

One of the horses neighed and stamped the ground restlessly. Caspan whispered soothingly in its ear and stroked its neck, calming it down. He pointed at the leaders. 'How do you think this will go?'

'Ah think it's safe tae say they both want peace, otherwise they wouldnae hae agreed tae this meetin',' Skye replied. 'Hopefully they can find a middle ground an' come tae an agreement that meets the needs o' both parties.'

'Which is easier said than done,' Master Scott muttered wryly.

Skye regarded him flatly. 'Ah donnae see why it's such a difficult thing tae do. They're nae bickerin' children. All they hae tae do is put on the table what they'd each like tae gain from a possible alliance an' come tae a mutual agreement.'

'And that's where the problem lies,' Scott replied. 'Agreements of this nature are not made without concessions.'

Skye arched an eyebrow at the Master. 'Maybe the problem lies nae in the concessions that must be made, but more so in the fact that they are *men* an' are too proud tae take a step back. Hae ye ever considered that?'

Scott smirked and turned to Caspan. 'She's not related to Kilt, is she?'

Skye glanced questioningly between the treasure hunters. 'Kilt?'

'One of our friends,' Caspan explained. 'She's quite, well, strong-willed.'

Skye held her chin high. 'Ah'll take that comment as a compliment.' She considered Caspan for a moment. 'How's General Brett? Ah hope nothin' untoward happened tae him durin' yer flight last night — like fallin' out o' his saddle.'

Caspan chortled. 'I hate to disappoint, but no, we made it safely to Duke Bran's camp. He's now kept under guard.'

'Keep a close eye on him,' Skye warned. 'Ah've never trusted that man. He reminds me o' a snake, full o' venom.'

It was about an hour later that Bran and Roy finished talking. Flecks of snow began to drift from the sky. Caspan was thankful he'd put on his warm tunic and Brotherhood cloak as he and the others led the horses over to their leaders. They mounted up, bid farewell and rode back down the hill in opposite directions.

'Well?' Scott asked the Duke as they approached the forest.

'It went much better than I thought it would,' Bran replied. 'Roy Stewart seems an honourable man. I'm sure, had fate not seen us born on different sides of the border, we could have been close friends.'

'It's not too late yet,' Caspan commented.

Bran nodded thoughtfully. 'We'll see. It's a shame, though, that Roy and I had to wait this long to meet.

If we had, our countries might never have gone to war in the first place.' He brushed the snow from his cloak as they rode, three abreast, along the forest trail. 'Roy's terminated his alliance with the Roon. He's going to join forces with us.'

'An alliance between Lochinbar and Caledon!' Scott whistled. 'I never thought I'd live to see the day that happened.'

Caspan could barely control his excitement and he reached across to pat the Duke commendably on the shoulder. 'Well done, my lord.'

The Duke smiled warmly in return. 'There are, of course, a few concessions and demands we both want met,' he said, prompting Caspan and Scott to exchange a wry glance, 'but they're reasonable, and we've already agreed upon most of the terms. The rest we can settle over the coming weeks.' He steered his mount around an exposed root and settled more comfortably into his saddle. 'As soon as Roy returns to his camp, he's going to send a false report to the Roon that a major battle was fought this morning, and that he has defeated the legions in Lochinbar. He's also going to tell the Roon that he's now marching west, and the giants are to hold off from fighting the remaining Andalonian army until reinforced by the highlanders. When the final, decisive battle is fought, Roy will move his force around to the rear of the Roon, cut off their retreat and attack them in the rear. Combined, our armies should be enough to defeat the giants.'

'It all sounds so simple,' Scott commented.

Caspan sighed longingly. 'And then the war will be over.'

'Not only *over*,' Scott said, 'but more importantly *won*.'

'Roy's also agreed to my demand that he withdraw from Darrowmere,' Bran added. 'His troops will begin leaving the city later today.'

Scott cocked an eyebrow in question at the Duke. 'And what does he want in return? One does not give up such a possession without recompense.'

'I've agreed to grant him control of the north-western section of Lochinbar. The region contains rich farming land, so the highlanders will be able to sow their own crops. It will put an end to the border raids every winter. The only problem, of course, is that I will have to persuade the people living in the area to relocate south, making room for new Caledonish setters.'

'They mightn't take too nicely to that,' Scott remarked.

Bran nodded. 'I know, but this is too good an opportunity to turn down. All I can do is try to put it to them as gently as possible and hope they see my reasoning. If not for this agreement, they might have lost their land and possibly their lives.'

Scott gave the Duke a gratifying look. 'So you avoided fighting a major battle this morning, got back your capital and made a new ally. Not bad for an hour's work.'

'I'll send word to my brother, the King, as soon as I get back to our camp.' The Duke gave a self-satisfied smile. 'I think he'll be a little excited by this sudden twist of events.' He peered up through a break in the canopy and kicked his heels into his mount's flanks. 'Now, let's hurry up. The wind's picking up and the snow looks like it's going to set in.'

CHAPTER 21

THE MARCH WEST

Duke Bran's army packed up and began the long march west shortly after midday. By now the wind had risen into a howling gale, which drove the snow in icy blasts that bit to the bone and made men curse and wish they were indoors before blazing hearths. Soon the countryside was blanketed in white swathes that made footing unpredictable, and the column crept like a lame lion across the land.

The Duke hadn't gone into much detail with his commanders about what had been discussed at the stone circle, but he did instruct them to tell his troops that today they would not be marching to battle the Caledonish army. Instead, they had formed an alliance with the highlanders, and were heading west to join the First Legion in what would prove to be the decisive battle of the war. In spite of this news, the ensuing battle and the blizzard gnawed at the men's morale.

Bran instructed special barrels of October Cider to be distributed amongst his soldiers before they set off. He'd been saving the kegs for a celebratory toast when they defeated Roy Stewart's army, but decided now was as good a time as any to crack open the barrels. Soldiers toasted to Lochinbar, to the health of the Iron Duke and King MacDain, and for the accursed snowstorm to pass. Then they packed up their tents, collected their belongings and headed west.

The troops tried to stick to forest trails as much as possible. The trees offered some respite from the wind, although care had to be taken to avoid falling branches. The canopy collected much of the snow, but the buffeting wind tore it free, blanketing the woodland paths in a thick carpet of white that hid rocks and roots, making footing treacherous and progress slow.

Caspan and Master Scott rode behind Prince Dale and the Duke, who were at the head of the army. Caspan peered down the trail, trying to spot the green-cloaked scouts who moved ahead of the main column. They drifted like ghosts through the woods, there one second and gone the next, clearing a safe route west. There was no longer any fear of attack from Roy Stewart's highlanders, but there might be bands of border reivers in the woods. These rogues came from Caledon, but acted independent of the Stewart Laird and were notorious for waylaying travellers through these parts of Lochinbar. Though it was highly unlikely they would dare make an assault on an army of this size, some might be hiding and staring down their drawn bows, unable to resist the opportunity of loosing a shaft that could hit the Iron Duke or his son.

Heavy on Caspan's thoughts was the welfare of his friends at Rivergate. With any luck the fire front had succeeded in driving the Roon back to the Pass of Westernese. If so, it would have forced them to cross the river at Westford and Hollen, buying the defenders at Rivergate much precious time. Caspan hoped that the First Legion had managed to journey to Chester Hill before the blizzard set in, and that his friends had moved south to join them. But short of a messenger raven arriving, which was highly improbable in this weather anyway, there was no way of telling what had become of them. All he could do was hope that General Liam was in position and his friends were safe.

Caspan was tempted to summon Frostbite and fly ahead of the army, but it would be far too dangerous. It would be next to impossible to navigate his way west in the blinding snow. With visibility reduced to little more than twenty yards, it would only be a matter of time until he got lost in the blizzard. Being a drake, Frostbite would have no problem surviving in the freezing conditions, but not so Caspan. No amount of clothing seemed to be able to ward back the biting chill. He feared he would perish if they failed to find adequate shelter. As frustrating as it was, it was safer to stay with the Duke and continue forward at a snail's pace along the protected, woodland trails.

Believing he could finally see light at the end of the long tunnel of war, Caspan relaxed for the first time in days. He rode slouched in his saddle, letting his mount choose its own path along the trail. The unrelenting pace and action of the past few days had caught up to him and hit him like a hammer, leaving him exhausted. Eyes heavy with sleep, Caspan was relieved when, an hour before dusk, they rode onto a section of field sheltered from the wind by the forest edge, and Bran gave the command to dismount and set up camp.

Caspan and Master Scott pitched their tent as close to the trees as possible. Caspan's cloak was soaked through. Even his tunic and breeches were damp, but he was beyond caring. Such concerns could wait until the morning. All that mattered now was that he rest. He stripped out of his wet clothes, rolled himself up in a makeshift bed of blankets and fell quickly into the deepest of sleeps.

He woke the next day to the sound of the howling wind and driving snow. Wondering where Scott was, Caspan wrapped himself in a blanket and peered through the tent flap. An icy blast buffeted the camp. Caspan shivered from head to toe and wished he had never stirred from his warm cocoon. Black clouds raced across the sky, driven by the shrieking gale. Snow had piled high against the windward sides of tents. Soldiers hurried around the encampment, preparing for today's march, but there was no sign of Scott.

Caspan closed the flap and yawned groggily. To his surprise, he found his clothes in a neat bundle at the base of his bed. Strangely, they were warm, as if they'd been hung to dry before a fire all night. Saying a silent thank you to Scott, Caspan dressed and, lured by the smell of cooked bacon, pulled his cloak tightly around him and hurried to a nearby tent. The soldiers welcomed him inside and treated him to a plate of bacon rashers and fried eggs. It was only now that Caspan realised he'd skipped dinner last night. He greedily devoured three platefuls before a horn bellowed, giving the command to break camp.

It wasn't until after Caspan had pulled down his tent and readied his saddle bags that he found Scott. The Master was already mounted, and was chewing on a piece of bread as he made his way slowly through the camp towards Caspan.

'Here,' Scott said, ripping off a generous portion and tossing it to Caspan. 'It's not a bowl of warm porridge but it's better than nothing.'

Caspan caught the food. 'Thanks, but I've already eaten. Some soldiers cooked bacon and eggs.'

'Bacon and eggs! And here I was thinking you'd be starving.'

Caspan proffered the bread back to the Master, but he waved it aside. Caspan tucked it inside a leather saddle bag for later. 'I would have invited you, but I didn't know where you'd snuck off to.'

'While you were happily sleeping in and then gorging yourself, I was summoned to a meeting in the Duke's tent, thank you very much,' Scott said with an ironic smile. 'We're going to press on ahead and put in a full day's travel, then set camp once night falls. We'll continue at dawn, and should reach the First Legion before midday.

Some of the officers wanted to continue travelling through the night and reach Chester Hill in the early hours of the morning, but it would leave the men exhausted and in no condition to fight a battle.' Scott swung easily out of his saddle and started to untie a leather tarp from the rear of his mount. 'Hopefully the message Roy Stewart sent to the Roon will stall the giants, holding them back until reinforced by the highlanders. Given this weather, though, there's no guarantee the message will arrive safely or in time. All we can do is hope that everything falls into place.' He tossed the sheet to Caspan. 'Here, put this on. I don't want you getting wet again or you'll come down with pneumonia.'

What Caspan thought was a rug was in fact an oiled leather travelling cloak. 'Thanks,' he said as he pulled it on over his woollen Brotherhood cloak and drew the hood over his head.

'The rain and sleet will bead on it and run off, leaving your clothes nice and dry.' Scott took a pair of thick leather gloves from his pack and handed them to Caspan. 'Put these on, too. The last thing you want is to lose your fingers to frostbite. You won't be much use with a bow then.'

The gloves were lined with fur. Caspan nodded appreciatively as he pulled them on, but he doubted this all would be enough to stop the cold from seeping through to his bones. He'd only been outside for perhaps half an hour, and he was already freezing.

'I'm not looking forward to today,' Caspan moped as he climbed onto his saddle.

The Master gave him a solemn look. 'I don't think any of us are, but we don't have a choice. If we wait for this blizzard to pass we won't make it to Chester Hill in time, and the First Legion will face the Roon on their own.'

'I know, but it doesn't make this weather any more bearable.'

Scott leaned over and patted him sympathetically on the shoulder. 'Cheer up. Before you know it winter will have passed, we would have defeated the Roon, and we'll be sitting back in the House of Whispers, drinking some of Gramidge's cider.'

Caspan smiled half-heartedly. The House of Whispers seemed a world away right now. He flicked his reins and guided his mount through the camp, following the Master.

In spite of his dry clothes, new cloak and full stomach, it wasn't long before Caspan felt miserable again. Wishing this nightmare would hurry up and end, he trailed despondently behind the Duke and Dale through the white wilderness.

An eternity seemed to have passed before Duke Bran gave the order to stop. Caspan was so depressed that he hadn't even noticed it was approaching dusk, or that they were deep in a forest. Snow still fell heavily, but at least they were out of the wind. There were also some dry patches of earth, close to the tree trunks, beneath the spreading branches. This is where the men made their shelters, but rather than pitch their tents, they stretched their cowhide tarps between the trees. Sentries were posted, scouts sent out to forage for dry wood, and, after many failed attempts, fires lit. The weary men of the eastern legions then settled down for the night.

Caspan and Master Scott tied their leather canvas between the boughs of two towering elm trees. They blanketed, tethered and fed their horses, then set about starting a fire and cooking a simple chowder.

They prepared their meal in silence and waited patiently for the soup to cook. Soon their pot was full of flavoursome, simmering broth. Master Scott ladled them each a bowl. Caspan felt his spirits rise with each spoonful of the hot, yummy chowder.

'You must be enjoying this by the way you're wolfing it down,' Scott commented, glancing at Caspan. 'It's good to see you smiling for the first time today.'

'There hasn't exactly been much to be happy about. It's been the most miserable, longest day of my life. I didn't think it would ever end.'

The Master murmured in agreement as he poured himself and Caspan tankards of honey cider and placed them near the edge of the fire. 'The Duke pushed us hard, but we've seen the worst. Tomorrow will be a lot easier. By midday we'll be at Chester Hill.' He leaned out and peered through a break in the canopy to inspect the night sky. 'Besides, this blizzard won't last forever. Hopefully it will start to die down.'

'I'll believe that when I see it,' Caspan muttered dourly. 'I've never seen anything like this before.' As if to add credence to his words, a cold blast tore through the forest, buffeting the stretched canvas tarps and making campfires hiss and flicker.

They sat in silence for some time, savouring each mouthful of the soup, when they looked up to find Prince Dale approaching their shelter.

'Mmm, that smells fantastic,' he said, rubbing his belly and staring enviously at their steaming pot. 'What is it?'

'Shepherd's Chowder,' Scott replied, shuffling over to make room for the Prince. He ladled Dale a bowl and handed it to him.

Dale took a spoonful. Some of the liquid dribbled down his chin and ran into his beard. 'That hit the spot,' he beamed, wiping the fold of his cloak across his mouth. He shovelled down half a bowl before he arched an eyebrow curiously at Scott. 'I didn't know you were such a culinary master!'

The treasure hunter grinned. 'I much prefer *eating* to cooking.' He patted a small leather pouch attached to his belt. 'The trick is to never go on an adventure without a trusty supply of herbs and spices.'

'I wish that's all I had to worry about,' Dale muttered. He looked around the encampment, making sure nobody could overhear their discussion. 'Father's called a final meeting with his officers. I'm sure he wanted me present, but I've conveniently wandered off.'

Caspan left his spoon hovering near his lips. 'Is everything all right?'

Dale regarded him levelly for a moment. 'Not a word of this leaves this tent.' Caspan and Scott nodded. The Prince lowered his bowl. 'I need a break,' he whispered. 'I'm mentally and physically drained. I saw my reflection in a stream earlier today, and I could barely recognise myself. I'm only eighteen, but I saw my father staring back at me.'

'I thought you'd be proud,' Caspan commented.

'I am.' Dale stared distantly at the steam rising from the pot. 'But I don't want to become my father. Don't get me wrong — I think he's a great man, and I have the utmost respect for him. But war has consumed his life. It's zapped the merriment and joy from him, leaving nothing but a withered husk behind. And I don't want that to happen to me. Maybe I'm too much of a dreamer and an idealist, but I want peace for Lochinbar. I've seen enough bloodshed and suffering to last me a lifetime. Hopefully the agreement between Father and Roy Stewart will bring an end to any future conflicts between Andalon and Caledon. Then we can focus on strengthening ties between our countries, promoting stronger diplomatic relations and creating trade agreements. That's what I want for the future.' He glanced sullenly around the camp. 'Not this.'

'I'll drink to that.' Caspan filled the Prince a tankard of honey cider, then raised his in a toast. 'Here's to the end of the war and lasting peace.'

'To lasting peace,' Dale and Scott repeated, and raised their drinks to their lips.

Chapter 22

SHADES OF GREY

As the evening progressed, Dale and Scott entered into a deep conversation about hunting. Although Caspan found the topic interesting, he knew little about it and thought he'd use this as an opportunity to check on Brett. He filled a bowl, grabbed a spoon and headed off through the night.

He hadn't seen the prisoner since they'd first arrived in Bran's camp, and he couldn't help but feel partially responsible for his treatment. He had, after all, delivered Brett to the Duke. As much as he despised the traitorous former general, Caspan wanted to make sure he wasn't being beaten or mistreated.

He found Brett sitting against a towering oak at the far side of the camp, wrapped in a thick cloak. His hands and feet were tied, but not bound to the tree, allowing him some movement. Three guards sat close by, playing a game of cards.

'Do you mind if I talk to the prisoner?' Caspan asked.

One of the soldiers glanced up at him. 'You're the lad who handed him over to the Duke, aren't you?' he asked, and Caspan nodded. 'Normally we wouldn't let anyone near him, but I think we can make an exception for you. Just leave your sword here. Brett's hands are tied, but I wouldn't put anything past him.'

Caspan unfastened his sword belt and left his weapon with the soldier before striding over to Brett. He regarded him for a moment, noting that though he appeared cold and miserable, the prisoner didn't appear to have been mistreated. Brett studied Caspan with his piercing blue eyes, then snorted derisively and turned away.

Caspan placed the bowl near his feet. 'Here. Not even traitors deserve to starve to death.'

'Stop or you'll make me cry,' Brett replied icily. He looked at the food suspiciously. 'It isn't poisoned?'

'I'd never stoop to your level,' Caspan said curtly. 'Besides, that would be too easy. I'm sure the King has a cell ready for you to rot in.'

'How generous of him.' Brett shuffled closer to the bowl, picked it up and sniffed its contents. He turned up his nose. 'Smells like swamp muck. Still, it's better than nothing.' He glanced up at Caspan and motioned at his wrists with a jerk of his chin. 'You could make this a little easier for me.'

Caspan stared at him flatly. 'Don't push your luck.'

'Oh well, you can't blame a man for trying.' Brett rested his back against the tree and placed the bowl on his lap. He picked up his spoon and started wolfing down the chowder. He paused and glanced self-consciously at Caspan. 'What? You haven't seen someone eat before?'

Caspan knelt before the prisoner. 'I just don't understand . . . why did you join the Roon?'

'And you wouldn't, even if I told you.'

Caspan held the man's gaze. 'Try me.'

Brett shrugged. 'The opportunity presented itself, and I took hold of it. There, are you satisfied?'

'That explains nothing,' Caspan replied, his disgust for the former general building. 'You betrayed your own people!'

Brett left his spoon hovering near his lips. 'My own people! Don't make me laugh. And don't you dare judge me! You know nothing about me or of the history of this kingdom.' He shovelled the spoonful into his mouth and slurped angrily. 'You think the Roon are evil, and you can't fathom why I joined forces with them. But let me tell you this — there is a fare worse evil in Andalon than the Roon. You think you're fighting the ultimate battle of good versus evil, that you're fighting on the side of light, with King Rhys's noble legions defending the realm against the savage horde from The Wild. But there are shades of grey that you can't even begin to see.'

'Don't you dare try to mask your betrayal behind riddles!' Caspan said contemptuously.

'Riddles! I speak of truths, boy; truths as old as this forest.'

Caspan sighed impatiently, but part of him wanted to hear what the prisoner had to say. 'What do you mean?'

'You accuse me of betraying my people, of committing treason. But what of a king who seized control of the throne by slaughtering his rivals?' Brett pointed his spoon at Caspan. 'There's my shade of grey.'

'What are you talking about? King Rhys is a just ruler. He —'

'Stop before you make me sick!' Brett interrupted. 'He's a *MacDain*. The sins of his ancestors taint his crown.' He cocked his head at Caspan's baffled expression. 'You have no idea what I'm talking about, do you?

'What sins?'

Brett smiled enigmatically. 'More shades of grey, boy. Beneath the splendour of his crown, Rhys sits upon a throne stained in blood. His ancestor, Elric MacDain, seized it after defeating Ulther Bloodcrest at the Battle of Morton Spike.'

'But that was a fair fight,' Caspan retorted. 'Besides, Elric had nothing to do with Ulther's death. He was thrown from his horse and trampled on the battlefield.'

'But what of Ulther's family and his bloodline?' Brett asked. 'History is written by the victors. It has a tendency to omit certain acts that might present its fabricated heroes in a negative light. Elric's scribes did a fine job in recording his exploits during the Battle of Morton Spike.' Brett's lips tightened. 'But find me an official historical text that tells of how Elric ordered assassins to hunt down and murder Ulther's wife, children and relatives. There are two sides to every story, boy. A wise man learns to listen to both.'

Caspan was shocked by this. He didn't know much

about the history of Andalon, but he'd only ever heard people talk of the MacDains with the highest regard. And he'd certainly never heard any stories of Elric ordering the elimination of Ulther's bloodline. 'Even if what you're saying is true, it happened over three hundred years ago,' he said. 'And what's any of this got to do with you?'

Brett glared at him. 'It has *everything* to do with me! In spite of Elric's attempt to wipe out the Bloodcrests, one of Ulther's sons managed to escape and was spirited away to Saxstein. He was my great-great-grandfather.' He squared his shoulders proudly. 'I am Ulther's sole, direct descendant. Revenge courses through my veins. I won't stop until I've reclaimed what is rightfully mine. One day, I'll sit upon my throne in Briston.'

Caspan stared at the prisoner, dumbstruck. He took a moment to compose himself before asking, 'But at what cost?'

'I'll side with any army that rises against the MacDains.' Brett studied Caspan intently, his blue eyes narrowing. 'You're still wondering how I could do such a thing; why I refuse to bury the past and am prepared to go to any length to achieve my goal. So you would have me deny my heritage? You'd have me feign fealty to the descendant of a butcher? I may be many things, boy, but I'm no hypocrite.' He lowered his gaze and stirred his broth. 'Now, if you don't mind, I'd like to eat the rest of my meal in silence. It's one of the few pleasures I have remaining in life.'

Taken aback by what he had heard, Caspan collected his sword from the guards and made his way slowly through the camp. Snow drifted down between the trees, but he was oblivious to it, lost in his own thoughts.

He hadn't really known what answer he'd receive from Brett to explain his alliance with the Roon. But he was most certainly not expecting to hear that Brett was a direct descendant of Ulther Bloodcrest, or that King Elric MacDain had tried to eradicate Ulther's bloodline. Only a few minutes ago everything had been so clear — Brett was a traitorous dog who had turned on his people and betrayed his king. But now Caspan wasn't so sure. He hated to admit it, but Brett was right. There was another side to this story: a shade of grey that lay hidden between the forces of good and evil. It by no means justified Brett's actions, but it made Caspan realise that you never truly understood somebody until you'd walked in their shoes.

Scott and Dale were still chatting quietly when Caspan returned to the shelter.

'Where have you been?' Scott asked, shuffling over to make room for him by the fire. He handed him a cup of warm, honey cider.

'I went to check on Brett,' Caspan replied as he tossed his sword onto a spare blanket.

Dale turned up his nose. 'What for?'

'He might be our prisoner and all, but I wanted to make sure he's being fed and treated fairly.'

'You're far more compassionate than me. As far as I'm concerned, he gets what he deserves. Even life in a dungeon's too lenient a punishment for him.' Dale raised an eyebrow at Caspan. 'And what did he have to say?'

There was a side of Caspan that wanted to ignore what Brett had told him, for nothing could justify joining forces with the Roon. But there was also a part of him that sympathised with the prisoner, and the treasure hunter wondered how he would feel if he were in the same situation. He doubted Dale would share the same sentiment, though. Not only had Brett betrayed King Rhys, he had also tortured Dale's father. Darrowmere, the capital of Lochinbar, had fallen due to Brett's treachery. Caspan had heard that Dale's bodyguards, the Crimson Blades, had given their lives in order for the Prince to escape. Dale had been born and raised in the city, and Caspan imagined the Prince held the former General of the Eighth Legion's betrayal close to heart. Caspan also didn't know how the Prince would react upon hearing that one of his ancestors was responsible for slaughtering Ulther's bloodline. For all Caspan knew, it was a great lie, but he wouldn't be certain until he returned to the House of Whisper's archive and investigated the matter for himself.

'Not much,' Caspan replied, taking a sip of his cider. He glanced at Scott and smirked. 'Although, Brett thought your chowder tasted like swamp muck.'

The Master bristled. 'Did he now! Don't go giving him any more of my food. What a waste of Shepherd's Chowder!'

Dale scowled. 'I would have thrown it at him. That would have given him something to whinge about. But enough talk about that traitor.' He regarded Scott. 'Now, where were we?'

'You were about to tell me about the time you went hunting near Mance O'Shea's Break,' Scott replied.

The Prince clicked his fingers and smiled. 'Ah, that's right.'

Caspan finished his cider, wrapped himself in a woollen blanket and lay down by the fire. He drifted off to sleep listening to the howling wind.

CHAPTER 23

THE FINAL BATTLE BEGINS

Caspan woke with a start. Someone was shaking him, and he looked up to find Master Scott kneeling by his side. It was still night, but the fire had died low.

'Get up,' Scott whispered urgently. 'Something's happened.'

Caspan jumped to his feet and strapped on his sword. 'What?'

It was then that he heard the signal horn from the far side of the camp. All around him soldiers were grabbing their swords, lighting lanterns and hurrying out from beneath their shelters.

Scott shook his head grimly. 'I don't know, but it can't be good. Come on. Let's find out.'

The treasure hunters raced through the forest, heading through the trees to where the alarm had been raised. A large group of soldiers had already gathered there. Caspan had to stand on a stump to peer over their heads. In a clearing at the base of a tree, a soldier was being berated by an officer. There was too much commotion for Caspan to hear what was being discussed, but his eyes flashed with surprise when he noticed that the soldier being scolded was one of the guards who had kept watch over Brett. Looking beyond them, Caspan saw the towering oak where Brett had been bound, but at the base of the tree were several frayed lengths of rope.

Caspan glanced down at Scott, stunned. 'Brett's escaped!'

Scott's eyes widened in alarm. 'Are you sure? I can't hear what they're saying.'

'Trust me. He's gone.'

Duke Bran and Dale arrived shortly at the clearing. The entire camp was alerted and search parties organised. Caspan and Scott assisted Dale and a band of soldiers search through the woods, but they could find no sign of the prisoner. It wasn't until scouts checked the perimeter of the camp that they discovered Brett had crept his way through the sleeping troops, stolen a horse and headed south through the forest. A band of scouts were sent out to hunt him down.

'You didn't see anything suspicious when you spoke to Brett last night?' Scott asked Caspan once they arrived back at their shelter.

Caspan shook his head. 'No. His hands and feet were bound. Mind you, I didn't think the guards were doing a particularly good job of keeping an eye on him. They were a lot more interested in their card game.'

Scott clicked his tongue. 'I wouldn't want to be in their shoes. Bran won't let them off lightly. Still, Brett will be easy to track in the snow. We just have to hope the scouts can catch him before he joins up with the Roon and tells them that Roy Stewart has switched sides.'

Caspan nodded gravely. 'I never thought of that.'

He had been so busy searching for Brett he hadn't realised that it was now morning. The blizzard had passed, and golden pillars of sunlight streamed down through breaks in the canopy. The sky was a perfect screen of blue. All around the forest patches of snow glistened like scattered diamonds. It was still cold, but not bitterly so, and Caspan stripped off his leather cloak and gloves and packed them in his saddle bags. He breathed in the crisp morning air and rolled his shoulders. In spite of having been woken early, he felt rested and ready for the day ahead.

'Here,' Scott said, handing Caspan a fresh bowl of Shepherd's Chowder. 'Didn't I tell you the storm wouldn't last forever?'

Caspan nodded. 'I never knew the sky could look so beautiful.'

'It's just what we all needed.' The Master motioned with a wave of his hand around the camp. 'Look at the men. They're refreshed and full of energy. They're a little on edge after what happened with Brett, but that should help keep them on their toes. The Roon won't know what hit them.'

Caspan's stomach tightened at the thought of today's battle. 'There's been no sign of Roy Stewart's army?'

'I heard that the Duke posted a band of scouts at the edge of the forest last night. When the wind abated in the early hours of the morning, they reported seeing a red glow in the distance, far to the north. They must've been the fires from Roy's camp.' Scott smiled encouragingly. 'The highlanders have been keeping pace with us. Rest assured, they'll be there when the battle starts.'

Caspan breathed a sigh of relief. He'd been worried that the highland army might have been delayed or lost in the storm.

'But we need to hurry up and pack,' Scott said as he started to untie their tarp. 'Duke Bran wants to make an early start.'

Around him Caspan noticed soldiers stamping out their campfires, strapping on their swords and hoisting their packs over their shoulders in preparation to march. He scoffed down his breakfast, then saddled and bridled their mounts. 'Why don't we fly ahead on our Wardens?' he asked Scott. 'We could join the First Legion in no time at all. We can also find out what's happened to our friends.'

'As tempting as that is, it wouldn't be the wisest thing to do,' Scott cautioned. 'We're dangerously close to the Roon army. We don't want to alert them that we're in the area. General Liam might have sent out advance units to ambush and harass the Roon, to slow them down until we join forces. Our drakes can be seen from miles away, and we could destroy their element of surprise. It's better we stay with the Duke. I know you're keen to see our friends, but we'll be with them soon enough.'

Caspan nodded reluctantly. 'I guess you're right.'

A few minutes later they joined the head of the army and rode out of the forest. The snow was thick, hampering their progress, but nobody complained. They were all just relieved that the storm had passed and they could travel with the sun on their faces. As they had done for the past two days, they stuck to forest roads where possible, where the canopy had collected most of the snow.

They had covered several miles and were crossing an open field when everybody froze. Soldiers loosened their swords in their scabbards. One of the officers to Caspan's right fought to control his mount. Its nostrils flared as it tried to buck him off. Pulling hard on the reins, the officer brought it under control, then patted its neck and made a soothing sound to calm it down.

Caspan scanned the open stretch of land, searching for the source of alarm. Then he heard it. His pulse quickening, he craned his ear to the west, focusing on the errant breeze that carried the faint yet unmistakeable sound of bellowing horns, trampling hooves and clanging blades.

The battle between the Roon and the First Legion had started.

Caspan shifted anxiously in his saddle and turned to Master Scott. 'That doesn't sound too far away.'

Scott nodded, his expression grim as he stared to the west. 'Maybe in the next valley.'

The wind abated, leaving the field silent and still.

'General Liam will be outnumbered!' Prince Dale warned his father, keeping his voice low so as to not be overheard by the soldiers. 'We have to hurry and join the battle before it's too late!'

Bran nodded, but his features were as fixed as stone. 'It's no use charging the infantry ahead. We might have a mile yet to cover, and it's no good having them arrive at the battlefield exhausted.'

'But we can't just stand here!' Dale protested.

'I never said anything about just standing here,' the Duke retorted. 'We'll send companies of riders ahead. They can assist General Liam until our infantry arrives.' He gave his son a sympathetic look. 'I'm as keen as you are to help the First, but we have to be patient. We'll advance the main army forward at a quick march. That way they'll still have the energy to battle.'

As if reading the Duke's mind, a mounted knight galloped up from the main column. The lion brooch attached to the lapel of his cloak identified him as an officer. Caspan and Scott moved aside, allowing him to draw rein before the Duke.

'I'll ride ahead with my company of lancers, my lord,' the officer announced.

'Go,' Bran said resolutely. 'Offer General Liam whatever help you can. We'll be right behind you.'

The commander saluted, wheeled his horse around and hollered for his company to follow after him. They thundered across the field, their mounts' hooves kicking up white clouds in their wake.

The Duke turned to the leader of his scouts, who rode near the Prince on a black gelding. 'Ride ahead too, Andy. Take your trackers with you and find high ground. Form a skirmish line and harass the enemy with your bows. Try to draw as many of the giants as far away as possible from the First, but don't engage them in close-quarters fighting. Stay mounted and ride away when Roon get close.'

'Of course, my lord.' The leather-clad, grizzled scout commander raised two of his fingers to his lips and gave a high-pitched whistle, summoning his band of cloaked trackers to his side. Their bows gripped in their hands, they set their heels to their mounts, spurring them across the snow-covered field.

Duke Bran nodded grimly as he tugged at the hems of his gloves and watched the cavalry units ride ahead. 'Now, it's time for us to move. We've got a war to win.'

He nodded at one of his commanders, who signalled for the main column to move forward at a fast march. Shields slung across their backs, their breath forming plumes of grey mist, the infantry of the Sixth, Seventh and Eighth legions trudged through the snow, following the compacted trail left by the advance riders. Units of heavy cavalry moved into position along their flanks, and a second unit of lancers formed a vanguard, the red pendants of their spears stark against the snow.

They covered perhaps a mile before a group of advance trackers, who were lying on their bellies on the crest of the hill, signalled that they had reached the battle. Caspan and Scott swung out of their saddles and, along with Duke Bran, Prince Dale and a band of officers, hurried up the slope. Not wanting to be spotted by the enemy, they dropped to their hands and knees as they approached the crest. The earth trembled beneath them. The squeal of steel on steel, the thud of steel-shod hooves and the bellow of war horns surged over the hill and seemed to make the very air vibrate. Caspan shuffled forward on his belly until he reached the top, swallowed and peered down into the valley.

His blood turned to ice. The greatest battle in the history of Andalon was being fought on the grassy plain below.

The combatants were arrayed in battle formations that stretched from one side of the mile-long valley floor to the other. General Liam's First Legion was deployed in a long, central shield wall, ten men deep, reinforced on the wings by cavalry and supported by a reserve unit of archers. A further mounted company waited back at the entrance to the valley, guarding the baggage-train.

The Roon were arranged in a similar formation, minus the cavalry. Their central shield wall was over twenty giants deep and grinded forward like a mobile fortress. On the flanks, where they faced enemy horsemen, the Roon curved their shield wall back and reinforced it with a façade of bristling spear-points. At the rear of the army, several hundred yards away from a company of archers positioned behind the shield wall, was a reserve force of over a thousand giants.

Snow lay thick on the flanking hills, but only a light dusting covered the valley floor. This favoured the Andalonians, Caspan believed, who relied heavily on their cavalry to move quickly from one side of the battle-field to the other to support the infantry and deliver devastating charges against the enemy. But watching the scene unfold, Caspan quickly realised that not even the fury of a hundred heavily armoured knights riding war-trained destriers was strong enough to break through the enemy lines. Their shields locked together, the giants braced themselves against the impact, then thrust with their spears and thick-bladed broadswords, cutting down many of the riders before they could withdraw.

Duke Bran's company of advance lancers, two hundred strong, had joined the cavalry on the right flank. Andy's band of green-cloaked scouts had dismounted near a clump of trees at the base of a hill. They fired an endless stream of shafts at the giants that charged towards them, stalling their advance and forcing them to form up behind their shields.

Even from this distance Caspan could spot General Liam. He sat atop his black stallion in the front rank of the shield wall, waving his gleaming sword above his head, rallying and spurring his troops. Beside him fought Maul. The great bear stood on his rear feet, towering over the Andalonians, skittering aside the enemy with swipes of his claws.

Caspan studied the battlefield, searching desperately for his friends. After a moment, he spotted Morgan and Raven atop their giant wolves amidst the Andalonian cavalry on the far left flank. Raven was wheeling Shadow around in a caracole and firing shafts at the giants. Meanwhile, Morgan was in the thick of the action, driving Fang hard against the enemy, hacking with his blade into their iron-rimmed shields.

Roland, Thom and Captain Jace rode close by, clad in chainmail vests and armed with broadswords and shields. Easy to spot in his blue bonnet, Roland sat atop a towering brown horse, which Caspan identified from its distinct white markings as Georgina. Roland fended off incoming spears with his shield and rained blows with his blade, trying to break through the enemy line.

It took Caspan a while longer to spot his remaining friends. They were in the reserve unit of the cavalry, protecting the baggage train. Shanty sat atop his faun, Ferris. Beneath his black Brotherhood cloak he wore an open-faced mail coif that also protected his neck. His chainmail vest was too large and bunched up around his waist over his belt. The dwarf stared grimly ahead, his sword resting across his thighs, and leaned forward to stroke Ferris reassuringly on the neck.

Off to his side stood Sara. She wore a thick leather jerkin reinforced with small iron plates, and fired arrows at a high trajectory over the heads of the Andalonian soldiers into the rear ranks of the Roon. Several yards to her right, Cloud Dancer spread her wings and stamped the earth restlessly. Then there was Oswald, wearing only a tunic and breeches beneath his Brotherhood cloak. He stood on a wagon, his head craned in the air, as he watched the battle unfold. His magical unicorn, Legend, waited obediently off to the side.

Caspan stared in awe at the Warden. For some reason he had imagined Legend would be white in colour, but he had a coat of deep grey, like soot. He was a powerful and majestic creature, standing taller than a draught horse. His black mane cascaded over his neck in silken ripples and faded to silver-grey on the forelock, where it parted around the spiralling horn that projected from his forehead.

Caspan felt the greatest sense of relief that his friends were alive. He had feared they might have fallen defending Rivergate, but now they were all in terrible danger. He was consumed by a desire to gallop down to the battlefield and guard them. It took all of his self-control not to draw his sword and spur his horse down the hill.

It was apparent to Caspan that the Andalonians were fighting a losing battle. The Roon outnumbered the Andalonians three to one. The First Legion's centre was starting to falter, being pushed back by the Roon. Their line still held, but a salient was forming in the middle of the Andalonian ranks. Caspan was no master tactician, but even he knew that if the Roon were to break through and the breach not quickly patched by reserves it would lead to the collapse of the entire First Legion. Wholesale slaughter would result.

His throat dry, Caspan glanced anxiously at Duke Bran. He was as rigid as a statue, his expression grim as he weighed the situation. Then the Duke signalled for the small band of officers to withdraw back to their horses and mount up.

'Ride to the north-east and find Roy Stewart,' Bran said, turning to a mounted ensign. 'They cannot be far behind us. Tell him the battle's started and he needs to get here — fast!' The soldier saluted and spurred off down the hill.

'We've planned for this battle and you all know your roles,' the Duke addressed his officers, his voice firm and commanding, rising above the clamour from the valley. 'It's going to be chaotic, but we must prevail. Losing this fight is not an option. Keep your lines of communication open with messengers. If you feel your section is going to falter, send for reinforcements. We have reserve units that can patch breaches in our lines. But don't wait until it's too late. The Roon only have to break through one section to rout us. As soon as that happens, this battle is lost.' He flexed his fingers and drew his blade. It hissed like a serpent as it brushed against the sides of the leather scabbard. 'Now, get your men into battle formation. Let's end this war.'

Horns bellowed and the officers barked commands as they rode amongst the troops. The Duke and Prince steered their stallions forward, and peered over the crest of the hill into the valley below.

Caspan clicked his mount alongside them. 'Where do you want Scott and me?' he asked.

'You're not officially under my command, so I'll leave that up to you.' Bran's hard features softened. 'You have a knack for popping up at just the right moment. I'm sure you won't let us down.'

Caspan nodded and stared determinedly at the left cavalry flank, where Roland, Thom, Raven and Master Morgan were in the thick of the fighting. Dale followed Caspan's gaze.

'It looks like you might be joining me,' The Prince remarked. He removed his helmet from where it hung

over his saddle horn, and put it on. 'I'll be commanding the attack on the left,' he said. 'Our objective is to
puncture through the side of the Roon army and encircle
the giants.'

'What of their reserves?' Scott asked as he drew his
mount alongside them. 'If you're not careful, they'll move
forward and you'll find yourself trapped.'

Dale tightened his helmet's leather strap. 'Captain
Hugh's company of lancers is going to cover our left
flank to block their advance.' He turned to consider
Scott and Caspan. 'It's not going to be easy. It doesn't
look as if the First has been able to outflank the Roon
yet, but that doesn't mean we're not going to try. The
one thing the Roon don't have is cavalry. Hopefully it
will determine the outcome of the battle.' He drew his
blade. 'Now, are you with me?'

Caspan and Scott shared a knowing glance before
nodding. Then they swung from their saddles and
summoned their Wardens. A great cheer rose from the
soldiers as the magical beasts materialised from clouds
of blue smoke. Frostbite and Shimmer stretched their
leathery wings and flexed their claws before waiting
dutifully by their masters' sides.

Caspan quickly saddled Frostbite, climbed atop the
drake and strapped himself into the harness. 'Master
Scott and I will provide cover from the air,' he said.
'We'll swoop down and try to cause as much damage
as possible.'

Dale nodded appreciatively. 'That'd be great. It
might make my task a little easier.' He beckoned for his

second-in-command to come closer. 'Make sure the men hold the line. No gaps, and swords drawn. We'll gallop when we reach the valley base, but not before. We don't want to risk any of our horses stumbling down the hill.'

The soldier saluted and rode along the length of the Prince's cavalry unit, which was spread out in a line, five riders deep, just behind the crest of the hill, hidden from the enemy.

'Make sure you keep an eye out for the Roon archers,' Scott cautioned, winding up Shimmer's reins around his left hand. In his right he gripped his longsword.

Caspan grimly recalled the time Frostbite had nearly been killed by an axe hurled by a Roon warrior during their first mission north. His heart racing, he waited for Duke Bran to give the command to attack.

CHAPTER 24

IN THE THICK OF BATTLE

Duke Bran thrust his sword forward, sending his army surging over the crest of the hill.

Riding at a canter, Prince Dale's cavalry pushed ahead of the infantry. They dug their heels hard into their mounts once they reached the valley floor and, with the Prince leading, galloped around the rear of General Brett's army, then swung right to join the cavalry on the far left flank. The Prince sent half of his men to reinforce the Andalonian horsemen fighting alongside Morgan, Roland, Raven, Thom and Jace, and led the rest of his unit, over two hundred strong, out past the enemy shield wall. The Roon tried to stretch their line to counter the advance, but they couldn't keep pace with the riders. Having outflanked the giants, his left flank guarded by Captain Hugh's cavalry, the Prince swung hard to the right again, bringing his unit around in a valiant effort to get behind the Roon.

It was a bold move, but it left his unit out in the open, exposed and vulnerable to the ranks of enemy archers. Their commander pointed his battleaxe at the horsemen and ordered his archers to redirect their fire at them. The group of six hundred Roon warriors hurriedly rearranged their lines, set arrows to bowstrings and took aim . . . only to be hit from behind by Frostbite and Shimmer.

The drakes swooped out of the sky and raked their claws through the enemy, destroying their formation and buying the Prince and his cavalry the time they needed to charge into the rear of the Roon shield wall. Before the archers could scramble back into line, Caspan and Scott turned their Wardens around and sent them in for a second attack. This time Frostbite breathed fire, forcing the giants to run for their lives. A few Roon managed to loose shafts at the drakes, but the Wardens moved too fast, the arrows zipping harmlessly through the air.

For the next hour the battle raged. Caspan and Scott used Frostbite and Shimmer to great advantage, flying over the battlefield to identify enemy strongpoints, or where the Andalonian lines looked like they might crumble, then diving down to attack the Roon. But not even their aerial assaults or the combined strength of the legions were enough to turn the tide of the battle in their favour.

Prince Dale's tactic of routing the enemy failed. Not long after Caspan and Scott had scattered the Roon archers, half of the giants on the right flank of the Roon army formed a second shield wall that countered the Prince's attack. For a while it looked as if the cavalry might puncture through the tattooed horde, but no sooner did one of the giants fall than another hurried forward to take his place. After perhaps half an hour of sustained fighting, the Prince, exhausted and streaked with sweat, abandoned the attack and led his men back to join the main left flank. Only half of his company remained.

The bulk of the eastern legions' infantry reinforced the centre of General Liam's army and pushed back the salient. But then a core unit of Roon berserkers tore into them. Foaming from the mouths, their bare torsos covered in swirling tattoos, they formed a wedge that broke through the Andalonian centre. Roon warriors swarmed into the breach, wreaking carnage and further widening the gap. Unable to unleash arrows for fear of hitting their own men, the Andalonian archers drew their swords and charged forward. But not even they could drive back the giants. Caspan and Scott tried desperately to help the defenders, but in the close-quarters fighting it was nearly impossible for their Wardens to single out enemy warriors. The Roon also hurled spears and axes at the drakes whenever they came near, forcing the Wardens back into the sky.

The battle raged in a storm of slashing steel and grinding shield walls, until the giants broke through the Andalonian infantry and spread out to encircle them. The cavalry units on the wings tried valiantly to stop the Roon, but even they were driven back. The giants surrounded the Andalonian army in a figure-eight formation, cutting off any hope of retreat or escape. All that remained was Andy's band of scouts, who held their ground near the copse of trees, and the reserve company of cavalry guarding the baggage train.

Flying high above the battlefield, well out of bow-range, Caspan searched desperately for his friends. Fortunately, there had been a reprieve in the fighting, during which both sides hastily reorganised their ranks. The outer rim of defenders in each encircled group formed a defensive shield wall, twenty men deep. Behind this milled the archers and cavalry in a chaotic mess. Still atop his black stallion, Maul by his side, General Liam thrust a spear with a shredded banner above his head and barked commands to the soldiers trapped with him in the easternmost section.

The second encircled group was under Duke Bran and Prince Dale's command. The hair on Caspan's neck prickled when he spotted his friends not far from the Duke. Thom's head and torso were wrapped in bandages, and Morgan clutched the left side of his chest, where his mangled mail vest was stained red. His Brotherhood cloak was shredded and the right sleeve of his tunic had been ripped off. Still, both he and Thom sat rigid in their saddles, their drawn swords glistening brightly.

Roland rode beside Jace, his battered shield slung across his back. He'd swapped his beloved bonnet for a conical helmet with a protective nasal guard. Georgina turned about restlessly, forcing Roland to pull hard on the reins to keep the massive draught horse in check. Raven sat nearby atop her dire wolf, Shadow. She stood in her stirrups, an arrow set to her half-drawn bow.

Caspan wanted desperately to fly down and spirit his

trapped friends safely away, but he knew it would be far too dangerous. In spite of flying low to the ground when they attacked the enemy so as to protect their drakes' exposed undersides, Frostbite and Shimmer had been hit many times already by arrows and spears. Fortunately all had bounced off their armour, leaving silver scars on their natural coats of blue, iron-like scales. But Caspan feared it would only be a matter of time until one tore through their leathery wings or pierced the soft scales on their bellies. If that were to happen, the drakes would be severely injured — possibly killed — and it was a gamble he wasn't prepared to make.

He looked to the east, searching for Roy Stewart's highlanders, but only the bleak, white hills gave answer.

'What are we going to do?' he asked Scott, who hovered a few yards off to his right.

The Master shook his head grimly. 'It isn't good. I don't know what's become of Roy Stewart. Maybe he's changed his mind and decided he doesn't want any part of this war.' He studied the battlefield, his gaze pausing on Andy's scouts. There were only a dozen of them left, and they were being chased up the valley slope by a band of giants. His gaze shifted to the reserve unit of cavalry waiting back with the supply wagons. 'They're our only hope,' he remarked. 'There must be close to fifty riders in that company. They need to puncture through the giants and create an opening for the others to escape through.'

'Which is easier said than done,' Caspan muttered, staring at the Roon amassing between the trapped

Andalonians and their baggage train, ready to repel any attempt made by the riders to break through.

The Master slapped his thigh in frustration. 'Blood and thunder! Look at them — just sitting there on their horses! What are they waiting for — an invitation? Why don't they attack?'

'Maybe there's no one to command them,' Caspan suggested, pointing at a group of dismounted soldiers gathered around a wagon, inside which a man lay. It was difficult to tell from this distance, but they were waving their hands about animatedly, as if in a heated argument. The rest of the cavalry waited idly on their horses by the dirt track leading into the valley, watching the spectacle. Caspan searched the group for Sara, Shanty and Oswald, but failed to find them.

'Commander or not, common sense should tell them to attack.' Scott yanked hard on Shimmer's reins, sending the drake shooting downwards. 'Come on,' he yelled over his shoulder, 'we need to find out what's going on.'

Caspan dug his heels into Frostbite's flanks, urging the drake after them. They flew down to the baggage train and landed.

'Who's in command here?' Scott demanded as he swung out of his saddle and strode to the soldiers surrounding the front wagon. Caspan followed close behind.

Sara pushed her way through the crowd to greet them, a distraught look on her face. A beefy soldier with yellow teeth and a sergeant's insignia stitched to his cloak grabbed her by the sleeve and yanked her back.

'Don't you dare touch me!' Sara protested, slapping his hand away and hurrying to Caspan's side.

The sergeant sneered at her. 'Or *what*?' He glared contemptuously at Caspan. 'Don't think that runt's goin' to stop me.'

Caspan had no idea what was going on, but he wasn't going to let the officer talk to him and Sara like that. He squared his shoulders, stared boldly at the sergeant and was about to cut him down to size with a sharp retort, when Scott placed a restraining hand on his shoulder.

'Let me deal with this,' the Master whispered, then addressed the sergeant. 'Where's your commanding officer?'

The sergeant looked Scott up and down and screwed up his nose. 'Not that I need to explain this to you, but *I'm* in charge here.' He jerked his double chin at the wagon. 'The Captain's been hit by an arrow. He can't even talk, let alone ride.' He snickered. 'He thought he was so brave and handsome, sittin' out there on his horse. And now look at him. He should have listened to me and stayed back.'

Scott drew a patient breath. 'Then why aren't you moving? Thousands of your countrymen will die if you don't help them. You're their only hope.'

'We ain't movin'. We were told to guard the baggage train, and that's exactly what we're goin' to do.'

Scott's lips tightened. 'Of what use will the baggage train be if there's no army left to use it?'

The sergeant stepped forward and pressed his face up against Scott's until their noses almost touched. 'That ain't my problem, little man. You pull no rank here. You're not even part of the military. Get back on your dragon and fly away.' He sneered at Sara and Oswald, who Caspan only now noticed. The elderly treasure hunter knelt beside a soldier lying on the ground, holding a damp cloth against the man's busted lip. 'And you can do the same,' the sergeant continued, jerking his chin at Sara and Oswald in turn. 'You might think you're all grand in your black cloaks, but I've had a gut-full of your back-chattin'. Open your mouths again,' he pointed at the injured soldier, 'and you'll get the same as he got.'

Scott shouldered past the officer and stood on a wheel spoke to inspect the Captain. Then he looked across at the band of mounted soldiers. Many had their swords drawn, ready to charge the Roon, but the uncertainty in their eyes revealed that they were reluctant to disobey the sergeant.

A roar rose from the ranks of the Roon. Everybody turned and watched as the reserve band of giants, which had waited at the far side of the valley, charged forward to join the main army and tore into the encircled Andalonians. The horsemen glanced at one another and shifted restlessly in their saddles.

'Leave your post and I'll flog each and every one of you!' the sergeant threatened them. 'You know I'll do it.'

It was more than Caspan could stand. He crossed angrily to the officer and stared hard at him. 'You're an absolute disgrace! Your countrymen are going to die, and you're hanging back here like a coward! I wonder if you even know which side you're fighting on!'

The sergeant's cheeks flushed red with rage and he reached for his sword. 'Why, you little . . .'

There was a loud clunk and the officer dropped unconscious to the ground. Shanty stood behind him on the wagon rail, gripping a plank of wood in his hands. He looked at Caspan and shrugged apologetically. 'He shouldn't have called you little. Some people might take offence.'

There was a celebratory cheer from the mounted soldiers.

'Thank goodness,' Sara said as she hurried over to assist Oswald help the hurt soldier back to his horse. She glanced at Shanty. 'What took you so long?'

'I was moving as fast as I could,' Shanty explained. 'It's not easy trying to climb a wagon when you're only four feet, two inches tall. It's a bit like trying to scale a mountain. Maybe next time I should do the distracting, and one of you the clobbering.'

'I think you did just splendidly,' Oswald said.

'We won't get into any trouble about this, will we?' Sara asked Master Scott. 'I don't know what else we could have done.'

'And nothing quite ends an argument like a good old-fashioned plank of wood,' Shanty remarked.

Scott clapped Shanty on the shoulder and jumped down from the wheel. 'Like the sergeant said, we're not part of the military, so we can hardly be arrested for resisting an order. Not that I'm in the least bit concerned about any of that right now.' He stared ahead at the encircled legions. 'We've got a far more important matter

239

to deal with.' Scott raced over to Shimmer, climbed up and kicked his heels into the drake's flanks, sending her into the air. He flew to the front of the cavalry column and hovered a few yards above the ground, buffeting the riders' cloaks with each powerful beat of Shimmer's wings. He drew his sword, thrust it above his head and roared, 'Will you follow me?'

Fifty voices answered as one in a loud cheer. The Master nodded proudly and pointed his sword at the company of Roon that had separated from the main battle to block them. 'I'll lead and carve a path through the giants. Then we'll head straight for the trapped Andalonians. Maintain a wedge formation, stay close and don't stop. There aren't that many of us, but all we need to do is puncture a hole through the Roon lines and keep it open long enough for our men to escape through. If we fail, this war is lost.'

Determined not to get left behind, Caspan climbed atop Frostbite and rode out to join Scott. 'Where do you want me?' he asked.

'Right by my side,' Scott said, then turned to consider the Roon they were about to charge. There were perhaps a hundred of them, formed up behind a shield wall, their spears pointed at the cavalry. 'I think one blast of fire should be enough to scatter them. What do you think?'

Caspan leaned forward in his saddle and patted Frostbite on the neck. 'It will be our pleasure.' The drake craned his head around to give Caspan a knowing look that suggested he could understand every word Caspan said.

'Just don't fly too ahead of the cavalry,' Scott cautioned. 'Otherwise the Roon might close the gap, stopping the cavalry from coming through after us.'

Caspan nodded and drew a deep breath, girding himself for what was to come. Scott commanded the cavalry into a wedge-shaped formation. Then somebody cleared their throat loudly, prompting Caspan and Scott to turn around.

Sara, Shanty and Oswald were waiting behind them, sitting atop their Wardens. Sara had an arrow set to her bowstring, and Shanty and Oswald gripped swords in their hands. Shanty had also acquired a large metal shield, which stretched from where his left foot rested in a stirrup to the tip of his nose. Caspan marvelled at how he could carry it.

'I hope you weren't planning on leaving us behind?' Sara asked.

Scott smiled proudly. 'I wouldn't dare dream of it.' He cocked an eyebrow questioningly at Shanty. 'You'll be able to keep pace?' The dwarf mumbled something in return, but his voice was muffled by the shield and the distant sounds of combat. Scott smirked as he raised a hand to his ear. 'I'm sorry, did you say something?'

The dwarf snorted as he lowered his shield, allowing him to see the Master properly. 'I said, you don't need to worry about us. Ferris can run as fast as a galloping horse over short distances. Just make sure *you* don't fall behind *me*.'

Scott grinned as he waited for his friends to join the company of riders. When they were ready, he raised his sword and thrust it at the enemy. With a mighty cheer and bellowing horns, the reserve cavalry set spurs to mounts and thundered across the field.

CHAPTER 25

HIGHLAND ALLIES

As their drakes streaked away from the ground, Caspan and Master Scott led the charge at the Roon shield wall. The pounding of steel-shod hooves across the earth only a few yards below them was deafening. Caspan felt as if he was at the head of a tremendous avalanche that would smash through any opposition. At the back of his mind, though, was the fact that although the battle had raged for several hours now, no Andalonian cavalry charge had yet been effective in breaking through the enemy's shield walls. He gritted his teeth and vowed that this was about to change.

As they neared the enemy some of the giants parted their shields, allowing archers to step into the gaps. Caspan and Scott hunkered down across their Wardens' backs and directed them to fly lower until the drakes' feet, tucked up under their bellies, almost brushed across the ground. Bowstrings twanged and arrows zipped through the air. Some ricocheted off the steel-like scales that covered the drakes' shoulders and the tops of their heads. One even tore through Caspan's billowing cloak. Gargled cries rose from behind as some of the riders, hit by feathered shafts, toppled from their saddles and disappeared in clouds of dust. But there could be no turning back now, and so the Andalonians charged forward until the shield wall closed again and the giants braced themselves for the impact.

Thirty yards from the enemy, Caspan commanded Frostbite to deliver his deadly fire-storm. Frostbite reared back his head, his nostrils flaring as he sucked in air, filling his lungs. Then he thrust his head forward, targeting the middle section of the enemy line. A stream of brilliant blue fire shot from the drake's nostrils, engulfing the Roon.

A hurled axe came out of nowhere. Caspan saw it as a blur of movement in the corner of his eye and yanked instinctively on Frostbite's reins, cutting short the drake's fire attack as they tried to steer clear of the weapon. But it was too late. The axe ripped through the soft membrane of Frostbite's left wing. Before Caspan knew what was happening, he was hanging on for dear life around Frostbite's neck as they crashed into the ground. They tumbled along the earth in a mess of twisting limbs and wings until they ploughed into the enemy.

Fire raged all around them. Bodies and shields flew through the air. Caspan was thrown clear and rolled across the singed and burning ground for what seemed like an eternity before he finally stopped. He lay on his chest, spitting dirt and blinking clarity into his spinning vision, vaguely aware that the ominous sound of thundering hooves was getting closer and closer.

He pushed himself up onto his elbows and looked back towards the shield wall. His blood turned to ice. Through the dissipating cloud of blue fire the cavalry emerged, charging straight towards him, their steel-shod hooves chomping into the earth like the jaws of a great beast. He scrambled frantically to his feet and dived to the side, narrowly avoiding the riders who galloped past him. He rolled across the ground until he was clear of their trampling hooves, then lay there, gasping for air. He waited until the last of the horsemen rode by, then, as the dust settled around him, he clambered to his feet and searched desperately for Frostbite.

To his relief, Frostbite had also rolled clear of the enemy and managed to avoid the cavalry. The drake was lying on the opposite side of the trail of churned earth made by the horsemen. But Caspan's heart sank when he saw the injuries Frostbite had sustained. The drake was licking his left wing, which hung limp by his side. A hole over a foot long had been torn through the leathery membrane. Frostbite would never fly with such an injury. The collision into the enemy had also ripped scales out of the Warden's brilliant blue coat, leaving patches of soft, pink flesh. Whereas Caspan's cloak was singed from when he had rolled through the fireball, Frostbite fortunately appeared to be immune to his own fire.

Caspan called out as he staggered towards Frostbite, who looked up and tried to rise. The drake placed his rear right leg tentatively on the ground, but was incapable of bearing his weight on it. Only now did Caspan realise that there was a large patch of exposed flesh, raw and grazed, on Frostbite's right thigh. Moaning in pain, the drake nursed his injured leg against his chest and lay down on his side.

Close to tears, Caspan hurried over to Frostbite and wrapped his arms around his neck. 'Oh, buddy, aren't you in a fine mess. Don't worry — I'll get you safely out of here. Everything will be fine.'

The drake looked deep into Caspan's eyes and, whimpering, licked the boy's cheek.

A battle cry from behind forced Caspan to spin around to discover that the Roon had re-formed their shield wall. They were advancing slowly towards him and Frostbite, peering warily over the rims of their shields, no doubt wary of the drake's lethal fire attack.

Abandoned by the cavalry who had charged ahead as planned, Caspan stared in horror at the approaching horde. Flight was foremost on his mind, but he knew they'd never be able to escape in time. Frostbite could barely stand let alone walk or fly. Grimly accepting what needed to be done, he turned to give his Warden a final hug and kissed him tenderly on the snout.

'Goodbye, my dear, dear friend,' he said, tears streaming down his cheeks. 'I'll miss you so much.'

His sword gripped in his hand, his teeth bared, he turned to face the giants. He was about to reach for Frostbite's soul key, when a familiar voice called from behind.

'I hope you're not planning on doing something silly?'

Caspan turned to find that Sara had reined Cloud Dancer alongside Frostbite. Shanty, Oswald and a dozen horsemen had also withdrawn from the main cavalry charge to join them.

Never before had Caspan been so happy to see his friends. He stared at them, speechless, wiping the tears from his eyes.

'We'll escort you back to the main group,' one of the horsemen said. Caspan recognised him as the soldier with the busted lip.

'Don't just stand there gawking at us!' Shanty warned Caspan. 'Hurry up and get out of here!'

Sara dexterously reached into her quiver, set an arrow to her bowstring and loosed the shaft at one of the giants. It thudded into the Roon's shield, just above its iron boss.

'Frostbite's injured,' Caspan said. 'He can't fly.'

Shanty ducked as a spear soared past his head. 'Then dismiss him. And be quick about it!'

Caspan reached under his tunic for Frostbite's soul key and froze. It was missing. Panicking, he patted his chest frantically, checking if it had slipped off its chain and fallen down inside his clothing. But he still couldn't find it.

'It's gone!' he cried, looking helplessly at his friends. 'Frostbite's soul key is gone!'

He started to sprint back to where he had rolled across the ground to check there, when Oswald spurred Legend alongside him.

'There's no time for that, Caspan,' he warned. 'We need to get out of here, fast.' He offered Caspan his hand. 'Climb up.'

Caspan swatted the elderly treasure hunter's hand aside and stared at him defiantly. 'There's no way I'm leaving Frostbite behind. Now get Shanty and Sara out of here before it's too late!'

He glanced over at Frostbite, who was trying to struggle to his feet, but his rear right leg gave way again. The drake pushed himself up on his front legs and faced the approaching giants. He drew his right wing back threateningly, bared his dagger-like teeth and roared. The Roon stopped dead in their tracks and retreated a few steps, but a muscle-corded warrior with snake tattoos on his arms and chest pushed through the shield wall and barked a command, restoring order. Another command from the burly giant saw the Roon on the flanks of the shield wall move forward, while the centre held steady, evidently in an attempt to encircle the small group of defenders and their Wardens.

Caspan stared beseechingly at Oswald. 'Please leave! You can still ride away. Now go!'

Oswald looked down at him and smiled softly. 'The Brotherhood never abandons one of its own.' A spear thudded into the earth barely a foot from Legend's front hooves, making the unicorn neigh and stamp backwards. Oswald tugged on the reins, holding the Warden in check. He extended his hand to Caspan again. 'Climb up. You won't stand a chance down there.'

No sooner had Caspan grasped Oswald's hand and swung up onto the unicorn's back than a spear sailed out from behind the Roon ranks and sliced across Caspan's shoulder. Crying out in pain, the treasure hunter dropped his sword. He had the presence of mind to dexterously manoeuvre his foot to hook the sword's crossguard on the toe of his boot. Caspan reached down to grab it, when he was startled by a bloodcurdling war cry. His sword slipping from his fingers, he looked up to see the Roon lower their shields and charge.

Sara fired four arrows swiftly, bringing down two Roon and making those behind stumble and pile on top of each other. But her feathered shafts were never going to stop so many giants. They rumbled forward in a landslide of black steel and rippling muscle.

Caspan feared this was the end, for there was nothing they could do to stop such a large force, when the centre of the Roon line was hit by a cone of magical blue fire. Frostbite turned his head slowly to the right, directing his blazing stream along the entire left flank of the attacking giants. Those lucky to have hunkered down behind their shields waited for the blue cloud to dissipate, then, tossing aside their burning shields, tore towards Frostbite, determined to slay him before he could deliver another devastating jet of fire.

Sara brought down three of the giants with carefully aimed shots of her bow. Then she joined Caspan, Shanty, Oswald and the horsemen in forming a protective circle around the injured drake.

'Here!' she yelled, resting her bow across her thighs as she nimbly untied her sword belt from around her waist. She tossed the weapon to Caspan.

He caught it and drew the blade clear of its scabbard just in time to meet a giant's double-headed axe. The jar almost knocked Caspan off Legend's back, but he held on tightly to the saddle blanket's grip with his free hand and kicked the giant hard in the neck. The Roon staggered back, but another giant rushed forward to grab Caspan by the tunic and tried to drag him off Legend. Squeezing his legs around the unicorn's waist, Caspan twisted around and hammered the pommel of his sword onto the giant's leather skull cap. There was a dull thud and the Roon slumped to his knees.

Giants swarmed around them. Legend reared up on his hind legs and clobbered the giants with his front hooves. No sooner would he land back down on all fours than he'd lash out with his hind legs, delivering bone-crunching kicks. The giants moved back warily, their shields raised, and stabbed with their spears and swords at the unicorn's exposed flanks. Caspan and Oswald parried aside the enemy thrusts, but Caspan knew it would only be a matter of time before a sword or spear-point snaked past their defences.

Caspan glanced over to the right. Shanty, Ferris and five horsemen charged into a group of giants. The faun lowered his horns as he smashed into the Roon. In spite of being only half their size, the faun's powerful headbutt splintered their wooden shields and sent three of the enemy sprawling on the ground. Two of the horsemen were cut down, and the dwarf and faun quickly retreated with the remaining riders to join Frostbite, who kept the enemy at bay with bursts of fire and swipes of his tail.

Sara and Cloud Dancer, meanwhile, took to the sky. Fortunately, the Roon archers appeared to have exhausted all of their arrows, for they had drawn their swords and joined the other giants in the melee. But many were armed with spears, which they threw with deadly accuracy. Already five of the horsemen had toppled from their saddles, clutching spear hafts. Sara kept Cloud Dancer hovering high above Frostbite, well out of spear-range. She loosed shaft after shaft down at the Roon, picking them off as they lowered their shields to attack her friends and the cavalry.

Sweat trickling down his forehead, Caspan saw the burly commander with the snake tattoos push through the press and prepare to attack Legend. The giant wielded a massive broadsword in a two-handed grip, its black blade engraved with runes and strange symbols. He heaved it back behind his shoulder, and, when Legend wheeled around to lash out with his rear legs at two attacking Roon, rushed forward. His great sword sliced through the air as it carved down towards the unicorn's neck.

Caspan cried out in warning. He leaned past Oswald and thrust with his sword, deflecting the giant's blade and sending it thudding into the earth. The Roon roared with rage, yanked his sword free and hoisted it back for another swing.

Caspan's right hand was numb from the vibration of the first blow. Gripping the leather-bound haft of his sword with both hands, he leaned out to the right, moving clear of Oswald, and tried to parry aside the next attack.

Legend reared suddenly to avoid a spear-thrust. Caspan was caught off balance and toppled backwards over the unicorn's rump. He hit the ground flat on his stomach. The wind exploded from his chest and pin-pricks of dazzling silver besieged his vision. Every part of his aching body begged for rest, to just lay still and give in, but he knew that his only chance of staying alive lay in climbing back atop Legend. Leaning on his sword, he pushed himself dazedly to his feet.

The giants rushed in for the kill.

Caspan staggered back until he bumped into Legend's flank. Harnessing what strength he had left, he raised his sword high above his head, determined to get in one final blow at the giants. He singled out his target: the tattooed commander.

From high above somebody screamed Caspan's name and an arrow thudded into the Roon's chest. But it had no effect on the giant, who snarled savagely as he drew back his great sword and thrust it at Caspan's torso. Caspan gritted his teeth and brought his own sword down in a gleaming arc.

Time froze.

Then something large and blue swept between the combatants with a gush of wind that buffeted Caspan's cloak and swirled dirt in the air. It hit the Roon commander with incredible force, knocking him off his feet and sending him crashing into his fellow giants, bailing them over like skittles. Exhausted, Caspan lowered his sword and rubbed the dirt and sweat from his eyes. He gazed skyward, his heart filling with hope as he watched Master Scott turn Shimmer around for another attack.

Shimmer beat his wings powerfully, tucked them close to his sides and shot downwards. The giants who'd been knocked over by the drake's first attack clambered back to their feet and raised their shields above their heads, but they offered scant protection against the drake. Shimmer's raking claws left a trail of splintered wood, and dead and injured Roon in his wake. Those giants lucky to have dived to the side hurled their spears at the Warden, but Shimmer was moving so fast that none came close to hitting him.

Scott and Shimmer climbed high into the air and banked around again. The Roon commander ripped off his tattered mail coif and roared at the giants, ordering them into a defensive formation. Those with shields hurried to the front and locked their iron rims together; those at the rear held their spears and axes at the ready, poised to throw. And that's when they were hit from behind.

Caspan spun around, wondering what had happened. Through the misty panes of exhaustion he saw something that left him gaping, wondering if it was a trick played by his imagination.

Lachlan and Talon had swooped down out of the sky and were tearing into the Roon.

Lachlan's flesh was coated in the black metal armour, which spread out in writhing tentacles from his Dray armband. He also wielded a shadow blade that sliced through enemy shields and weapons as easily as a heated knife carving through butter. He leapt from Talon's back and fought on foot. In the chaotic press many enemy thrusts snaked through his defences, but the weapons glanced harmlessly off Lachlan's magical exoskeleton. Talon fought by his side, slaying all who came before them. They battled their way through the enemy horde until they reached Caspan, Oswald and Legend, then carved a path over to Frostbite, Shanty, Ferris and the remaining horsemen. Caspan noticed that the dwarf grimaced and clutched the lower left section of his torso, where his mail shirt was mangled.

'I couldn't be happier to see you, lad. Your timing's impeccable,' Shanty said to Lachlan as he tossed aside his splintered and useless shield. He pointed his sword at Lachlan's Dray armband. 'But was that a wise thing to do? You know what happened the last time you put that thing on.'

Lachlan parried aside a spear-thrust and grabbed the weapon by the haft. He yanked back, drew close the giant at the other end, and knocked him senseless with a punch to the jaw. 'We'll talk later,' he growled. 'Right now we've got a battle to fight and a war to win!'

Caspan lost track of time. He hacked and slashed until his breathing came in ragged gasps and he barely had the strength to lift his sword. The battle became a kaleidoscope of blurred images; a montage of slashing blades, trampling hooves and fireballs.

And through it all braved Lachlan. His tunic and breeches were singed and torn; his Brotherhood cloak a shredded mess pockmarked with smoking holes. Caspan feared that Lachlan would be overwhelmed by the sheer number of giants attacking him, but he cut them down in swathes. Soon he had slain dozens and none dared oppose him.

A horn sounded, signalling the Roon retreat. The remaining giants trudged over to join their burly commander, then jogged back towards the main battle.

Caspan stuck his sword in the ground, rested his hands on his knees and sucked in air. Finally, they'd been granted a reprieve. But he knew it would be brief, for the battle was far from over. A quick glance over at the encircled Andalonians revealed that the reserve cavalry was still trying to hack a path through the giants. Master Scott and Shimmer had joined them. They were meeting staunch resistance, though, and Caspan feared they wouldn't prevail.

He looked at his friends, their Wardens and the six remaining horsemen, wondering if they'd be able to muster the strength to join the cavalry. But they appeared even more exhausted than him.

Oswald climbed gingerly out of his saddle and clapped him on the shoulder. 'We gave it our best shot. We couldn't have done more.'

Caspan shook his head, refusing to believe that the battle was lost. 'But we can't give up. Not after everything we've been through.'

'Then what do you propose we do?' Oswald asked, kneeling and resting his sword across his thighs. 'If Frostbite could still fly we might have stood a chance. But Frostbite's injured, and we've had it. Shanty's hurt, and we barely have enough strength to lift a sword, let alone wield it. All we've got left is Lachlan, and we can't expect him to take on an entire army.' He cleaned his spectacles on a kerchief before pushing them back up on the bridge of his nose. He gave Caspan an encouraging look. 'Smaller forces have defeated larger armies by employing guerrilla tactics. We can take to the forests and mountain passes. We'll hit the Roon in lightning-fast raids and ambushes, then disappear before they know what hit them. We'll harass and harangue them until they realise we'll never stop, and that Andalon is more trouble than it's worth. That's how we'll beat them.'

Caspan eyes narrowed. 'And what of our friends? What of Roland, Raven, Thom, Master Morgan, Prince Dale and Duke Bran? Do we abandon them? Do we just give up?' He drew a deep breath, gripped his sword and climbed onto an abandoned horse. He looked defiantly at the elderly treasure hunter. 'The Brotherhood never abandons its own.'

'I'll second that,' Sara said as she set Cloud Dancer down near Frostbite. She swung out of the saddle and started scrounging through the battlefield for arrows.

'As will I,' Lachlan announced.

'And don't think for one moment that you'll be leaving me behind!' Shanty growled. 'My blood's up, and it's going to take more than a blow from an axe to keep me out of the action. Dwarves are made of hardy stock.' He looked quizzically at Lachlan's shadow blade. 'How'd you come by that?'

'Compliments of Gramidge,' Lachlan explained.

'He figured Foe Slayer could be put to better use than collecting dust in the Eagle's Eyrie.'

'Now why didn't I think of that,' Shanty said. 'You don't happen to have the ring, Swift Feet, on you?'

Lachlan shook his head. 'Sorry. Gramidge brought it over with him, but King Rhys thought it could be best used by one of his messengers.'

'Oh, well, I'll just have to rely on good old sweat and brawn,' the dwarf replied. 'Still, that's never let me down in the past, has it, Ferris?'

The faun stamped a cloven hoof on the earth and nuzzled against Shanty's shoulder.

Oswald regarded the dwarf disapprovingly. 'You should know better than this.'

Shanty frowned. 'What do you mean?'

The elderly treasure hunter pointed at Caspan, Lachlan and Sara. 'They're young and impetuous. They think they're invincible. Doing things that are brash is in their blood. But I didn't expect you to join them. You should well and truly know how dangerous it will be, charging back into the fight.'

Shanty stared fixedly at Oswald. 'I do. And that's exactly why I'll be with them every step of the way.'

Oswald sighed and opened his mouth to comment, when a blast of bagpipe music sounded. Everybody turned to the east. There, in a line that stretched for over a mile along the crest of the valley hill, was the Caledonian army.

Roy Stewart sat at the front of his highland force astride a chestnut stallion, its mane shining burnished gold in the sunlight. One side of the highlander's face was covered in black war-paint and he gripped a massive claymore in his mail-gloved hand.

Shadowing the Stewart Laird were his bodyguards, the Gall-Gaedhil. They were mounted on stocky, shaggy-maned horses, and wore shirts of black mail and carried small wooden bucklers in their off-hands. Behind them amassed the highland army, organised into companies based on their clans. Familiar with Caledonish tartans since his mission to Tor O'Shawn, Caspan indentified the Stewarts, Campbells, Macintosh, MacGillis, Camerons, Wallace and MacDonells. Their banners fluttered in the slight breeze, and their pikes and swords glistened like a silver forest.

Roy Stewart pulled back on his reins, making his stallion rear up on its hind legs. He shouted something to his army in Chaelic, the ancient tongue of Caledon, then thrust his claymore high above his head and gave the command to charge. To the accompaniment of their bagpipes, the highlanders gave a deafening roar and tore down the slope.

Ignorant of the secret alliance between Andalon and Caledon, the giants cheered and blew their war-horns in anticipated victory as the highlanders swarmed into the valley and formed up behind them.

Lachlan cursed under his breath and trudged boldly towards the highlanders. 'As if things weren't bad enough,' he growled before turning to look back at his friends. 'Get out of here while you can. And take Talon with you. I'll hold them off.'

Caspan had forgotten that Lachlan wasn't aware of the agreement made between Duke Bran and Roy Stewart. He hurried over and grabbed his friend by the sleeve. 'Wait. It's not what you think. Roy's fighting on *our* side.'

Lachlan blinked in disbelief. 'What? But he's our enemy.'

'It's all a bit too much to explain right now, but you need to trust me.' Caspan's heart raced as he stared at the Caledonish army. 'Let's just hope Roy Stewart stays true to his word.'

Lachlan lowered his sword and gazed blankly at the highlanders. 'So he's joined forces with *us*?' he muttered, his voice heavy with doubt.

Caspan nodded and pumped his fist. 'Come on, Roy Stewart!' he whispered, willing the highland laird, who stood erect in his stirrups for all to see, to honour his word. 'This is it!'

Caspan held his breath expectantly as Roy raised his sword high above his head and cried, 'Attack!'

The Roon cheered and drew aside, creating channels through which the highlanders could attack the Andalonians. The Caledonish warriors rushed forward, funnelling into the gaps, then turned on the giants. Hundreds were cut down before they even knew what was happening. By the time the giants had coordinated their defences and formed islands of shield walls, the combined armies of the highlanders and Andalonians swarmed them.

Caspan and his friends raced over to join the fight, but it was difficult for them to reach the giants over the hordes of Caledonish men. No doubt determined to enact revenge for their company of slain scouts, the highlanders fought in a thick press that prevented anybody from coming forward. Not even Lachlan could push his way through them.

Caspan darted to the rear of the Caledonish warriors, probing for a way to reach Roland and the other Brotherhood members. Eventually a gap opened before him and he hurried forward to join the Andalonian soldiers. He searched desperately through the sea of faces, hunting for his friends, but it was impossible to find them in the chaotic press. All around him men were surging forward, trying to fight the giants. A horse slammed into Caspan from behind, knocking him off his feet and sending his sword flying from his grasp. He rolled clear of its trampling hooves and staggered to his feet.

'Caspan! Over here!' a voice cried over the ruckus.

Caspan spun around and spotted Prince Dale twenty yards away, still atop his stallion. The treasure hunter pushed his way through the mass of soldiers until he reached the Prince and climbed up behind him.

'Thank goodness you're alive!' Dale yelled over the sounds of combat. 'It's been a while since I last saw you or Frostbite. I thought we'd lost you.'

'I've been with the reserve cavalry, trying to break through the Roon to save you.' Caspan continued to search for his friends in the crowd, hoping he might be able to spot them from this elevated position. 'Where are the others?'

Dale pointed with his sword to the left. 'Not long ago

I saw Roland, Raven, Thom and Morgan over that way. Don't worry; they're alive and well.'

Caspan scanned the groups of Andalonian soldiers and exhaled a relieved breath when he finally saw his friends. Roland and Thom were riding tandem atop Georgina, and Morgan and Raven still rode their magical dire wolves. Captain Jace fought on foot, wielding the broken haft of a spear. They were all streaked in sweat and dirt, their clothing torn and their blades notched. But they were alive.

Dale tried to turn his mount around to join them but couldn't push through the mass of soldiers. The Prince and Caspan eventually managed to reach Duke Bran, who barked commands to his soldiers, protected by a core unit of heavily armoured horsemen.

For hours the battle raged, the combined armies of Caledon and Andalon maintaining the upper hand, until a horn bellowed, signalling the Roon retreat. What was left of the Roon army abandoned the battlefield and tried to escape back along the valley. The Andalonian cavalry gave chase, pursuing the fleeing giants far into the hinterland.

Caspan dismounted from behind Dale and stared across the battlefield, struggling to comprehend that not only had they won the battle and saved Andalon, but that he had also survived. All across the valley, exhausted soldiers dropped their weapons and slumped to their knees.

'We did it!' Dale exclaimed, sliding off his saddle and clapping Caspan on the shoulder. 'We actually did it!' he yelled triumphantly, thrusting his sword into the air.

Caspan nodded, dumbstruck. 'It's hard to believe.'

'Now, I don't care what you say, but that was epic!' said a familiar voice.

Caspan and the Prince turned to find Roland behind them. The black-haired jester climbed gingerly from his saddle and tossed aside his sword.

'Come here, you great big puddenhead,' Caspan said as he hugged his friend, never more glad to see him alive and well.

Chapter 26

PEACE AT LAST

'And now, without further ado, I'd like to commemorate our victory at Chester Hill with a song I've composed specially for the occasion,' Roland announced from where he stood at the head of the table. He raised his bagpipes to his lips.

Shanty sprang from his seat with such urgency he knocked over a tankard of cider. 'Blood and thunder! Now look what you've made me do! Somebody stop him!' he yelled, pointing at Roland. 'I had to listen to him practise last night, and I can't take any more of it. My head will explode!'

'I'm sorry, Roland,' Dale called out from the royal table nearby, 'but Shanty's right. If I hear another tune from your bagpipes, I'll have to arrest you.'

Sara, who sat across the table from Roland, raised an eyebrow at the Prince. 'Tune? You're being generous.'

Roland laughed humourlessly and glanced at Dale. 'You're not serious, are you?'

The Prince's expression was deadpan. 'Oh, I am.'

Roland slunk back into his seat and placed his bagpipes on the table. 'That's the last time I go to any effort to make your lives a little more entertaining,' he moped. 'Some people just have no appreciation of the finer things in life.'

Sara pouted her bottom lip in mock sympathy. 'Oh, you poor diddums. Just remember: there's a time and place for everything.'

'And the place for him to play his bagpipes is on top of the furthest mountain,' Shanty commented, prompting Roland to snatch a bread roll from the table and pelt it at him. The dwarf dexterously caught it in his mouth, making everyone at the table roar with laughter.

'They seem to be enjoying themselves,' Caspan said to Lachlan.

The boys were standing over by one of the three hearths in the great hall of King Rhys's castle. It was a massive chamber, at least a hundred yards long and fifty yards wide, with an ornate, vaulted ceiling and walls bedecked with tapestries and banners. Hundreds of guests sat around the thirty long tables, which were packed with trays of suckling pig, glazed quail and roast chicken, plates of sliced turkey and venison, and baskets of freshly cooked warm bread. Caspan had attended several celebratory feasts since joining the Brotherhood, but nothing came close to the splendour of King Rhys's spread.

'They have every reason to,' Lachlan replied. 'I'm sure you heard earlier today that the last of the Roon were chased back beyond The Scar. The war is now officially over. And more importantly, we won!' He raised his tankard of cider in a toast. 'Here's to peace and leading a normal life.'

'I'll drink to peace, but I don't know if I want to live a normal life.'

'Oh?'

'Don't you think it would be a little, well, *boring*?'

'Our lives will never be boring. We might have defeated the Roon, but we're still going to continue exploring Dray tombs in search of magical items. I overheard Duke Connal tell Master Morgan that he's thinking of sending us down to Salahara.'

Caspan's eyes flashed with excitement. 'Salahara! I've always wanted to see the desert kingdom. Did he say when?'

'Sometime next month. So don't worry; you'll be getting your full dose of excitement soon enough.' Lachlan sighed. 'But my life will never be *normal* again.' He pulled back his sleeve to reveal the Dray armband attached to his forearm. 'I don't exactly blend in with the crowd anymore.'

It was warm inside the hall, but Lachlan insisted on wearing his black Brotherhood cloak. Its hood was drawn over his head and he wore gloves, to conceal the magical armour that covered his skin. He'd been dressed like this since the Battle of Chester Hill, one month ago.

Caspan gave his friend a sympathetic look. 'We're incredibly grateful for what you did, but you didn't have to do it.'

'What? And miss out on all the action? Don't be ridiculous. Nothing was going to keep me away from the final battle.' Lachlan pulled off a glove and inspected his hand. The black exoskeleton reflected the flickering fire light. 'I just have to learn to accept that this is how I'll look from now on.'

'So Arthur still doesn't think you should try taking the armband off?'

Lachlan shook his head. 'After what it did to me last time, he doubts I'd survive. And I'm not prepared to take that risk. We fought long and hard to defeat the Roon.' He smiled at Caspan. 'I'd like to be around to enjoy the peace.'

'I'll drink to that.' Caspan clanked his tankard against his friend's and took a long draught.

'It has its advantages, too,' Lachlan commented, inspecting his hand again. 'Weapons bounce off me, and I'd be almost impossible to spot in a game of hide and seek at night time.'

Caspan laughed, glad that Lachlan could make light of his situation. 'I hope Roland doesn't cotton on to that. There's no telling what mischief he'd try to get you into.'

'What's this about mischief and Roland?' Kilt asked as she joined them, arm in arm with Saxon. 'I thought the two were inseparable.'

Just like you and the Baron, Caspan thought wryly. Kilt and Saxon had been invited by the King to attend the victory celebration and arrived at the capital yesterday afternoon. Caspan was glad to see Kilt again. Never before had he seen her so happy. For someone who rarely smiled she positively glowed, her laughter filling the hall.

'I wonder if Roland's collected any more war trophies,' Saxon said. 'I heard he salvaged a wagon-load of Roon weapons from the Battle of Chester Hill.'

Caspan nodded. 'It was pitch black before we finally managed to drag him from the battlefield.'

'Where's he storing everything?' Kilt asked.

'He's rented a warehouse down by the docks,' Lachlan replied.

Kilt's eyes widened. 'A warehouse! Are you serious?'

Lachlan nodded dourly. 'Sadly, yes.'

'Well, I'm not too sure if his latest acquisition will fit inside there,' Saxon commented. 'He's now the proud owner of a Roon warship.'

Caspan almost choked on his drink. 'What?'

'Remember the Roon boat that managed to make it to the beach during the Battle of the High Coast? Well, he sent a messenger raven last week, asking if he could have it.'

Lachlan cocked an eyebrow. 'And you said *yes*?'

Saxon shrugged. 'I could hardly begrudge him. If it wasn't for the Brotherhood, the High Coast might have fallen.'

'With Roland aboard a warship, the High Coast might *still* fall,' Lachlan warned. 'I hate to think of what trouble he'll get up to, sailing around the west coast in a Roon galley.'

Kilt scratched her head in wonder. 'What's he planning to do with all this stuff? Open a museum?'

Caspan chuckled. 'Beats me. The way he's going, he'll be able to equip a small army.'

'Have you heard about what happened to him last night?' Kilt asked the boys.

Lachlan moaned. 'I'm not sure I want to.'

'As you know, Roy Stewart and his contingent of highland lairds arrived here yesterday,' Kilt explained. 'Well, the laird of the Strathboogie Clan has made Roland an honorary member of his clan.'

Caspan shook his head and grinned. 'We'll never hear the end of his bagpipe playing now.'

'I think we've got bigger problems than that to deal with,' Lachlan said. 'Check this out.'

Everybody looked at a cleared space in the middle of the hall, where a group of highlanders had assembled in a line. A pair of Caledonish basket-hilted broadswords lay at their feet, their crossed blades forming an X. At first Caspan wasn't sure what had alarmed Lachlan — until he saw Roland standing in the middle of the line, wearing a Strathboogie kilt and shawl, his hands planted on his hips.

Caspan shook his head. 'Don't tell me he's going to —'

A highlander standing off to the side drowned his sentence with a burst of bagpipe music. Guests stood up and gathered around the group, curious expressions on their faces. When there was a large enough audience, the musician stopped, glanced at his fellow highlanders and nodded. Then he played a tune that Caspan recognised instantly — *Caledon the Brave*. To a roar of applause,

Roland and the Caledonish warriors danced a highland jig around the broadswords.

'Where did he learn to do that?' Kilt yelled over the music and clapping.

Caspan smirked from ear to ear, marvelling at how Roland's feet darted nimbly between the blades. 'I don't know. Although nothing surprises me much more about him. Mind you, I think he's improvising a bit.'

As if on cue, Roland skipped into the middle of the hall, pirouetted and leapt onto a table. He quickly arranged a knife and fork into an X and attempted to jig around them. It failed miserably, with the fork stabbing him in the heel and the knife knocking over a tankard. Still, it didn't stop Roland, who dived off the table into the arms of his fellow performers. No sooner had they placed him back on his feet then he planted his hands on his hips again and skipped, kicked and capered his way around the broadswords.

There was a chorus of cheering at the conclusion of the dance. Then the highlanders hoisted Roland onto their shoulders and did a lap of honour around the hall.

'Och, ye wee Jimmies!' Roland called as he was carried past his friends, waving his blue Strathboogie bonnet with pride.

'Personally, I blame Shanty,' Kilt commented, watching as Roland was escorted around the royal table, much to the amusement of King Rhys and Duke Bran. 'It was his idea to dress as highlanders to infiltrate Tor O'Shawn. I always said it was a bad idea. And now look at the monster he's created.'

Caspan smiled warmly as he regarded the Stewart Laird, who sat in a special seat beside King Rhys and his wife. Roy had remained true to his word and withdrawn his soldiers from Darrowmere. Duke Bran had likewise honoured his part of the agreement the men had made at the stone circle. A new duchy, Glengyle, had been created in the north-west of Lochinbar. It was a land of rich, rolling pastures and forests plentiful with game. Highlanders were already settling in the area. For the first time in several hundred years, Caledon and Lochinbar were at peace. Caspan couldn't also help but notice the strong bond of friendship that had been formed between Roy and Duke Bran, who sat to his right. They joked and laughed like old comrades.

Caspan also noticed how well Prince Dale and Skye were getting on. They sat beside one another at the royal table, smiling happily as they chatted. Caspan felt immense pride in having played an important role in solidifying the union between Andalon and Caledon. If he hadn't escorted Skye to Sharn O'Kare Glen and remained for the subsequent meeting with Roy Stewart, Lochinbar and Caledon might still be at war.

Caspan had also learnt that Lady Brook, General Brett's co-conspirator in forming an alliance with the Roon, had been caught at one of the southern city ports, trying to buy passage aboard a merchant ship bound for Salahara. She was now locked in a dungeon, facing charges of treason. Brett, however, was still on the loose, and Caspan was certain they hadn't seen the last of him. But looking at Dale and Skye, both of whom would chart the future course of their countries, Caspan had every confidence that the alliance between Caledon and Lochinbar would only get stronger. The Prince's desire for peace was no longer a distant dream but a reality and firmly within his grasp.

And Caspan was determined to play an integral role in maintaining the peace. Only yesterday he and his fellow former Brotherhood initiates had met with King Rhys to discuss their appointments as barons. This was a reward for their services to the King during their mission to Tor O'Shawn. The appointments would take place next week during an official ceremony, but the King wanted to know if the treasure hunters had a preference for a particular territory. Many lords had died during the recent war, and Rhys was eager to appoint new nobles to the estates. After his shock that he would soon have a title and a manor house, Caspan thought long and hard about which territory he'd like to control. Of course, advisors and managerial staff would be provided to assist the new young lords, who knew little, if nothing, about managing an estate. They would also remain members of the Brotherhood and spend most of their time at the House of Whispers.

Sara chose a territory close to Briston so she could see her family more regularly. Roland likewise selected an estate close to the village he grew up in, south of the High Coast. Lachlan was adamant he wanted a manor house somewhere in the north of Dannenland, up near The Scar, where he could protect the border should the Roon ever try to return. Caspan wasn't surprised when

Kilt selected an estate near Castle Crag, no doubt to keep in close contact with Saxon.

Caspan thought back to the first time he had seen the Caledonish highlands. It had been during the mission to Tor O'Shawn, when the treasure hunters had rested at Mance O'Shea's Break. Peering through a hole in the wall, Caspan had gazed in awe upon the snow-capped mountains and heather-flecked hillsides. Never before had he seen such rugged beauty, and it left an indelible impression on him. After much deliberation he decided to have an estate in Glengyle, the newly formed duchy in the north-west of Lochinbar. According to Duke Bran there was an old castle there that would suit Caspan nicely. It overlooked a loch and had strong walls that could be easily defended. It needed a little work, but to Caspan it sounded just perfect.

He would help the Caledonish settlers in Glengyle make a new home for themselves. He'd learnt a little about diplomacy during his adventures with the Brotherhood, and he believed his calm demeanour and patience would be valuable in resolving disputes. He also shared a close bond with both Duke Bran and Prince Dale, and he had earned the respect and trust of Roy Stewart and Skye. Caspan believed he'd be able to mediate between them should their alliance become strained.

'You look like you've got something on your mind,' a familiar voice said, drawing Caspan from his thoughts. He was surprised to find that Oswald and Sara were standing beside him; Lachlan, Kilt and Saxon had returned to the table.

'I'm thinking about everything that's happened since I joined the Brotherhood,' Caspan replied to the elderly treasure hunter. 'It leaves me a little numb at times.'

Sara smiled and pointed towards the far end of the hall, where Frostbite sat with his fellow magical guardians, who were neck-deep in a barrel of food. 'I've never seen a Warden eat so much,' she remarked.

Many of the guests were wary of the Wardens and kept well clear of them, but King Rhys had insisted that they be allowed to attend the celebratory feast. They had played just as important a role in defending the kingdom as had the treasure hunters, and he insisted that a section of the hall be reserved for the guardians. Blankets had been laid across the flagstones, and barrels of savoury meat and grain had been prepared for their sitting.

Caspan felt guilty every time he looked at Frostbite. If he'd taken better care of his soul key he would have been able to dismiss the drake to the astral plane to heal. He'd remained on the battlefield at Chester Hill until night fell, searching through the trampled earth and broken weapons that littered the valley floor. His friends had helped him, but they couldn't find Frostbite's soul key.

Fortunately, Arthur wasn't only skilled in healing humans, and quickly tended to Frostbite's wounds upon their return to Briston. The drake's injured leg was set in a splint, his left wing was supported by a massive bandage, and his missing scales had been patched with pieces of thick, hardened leather. Arthur insisted that, with rest, Frostbite would soon be fully healed and soaring through the sky once more. Still, it was bittersweet for Caspan.

Frostbite would recover from his wounds, but with his soul key lost the drake would never be able to return to his astral home. He was forever trapped in Caspan's world. Caspan was grateful for Frostbite's company, but he felt immense sorrow that Frostbite was now mortal.

Meanwhile, Bandit had made a full recovery. The friends had waited with bated breath yesterday evening as Roland summoned his manticore for the first time since the fight against the rocs. Caspan had feared that Bandit might have succumbed to the injuries he'd sustained during the ferocious encounter and be lost forever. Words could not express the joy he felt when the manticore had materialised out of the blue smoke. The Warden had stretched out his wings slowly and, with a mischievous glint in his eyes, tripped Roland over. Tears of joy streaming down his face, Roland climbed to his feet and embraced his Warden in a great hug that lasted for minutes.

Caspan had feared that the war would tear his friends apart, but they were all now back together, ready to return to the House of Whispers. Their lives would never be the same again, with new titles and responsibilities, but they were still proud members of the Brotherhood. There was a world for them to explore, of Dray tombs and burial mounds to investigate, but the House of Whispers held a special place in Caspan's heart. It would always be his home.

His heart swelling with pride, he glanced at his friends; at the small gathering he now called family. Gramidge was wearing an old coat he'd found in the small chamber that had once served as his private quarters when he had worked in the castle. The steward extracted a piece of parchment from his pocket and studied it curiously. He leapt suddenly to his feet, startling those seated around him.

'I can't believe it!' he yelled, waving the parchment above his head for all to see. 'I found it! I found it!'

'You found what?' Roland asked.

'The lost recipe for Lip Smacker!' Gramidge hollered. He sought out Caspan and beckoned him over. 'We'll start production tomorrow, Cas. What do you reckon?'

The members of the Brotherhood cheered and banged their tankards on the table.

Smiling broadly, Caspan put his arms around Oswald and Sara, then went over to join his other friends.

ACKNOWLEDGEMENTS

As always, a special thank you to the wonderful team at Random House Australia, particularly Zoe Walton and Cristina Briones, and to my amazing family and friends — you all know who you are.

ABOUT THE AUTHOR

Stuart Daly is a History teacher in a private high school in Sydney. He is the author of *The Witch Hunter Chronicles* series, an epic tale of witch hunting and demon slaying set in the seventeenth century. *Brotherhood of Thieves* is his action-packed fantasy series about a secret order of treasure hunters. Stuart lives in Sydney with his wife and three children.

THE WITCH HUNTER CHRONICLES

BOOK ONE: THE SCOURGE OF JERICHO

No reprieve. No surrender.
This is the Hexenjäger.

It's 1666, and the forces of darkness are spreading across Europe. Dreaming of wielding a blade in epic battles like the father he never knew, Jakob von Drachenfels falsifies a letter of introduction to join the Hexenjäger – an elite military order of witch hunters. He soon learns a lesson in the dangers of ambition when he finds himself selected for a team sent to recover a biblical relic from a witch-infested castle. But when the team is betrayed from within, what was already a difficult mission turns into a desperate struggle for survival.

Out now!

(Also available in ebook format)